"Bill, look out!"

Cody looked sharply toward the station, trying to spot his friend. But Ethan didn't look that way. As he dropped instinctively into a crouch, his eyes quickly scanned the street, searching for danger. He saw the shotgunner step around the back of the wagon, saw the scattergun coming out from beneath the yellow duster. Other people saw the gun, too. He heard a woman scream, and a man ran directly across the line of fire in a panicked effort to get out of the way.

"Get down!" Ethan grabbed Cody as he shouted the warning, swinging Buffalo Bill roughly around. Buffalo Bill lost his balance and sprawled in the muck of the street. Ethan yanked the Colt out of the holster and threw himself sideways as the scattergun came up and flame belched from one of the barrels. The buckshot whistled over his head. He hit the ground and rolled and came up on one knee, firing a split second before the shotgunner could cut loose with the second barrel. A man on the boardwalk in front of the barbershop went down. The plate glass window behind him was shattered.

Ethan checked the shotgunner; he was down, but still alive, writhing in the mud. Rising, Ethan brought the Colt up, took careful aim, and fired a second time. The shotgunner's body jerked, and then was still.

Ethan felt lancing pain in his right calf, and his legs were knocked out from under him before he heard the next shotgun blast. He landed poorly, knocking the air out of his lungs. Another of Letcher's men was coming from another alley on the opposite side of the street . . .

St. Martin's Paperbacks Titles
by Jason Manning

LAST CHANCE

Jason Manning

St. Martin's Paperbacks

LAST CHANCE

Copyright © 2003 by Jason Manning.

ISBN: 0-312-98204-6

Printed in the United States of America

St. Martin's Paperbacks edition / December 2003

St. Martin's Paperbacks are published by St. Martin's Press, 175 Fifth Avenue, New York, NY 10010.

10 9 8 7 6 5 4 3 2 1

PART ONE

1

It was cold, bitterly so. So cold that Ethan Payne's exhalations seemed to crystallize right in front of his face. The shaggy mountain mustang he rode had icicles on its chin. Ethan couldn't recall ever having experienced a winter like this one. Not even during his childhood in Illinois, where sometimes those Canadian winds would blow down across the frozen Great Lakes and lay a blanket of ice and snow across the Midwest, and where, when winter came early, it could turn so cold so quickly that cornstalks would become as fragile as glass. It was just his luck, thought Ethan, that he'd be in the high country of the Rockies when the coldest winter on record came howling down from the North. Even the old-timers at the gold camp of Leadville couldn't remember one this bad.

As the mountain mustang carefully picked its way down a snow-covered slope of shale, Ethan cast a bleak gaze at the scene before him. The high plateau upon which the town of Leadville had been founded was ringed completely by jagged peaks, blue in the distance and shrouded by wisps of cloud. The sky was overcast, as it had been for many days. The limbs of the conifers sagged with the burden of snow—Ethan calculated that several feet of the stuff had fallen in the past two weeks. The only sounds he could hear were the whisperings of the wind and the crunch of the mustang's hooves in the deep snow. He knew he could rely on the surefooted horse to get him home. The animal wasn't much to look at, but it had been born to this country and was accustomed to its dangers.

At the bottom of the slope they reached a creek that was almost completely frozen over, and a whiff of something noxious reached Ethan's nostrils. It was the effluvium of Leadville's denizens; the town was located a mile or so uphill. He turned in that direction, knowing that before long he would be confronted by more evidence of human habitation—acre upon acre of tree stumps, the mark of the lumber crews. It seemed to Ethan that at least one new structure was erected in town every day. Both gold and silver had been found in this country, and the dream of striking it rich was bringing newcomers on a constant basis—even in the middle of winter. Ethan shook his head, wondering how many gold seekers would perish in the snow striving to reach Leadville, or any one of a dozen other gold camps in Colorado. Having experienced a gold rush before, Ethan was well aware of the lengths men would go to on the slim chance of finding the mother lode. He'd been in California nearly thirty years ago, and he'd seen it there with his own eyes. Now he was seeing it again. It didn't look any better to him this time.

He and Julie had started talking about leaving Leadville months ago. He had an aversion to looking for gold, and he wasn't a good enough card player—or a good enough cheat—to make much money playing cards; besides, Leadville had plenty of professional card sharps who took most of the earnings of the prospectors. So it was more or less out of desperation that he had gotten into the business of providing the people of Leadville with fresh meat. It was a funny thing about gold seekers—they wanted to spend every minute of daylight panning for gold, and usually didn't pay much attention to what folks who didn't have the fever considered to be essentials, such as food and shelter. Ethan was an excellent shot with a long gun. He'd always been; back in Illinois he had spent much of his time hunting. His father had been too drunk, usually, to do anything of the sort. It was ironic, Ethan thought, that he had come to the gold fields in hopes of finding something to do besides make his living with the gun—and here he was doing just that. Though it wasn't much of a living, really.

He glanced over his shoulder at the mule that plodded along behind the mountain mustang, on the back end of a lead rope. There were two bulging deer hides lashed to a wooden rack that, in turn, was strapped to the back of the mule. In this weather a hunter had to clean his kill quickly, before the carcass froze harder than stone. Those hides held every last pound of edible meat. All Ethan had left behind was the offal and the bones. Even so, there wasn't much meat in the hides. Game had become scarce in the vicinity of Leadville. There were just too many people in the valley now, and they were cutting down the trees and fouling up the water and making too much of a racket. The game had moved elsewhere, which meant Ethan had been forced to trek farther and farther afield to find it. This time he'd been out for two days. And two days exposed to this kind of weather was very unpleasant. There had to be a better way to make a living.

Problem was, Ethan didn't know of a better way. He'd been offered the job of town marshal, but he'd passed on that. His reputation from his badge-toting days in Kansas had followed him. But he didn't consider law-dogging to be a better way. And that was why he and Julie were still in Leadville even though neither one of them was particularly fond of the place. They didn't know where else to go, or what to do when they got there. They were just a pair of drifters, living day to day, hand to mouth, with not much of a future and a past that neither one of them cared to dwell upon. All they had was each other. Julie never complained about her lot. She never dogged him about how it was his responsibility to take care of her. She had suggested working in one of Leadville's saloons, but he had opposed that idea so vigorously that she hadn't pressed the issue. Most of the percentage girls in the gold camp were also whores, and Ethan didn't care to see her subjected to that sort of attention from other men. She'd experienced plenty of that, in her time.

He had met her during his stint as troubleshooter for the
Overland Mail. She and her husband had run a waystation
called Wolftrap. Her husband had run off and left her, and
Ethan had taken up with her at that juncture. Then Joe Cathcott
had returned, and, looking back on it now, Ethan supposed it
had been inevitable that he'd had to kill Cathcott, a piece of
work who was partly responsible for the fact that, shortly
after, he ceased to be employed by the Overland. After that he
and Julie had gone their separate ways—his killing her husband, no-account though he had been, had proven to be too
much for their relationship to endure. Much later they'd met
again, in Abilene. He'd been the law in town, and she'd been a
prostitute addicted to laudanum. They'd survived all of that,
and now here they were. Still trying to survive.

He began to see the claims as he rode along the creek.
Downstream of Leadville there weren't that many. These
were the latecomers, the gold seekers who had arrived to
find that everything upstream had already been staked out
for a good two miles up into the mountains. As far as Ethan
knew, none of the men who had claims along here were getting anything at all out of panning the creek from sunup until
sundown. Still, they jealously guarded their claims—you
would have thought they were standing on a mound of solid
gold dust rather than mud and rock. So Ethan was careful to
swing wide around the claims, having no desire to be taken
for a claim-jumper and shot at. The prospectors lived in
lean-tos or tents; none of them had bothered taking the time
to build a substantial structure. Most of them were in the
creek, panning, and when they saw or heard Ethan they put
the pans down and reached for their rifles or shotguns. As
with most other mining camps in the West, Leadville was a
wild and wide-open place. There was a town sheriff, but
there was only so much law and order one man could provide. These men knew that it was up to them to protect not
only themselves but their possessions, and most of them
took no chances. It was a shoot-first-and-ask-questions-later
situation.

Ethan soon reached the edge of town, a collection of

clapboard buildings lining a major street and several minor ones, located on a high plain and visible from a fair distance away across a good quarter-mile of tree stumps. Smoke was rising from dozens of chimneys, and Ethan could hear the cacophony of hammers and saws as work crews labored to erect another slipshod building. No one much cared, mused Ethan, about whether a building would still be standing a decade from now. It wasn't about permanence, but utility—it was about getting in out of the bitter cold today and letting tomorrow take care of itself. Ethan doubted that there were very many people currently residing in and around the mining camp who expected to be here a year from now. He knew he didn't. But then again, with nowhere else to go—at least nowhere that had better prospects—he couldn't be sure that next winter wouldn't find him right here in the same place, doing the same thing.

His arrival attracted some attention, but that was only because he had fresh meat draped over the back of the mule. The people of Leadville didn't pay much attention to him personally. Most of them knew who he was, and knew he posed no threat to them, as a stranger might, just as long as they didn't cross him. That was the one good thing about having his kind of reputation, thought Ethan. People tended to leave him alone.

One man, though, did approach him, stepping out the door of a building with the word RESTAURANT painted in red across the front. He angled across the muddy street to intercept Ethan, who checked his horse. The man was tall and small-shouldered, but with a substantial paunch, and black hair slicked back with pomade. He was wearing an apron covered with dough and dried blood. When he spoke, it was with a broad German accent.

"Mr. Payne, I vill give you top dollar for vat you have brought today."

"Mr. Heflin, you know how this works. I sell the meat at auction to the highest bidder."

"I vill give you a dollar a pound more than Mr. Grant gave you last time."

"Good. Then you should walk away a winner at the auction."

As it appeared that the German intended to say more on the subject, Ethan tapped the mountain mustang with his heels and put it into motion. Heflin had to dance aside to keep from being trampled by the wild-eyed horse.

Ethan hadn't got much farther down the street before he noticed another man trying to cut him off. This one was the sheriff, Joe Simms. Simms was middle aged, with iron-gray hair and a noticeable limp. He'd told Ethan that he'd been shot in the leg by Apaches several times while scouting for the army, and Ethan had no reason to doubt that this was true. Simms had the look of a man who had seen the elephant, who had been all over and done just about everything worth doing, and maybe even a few things *not* worth doing. He wasn't shy about using the six-shooter on his hip—he'd killed two men that Ethan knew of, and both had deserved killing. But Simms struck him as a man who understood his limitations and who never bit off more than he could chew. He wouldn't have lasted a month as a lawdog in Abilene, mused Ethan. A mining town was one thing, a trail town another.

Once more Ethan stopped the mustang. Simms slogged through the muck until he was right alongside the horseman. He cast a quick look around to make sure no one else was within earshot, and now Ethan could see by the expression on the sheriff's face that something was seriously wrong.

"I think we've got a problem, Payne."

"We?"

Simms fired him a look of annoyance mixed with caution. "Don't worry. I'm not going to ask you to back me up in gunplay. I got the message a long time ago that you weren't the least bit interested in wearing a badge again, not even on a temporary basis."

"That's right," said Ethan.

"I just come from Doc Bingham's. A prospector by the name of Fanning died this morning."

"People die all the time, especially in places like this one."

"Yeah. But they don't usually die the way Fanning did."

"And how was that?"

Simms grimaced, and Ethan could see the grayness in his gaunt, stubbled cheeks.

"Doc says he's seen it before, so he's sure of his facts. That was back in Philadelphia, when he was still in medical school, and there was an epidemic."

Ethan felt a cold shiver run down his spine. He didn't like the sound of this. "Seen what before?" he asked, curtly.

"And Fanning isn't the first one. There have been four other cases in the past week. All but one's dead."

"Damn it, Sheriff . . ."

Simms looked up at him, and Ethan was surprised to see a bleak hopelessness in Joe Simms' eyes.

"It's typhoid."

2

The first thought that crossed Ethan Payne's mind was that he was going to be sorry—sorry that he hadn't taken Julie out of here, as he'd wanted to, before winter set in. Because now he had a feeling it was too late.

Ethan dismounted, and found himself taking a quick look around also, to see if anyone was within hearing distance. The main street of Leadville was bustling with activity, as it always was.

"Who knows about this?" he asked Simms.

"Far as I know, just you, me, and the doc, so far."

"Then this is noplace to talk about it. Anybody in jail?"

"Not this morning, no."

"Then let's go there."

They walked up the street to the jailhouse. Like all the other buildings in town, it was made of green timber. Strap-iron bars had been secured to the windows. They walked into the office, a room barely big enough to contain a pot-belly stove, a small kneehole desk, and a narrow canvas bunk in the corner. There was a gun rack on the wall and an old map of Colorado, back when it had been a territory. Of course Leadville wasn't on it, and Ethan wondered if, after the typhoid had finished with the town, it would be on any future maps, either.

"Want some coffee?" asked Simms, motioning at the blackened coffeepot atop the stove.

"Nope. But I won't turn down the offer of a drink from the bottle you've got stashed in that desk."

Simms smiled. He opened a desk drawer and tossed Ethan the half-empty bottle of sour mash. Ethan unplugged the bottle and took a long swig. The liquor exploded in his belly, and he felt marginally better about things. It was just an illusion, though. He knew that. If he drank enough sour mash he'd stop worrying completely about typhoid, or anything else. Still, sometimes illusion beat reality all to hell. He took another swig before surrendering the bottle to its rightful owner. Seeking the same escape, Simms took a long pull.

"I told the doc I'd send somebody to Camp Sheridan, tell the army what was going on here, that I'd need help keeping people out of town. Not to mention keeping folks from leaving. He said it was important to try to prevent the spread of the typhoid, but he doubted the army would want to have anything to do with it. He's probably right." Simms sighed, saw his chair, and sank into it with a weary sigh. He ran a hand over his face. "To be honest with you, Payne, I'm not sure what to do about this. I thought maybe you'd have some ideas."

Ethan shook his head. He didn't want the responsibility of coming up with ideas, not about something like typhoid, about which he knew next to nothing, except that it was deadly.

"All hell's going to break loose," he predicted. "It'll be interesting to see how many people around here put living above finding gold. There'll be a lot who'll try to get out, and I don't see how you can stop them. But there will be others, some who are already here and others who will come here despite the risk, just to jump claims." He shook his head. "I don't envy you your job."

"So you're not inclined to help me, I take it."

"Help you do what?"

"According to the doc, we've got to keep the disease contained. A lot of us could already be infected. Most of us will show symptoms. Some of us will die. But even the people who look well could have the disease. And the doc says it's highly contagious. So wherever they go, they could give it to other people. He said that back in Philadelphia, thousands of people died in a matter of weeks." Simms took another swig from the bottle of sour mash. "The way I see it, it's my responsibility to keep anybody from leaving Leadville until we're sure this thing has run its course."

Ethan shook his head. "Not possible. Maybe the army could do it, but you can't. You'd need fifty men with rifles and a willingness to shoot to kill to keep people in town if they don't want to stay. Where are you going to get fifty men you can trust? And are *you* willing to kill folks if they insist on going?"

"I would hope it wouldn't come to that."

"When word gets out—and you know it will—there's only going to be one law that matters. Every man for himself."

"And that includes you," said Simms.

Ethan gave him a long look. "I'm taking Julie out of here. Don't try to stop me."

He stood up, turned for the door.

"If you're looking for her, you'll find her at Doc Bingham's."

It was as though the blood in Ethan's veins turned to ice. He turned back. "Why is she there?"

"Oh, she's fine, so far. It's that gambler friend of yours. Seems he's come down with—"

Ethan was already out the door, so he didn't hear Simms finish the sentence. But then, he didn't really need to.

When Ethan walked into the doctor's office, Bingham called out from the back room that he would be right there. Ethan didn't wait. He went on through the curtained doorway, and found the doctor and Julie standing on either side of a narrow bed. Clooney was on the bed, fully clothed, and the way he looked scared Ethan clean through. The gambler was ghastly pale and glistening with sweat. He was moaning deliriously and only semi-conscious. Then, suddenly, he let out a sharp cry of pain. Rolling over on his side, he pulled his knees up, clutching at his stomach.

Bingham glanced at Ethan, then looked across the bed at Julie. "He's burning up with fever. We've got to try to break it. There's a rain barrel out back. Fill that bowl over there with water, please."

"Yes, doctor." Julie glanced at Ethan, too, and he could see that she was worried. Of course, she would be—Clooney was really the closest friend either of them had in Leadville. The gambler had known Ethan for years; they'd met in Abilene, and Clooney had backed Ethan on more than one occasion. A few months after Ethan's arrival in Leadville, Clooney had showed up, claiming that Abilene wasn't any fun anymore, now that Ethan Payne had tamed it, so he'd decided to look for excitement in the Colorado gold camps. It wasn't excitement but rather his old friend that Clooney had been looking for, and Ethan had been glad to see him. Now, though, he was wishing the gambler had stayed in Kansas.

When Julie had gone out to collect the water, Bingham turned to Ethan. "Just like Fanning and the others," he said grimly, passing a hand over his balding pate. "The worst part is there's just not much I can do to help him."

"There's no cure?"

"No. Hell, we're not even sure what causes typhoid, though I subscribe to the conventional wisdom that it's a germ of some kind that is ingested from bad water."

"Will he live?"

Bingham shrugged. "I have no way of knowing. Some do, and some don't. All I can do is try to bring the fever down."

"He was fine the day before yesterday."

The physician nodded. "It comes upon you suddenly, without warning. Severe stomach pain, then the fever, sometimes a rash. There may be vomiting and diarrhea."

"How long before we'll know?"

"If he'll live?" Bingham looked at his patient. "It won't take long. A few days, maybe sooner."

"It can kill that quickly?"

"Oh, yes. He's a friend of yours, isn't he?"

"That's right."

"Well, he's a young man. Appears to be a fairly healthy specimen. Perhaps he'll pull through."

Julie returned with the bowl of rainwater. Bingham provided her with a cloth, which she dampened and applied to Clooney's forehead, cheeks, and neck. Ethan stepped forward, holding out a hand.

"Here, I'll do that," he said.

"No, I'll do it," she said. "I don't mind."

"I don't think you should stay here, Julie." He looked at Bingham, hoping the doctor would back him up. "It's very contagious, isn't it?"

"Yes. But if she's going to contract typhoid, it's probably already happened."

"He came to our place yesterday," Julie told him, "complaining that he didn't feel well. He said he'd never been sick in his life. I had him lie down and made him some soup. But he couldn't keep it down. I could tell he had a fever, so I brought him here. He walked all the way, and then collapsed on the doctor's doorstep."

"You say it comes from bad water," said Ethan, addressing Bingham.

"I said I *think* it does."

"So if it's a germ, you could kill it by boiling the water, right?"

"Yes, I think so."

"Then you can't keep this a secret, Doc. You've got to spread the word. Make sure everyone boils any water they plan to drink or use for cooking." Ethan thought about the soup that Julie had made two days ago. Had it been safe to eat?

"I know you're right," said Bingham, anguished. "But there'll be mass panic. If we let the people leave the typhoid could spread to the next town, and the next. It could even hit Denver, God forbid."

"You've got to let them know," insisted Ethan. "I'll ride

to Camp Sheridan. I'll convince the army to get involved."

Bingham nodded, looking relieved. "Good. I'll keep it quiet only until you get back."

"Deal." Ethan turned to Julie. "I need to talk to you."

He took her by the arm and firmly led her out of the room. Once through the curtained doorway, she swung around and into his arms, and he held her close. She was trembling slightly.

"I'm frightened, Ethan," she said in a small voice.

"I know. So am I. Come on, I'm getting you out of here."

She pulled away from him. "I'm not leaving," she said, surprised. "I can't. Didn't you hear what the doctor was saying? I . . . " She hesitated, steeled herself. "I could be infected. We all could be."

"And you might not be—yet. But if you stay here you will be for sure."

"No. We can't do this, Ethan. We've got to stay here until this thing has run its course. And if . . . if we die, then mark it down to God's will."

"If we die," said Ethan grimly, "mark it down to the fact that we didn't leave."

3

Ethan reached Camp Sheridan the next day. He rode up to the gate where he was challenged by a sentry, who demanded to know who Ethan was and what he wanted.

"I've come to see your commanding officer."

"What business do you have with him?"

"I'm from Leadville," said Ethan. "There's been an outbreak of typhoid."

The sentry's reaction caught Ethan by surprise. He brought his rifle up and aimed it at the rider, taking several steps back. "Turn your cayuse around and get the hell out of here, mister," he snapped.

Ethan was cold and tired and worried, and he was in a hurry to get back to Julie. Though he knew that, logically, it made no sense, he couldn't help but feel that if he stayed with her she would stand a better chance of surviving the typhoid. And, besides, he'd lost count of the times men had pointed guns at him. He wasn't fazed.

"I'm not going anywhere until I talk to your commanding officer," he said.

"What's going on down there?"

Both Ethan and the sentry looked up. An officer stood looking over the log palisade.

"This man's come from Leadville, Lieutenant, and he's talking about typhoid. Wants to see the colonel."

The lieutenant disappeared from the wall. A moment later he emerged through the gate.

"There's typhoid in Leadville?" he asked, as though he couldn't believe he'd heard right. Or maybe, thought Ethan, he just didn't want to think he had.

"That's right," replied Ethan. "The local sawbones, Doc Bingham, is sure of it. He sent me here to get the army's help."

"The army's help!" The lieutenant sounded as if that was the most ridiculous thing he'd ever heard. "Look, mister. I want you to ride back toward that treeline yonder and wait there. Somebody will come out to talk to you."

"Fine," said Ethan. He could understand their caution. They had no way of knowing whether he was a carrier of the typhoid or not, and they couldn't take any chances. "But don't take too long."

The lieutenant was starting to turn away, but thought of something and looked again at Ethan.

"You venture up this close to the fort again, mister, and I'll order my men to shoot."

Ethan didn't dignify that with a response. He swung the mountain mustang around and rode away.

As instructed, he crossed an open meadow to the foot of forested hills before dismounting. Ground-hitching the mustang, he took a canvas bag and his canteen from the saddle and sat cross-legged in the snow and the dead brown grass. The altitude here was several thousand feet below that of Leadville, and there wasn't nearly as much snow, though it felt just about as cold to Ethan. The bag contained biscuits Julie had made for him. She made the best biscuits he'd ever tasted. He wasn't hungry but he knew he had to eat. His body needed nourishment. As soon as he'd delivered the message to the army he was heading back to Leadville, and he wasn't going to be taking his sweet time about it, either.

He was on his second biscuit when he saw a detail emerge from the fort—four men on horseback. When they were closer and he could see them better he felt comfortable in assuming that the man in the lead was the garrison's commanding officer. He wore the braid and the epaulets of a high-ranking officer on his blue tunic, and he carried himself like a professional soldier, perhaps even a West Point product. The lieutenant who had spoken to Ethan at the gate was with him, and the other two horsemen were privates. As they checked their horses ten yards away, Ethan stood up and put the canvas bag and canteen back on his saddle. He remained standing beside the horse, on the right side where his Henry repeater was snugly encased in a leather scabbard.

"I am Colonel Bainbridge, commanding officer here," said the older man. "The lieutenant tells me you've reported an outbreak of typhoid in Leadville?"

"The army needs to quarantine the town, Colonel, and keep it from spreading."

"Damn it, man," breathed Bainbridge, exasperated. "Why did you have to come here?"

Ethan smiled faintly. He felt sorry for the colonel. Bainbridge knew where his duty lay—that was evident from the tone of his voice. But obviously he would have much preferred leading his command straight through the gates of hell.

"You were the closest, Colonel. It can't be kept quiet much longer. So should I tell the doc that you're coming?"

Bainbridge looked at the lieutenant, at Ethan, and then at the trees beyond, but he could find no way out of his predicament.

"I suppose so," he said, sourly. "Are you saying you're going back to Leadville?"

"Yes, I am."

"Most men wouldn't, under the circumstances."

"I don't have a choice."

Bainbridge nodded. He understood. "I hope whoever it is will come through this."

"Beg your pardon, Colonel," said the lieutenant, "but can we really take the chance that he's telling the truth? He might head for Denver as soon as he's out of sight. And if he carried typhoid with him . . . well, all hell would break loose, sir."

"What do you suggest we do with him, Lieutenant?"

"We should detain him, sir."

"It would be a mistake to try that," warned Ethan.

Bainbridge looked at him. "Yes," he said slowly, sizing Ethan up. "Yes, I suspect it would be. I think we can take this man at his word, Lieutenant."

"But, sir . . . "

"I appreciate your concern for my career, Lieutenant," said Bainbridge, with an icy underpinning to his voice. "But I'm not worried about this man going to Denver. He's returning to Leadville, just as he said. I'll stake my career on that."

Ethan fit foot to stirrup and swung aboard the mountain mustang. "Thank you, Colonel," he said. "What do I tell the doc?"

"I'll be leaving in an hour with a detachment sufficient to the task. Good luck to you, sir."

Ethan nodded. The colonel was looking at him in the way of someone who knew that the other person was doomed, and that this would be the last time he'd be seen alive.

Ethan got back to Leadville in time to bury his friend Clooney.

According to Doc Bingham, the gambler had never regained consciousness. The fever would not relent, and, three days after showing up at Julie's door complaining of feeling ill, the man was dead.

When Ethan told Bingham that the army was on its way, the physician was immensely relieved.

"People have started to talk. Spread rumors. Every time I go out that door I get questions from nearly everyone I meet. Frankly, I'm tired of lying. Besides, I don't think I'm very good at it." He looked morosely at the sheet-covered corpse on the bed in the back room of his office. "One more body gets carried out of here and that will be it. The panic will start."

"Then we'll wait," said Ethan woodenly. He'd considered

the possibility that Clooney would succumb to the typhoid, and had tried to prepare himself for that eventuality. But he wasn't prepared for just how hard the gambler's death hit him. He managed, in spite of this, to maintain his composure. He could mourn later. Right now he had to think clearly.

"Wait for how long?" asked Bingham.

"Until the army gets here. Then I'll bury him. Get some rest, Doc. You look like you haven't slept in a week."

"I don't think I have." Bingham shuffled into the front room. Ethan pulled the sheet back from Clooney's face. It was gray and gaunt, the cheeks hollowed, the eyes sunk deep in their sockets. While he was no stranger to death, Ethan was shocked by the speed with which the typhoid had snuffed out the gambler's life. Just a week before, Clooney had seemed as fit as a fiddle. There were better ways to die, figured Ethan. Standing up and fighting back, for instance. But there was no fighting back against this foe. It had no mercy. It did not distinguish between young and old, man or woman, adult or child.

Sitting in a chair in the corner of the room, Ethan stared at Clooney's uncovered face and wondered if the man had had what one could justifiably call a "good life." It occurred to him that they had spoken often of his own past, but he knew next to nothing of Clooney's. The gambler had been content to let the past alone, and maybe that was the smart way to live, the only way to be happy with one's lot. Clooney had seemed fairly happy, even though his life had been one of rootless wandering, much like Ethan's. He recalled that Clooney had once remarked that he'd like to someday find a good woman and settle down. The problem was, he'd added, that a man didn't find too many good women passing through a bucket-of-blood saloon, which was where the gambler spent most of his waking hours plying his trade. Still, if Clooney had had the wherewithal to consider his life in his last hours, Ethan decided that he'd have been fairly content. Because, above all, he'd been a practical man, willing to accept whatever life brought his way. Ethan missed him terribly.

A couple of hours later, Julie arrived. Ethan got up and went into the front room when he heard the door open, and she flew into his arms, overjoyed to see him. Doc Bingham was slumped in the chair at his desk, sound asleep.

"I'm so sorry about Clooney," she whispered into his chest, holding him tight.

"I know."

She looked up at him, wiping a tear from her cheek. "And now Jenny's little girl, Amanda . . . she's been throwing up all day. I just came from there."

"Good God," muttered Ethan. Jenny was a percentage girl who worked in a tent saloon on the edge of town, and Julie had often kept her child while she was working. The death of anyone, particularly a child, was a blow to Julie, but Amanda's death would be extremely hard on her.

"I'm scared," she admitted. "Not so much of the typhoid— I mean, that's in God's hands. But of the people, when they find out what's going on. I'm scared of what some of them will do when they think they have nothing to lose."

"I won't let anything happen to you," said Ethan, and then realized how empty that promise really was. He might be able to protect her from some things, but there was nothing he could do to save her from the disease that had killed Clooney and Fanning and would probably kill many, many more before it was done. The realization made him feel helpless, impotent—and he didn't like that feeling one bit.

They heard men shouting outside, the pounding of booted feet on the boardwalk in front of the doctor's office. Julie looked at Ethan with a silent question in her eyes.

"I think the army is here," he said quietly.

A few minutes later a man Ethan did not know came through the door. His eyes were wide with excitement, and his entrance was sufficient to rouse Doc Bingham from his much-needed slumbers.

"Doc! There's soldiers at both ends of town! Someone said somethin' about a quarantine. What the hell is going on?"

Ethan noticed that there was a lot of commotion in the street, men running this way or that, and more men gathering out in front of the doc's office. When Bingham hesitated, Ethan decided to take matters into his own hands. He advanced on the man who had entered.

"Get out of here. The doc will talk to you later."

"I ain't going nowhere until I get some—"

Ethan spun him around and, before the man could effectively resist, had him by the collar and the belt at the small of his back. In this manner he herded the man out onto the boardwalk and pitched him into the crowd. The others got out of the way and let the man sprawl facedown in the muck. Steaming mad, the man got quickly to his feet and his hand moved an inch toward the pistol stuck in his belt—only a fool went around Leadville without some kind of weapon. But then the hand stopped moving, because its owner realized that he was looking down the barrel of Ethan's Colt.

"What's going on here, Payne?" This was a man in the crowd, which had by now grown to more than twenty strong. "Why is the army here? What's this business about a quarantine?"

"How's that gambler friend of yours?" asked another. "I heard he was here, and real sick. Just like Fanning."

"Yeah, and we buried Fanning yesterday." This was yet a third member of the congregation. "What about it, Payne? Is Clooney still on the right side of grass, or not?"

"He's resting," said Ethan stonily. "And I'd sure hate to disturb him." To emphasize what he meant, he thumbed the Colt's hammer back.

"Ease up, gunslinger," said the first man. "We just want some answers. We have a right to know if there's something bad going around."

Ethan had been waiting for that. Bingham had said that the rumors about an epidemic had already begun. These men weren't fools.

"It's all right, Mr. Payne." Doc Bingham had come outside. Now he stood beside Ethan and gravely surveyed the faces of the men standing in the street. Ethan lowered the hammer on his sixshooter, but he didn't put the pistol away.

"They do have a right to know," continued the physician, "and I apologize to all of you for keeping it quiet these past few days. I hope that, in time, you'll come to understand why I did what I did."

"Stop beating around the bush, Doc," said one of the men.

Bingham nodded. "Of course. It's my professional opinion that Mr. Fanning and Mr. Clooney, as well as several others in the course of the past eight or nine days, have died of typhoid."

"Typhoid!" The dreaded word was breathed by several men almost simultaneously. They exchanged looks of growing horror.

"Now listen, please!" begged Bingham. "Let's all keep our wits about us. There are certain precautions—"

"My God," said one of the men in a strangled voice. "We're all gonna die."

"No! No, we're not all going to die!" exclaimed Bingham. "That's just the sort of wild talk we don't need. There are certain precautions you can take. First and foremost, you must make sure that you do not ingest any water that hasn't been thoroughly boiled. Do not eat or drink after anyone else. And—"

"How long have you known about this?" asked one of the men, his tone truculent enough to make Ethan tense up.

"I've suspected it for about a week," confessed Bingham.

"And you kept quiet about it just long enough for the army to get here."

"That's the size of it," said Ethan. "Because some of you would be fool enough to try to run away from this thing, and you'd wind up carrying it to other towns, and before long everybody in the state would be in the same fix we're in."

"They can't keep me here if I don't want to stay," said another man, panic creeping into his voice. "By God, I'm getting the hell out of here right now."

"Yeah, me, too," said another.

The crowd began to disperse. Several of the men threw angry, glowering looks at Bingham. But none of them were

inclined to act on their anger. Not with Ethan standing there
with a Colt revolver in his hand.

"Don't worry about it, Doc," said Ethan, noticing the
expression of dismay on Bingham's face. "You did the right
thing."

"Did I?"

As if in answer, several shots rang out at the north end of
the street. They couldn't see anything from this far away, but
Ethan had a feeling that at least one person had just found
out the hard way what the army was doing in Leadville.

4

Colonel Bainbridge was as good as his word—he'd brought enough men to do the job. He effectively quarantined Leadville, surrounding it with heavily armed troops. That first day, half a dozen men tried to get out, all the same. Two were killed, another wounded, and the other three turned back after the first warning shots were fired over their heads. Meanwhile, detachments went up and down the creek, rounding up all the prospectors they could find. While the men forming the cordon around the town had some hope of avoiding close contact with possibly infected civilians, the soldiers in the detachments did not. Most of the prospectors were not predisposed to abandon their claims, despite assurances issued on Bainbridge's authority that all claims would be recorded by the army and protected by troops. That meant that the men in the detachments often had to physically restrain the gold seekers and escort them through the cordon into Leadville. Once inside the town limits, the prisoners were released.

Ethan accompanied Doc Bingham and Sheriff Simms when the latter went calling on Bainbridge. Their approach elicited the same sort of reaction Ethan had experienced from the soldiers at Camp Sheridan. They were kept at bay with a dozen rifles trained on them until the colonel could be sent for, and when Bainbridge arrived on the scene he was careful to keep his distance. The colonel was courteous but businesslike. He promised to give what assistance he could, but made it clear that his first priority was to contain the outbreak. He urged Simms to make certain everyone in Leadville understood that this meant they could not leave until the quarantine was lifted. Anyone who did would be killed. He agreed to provide as much fresh water as possible for the townsfolk; he would have his men melt snow, boil it, and put it in casks for civilian use. Ethan pointed out that since no one knew how long this situation would exist, the people imprisoned in the town would also have need of food. Bainbridge promised that he would send details out into the mountains to hunt for game.

"Is there anything else I can do for you gentlemen?" asked the colonel.

"Yes," said Bingham grimly. "Pray."

"I've been doing that, sir, and will continue."

"There is one other thing," said Ethan. "We have dead to bury now—and more to come, I'm sure. We can't have the bodies piling up in the streets."

"Burn them," said Bainbridge curtly. "It's the safest way to dispose of them."

Ethan thought about Clooney, and shook his head. "We don't want to *dispose* of them. We want to give them decent burials."

"What do you suggest?"

"Give us access to the cemetery," said Simms. "It's just beyond your cordon on the other side of town."

Bainbridge thought it over, and nodded. "Consider it done."

Simms looked bleakly at Bingham and Ethan. "Then I guess that just about covers it."

"God be with you gentlemen," said Bainbridge.

As he walked back into Leadville with the doctor and the sheriff, Ethan wondered whether God was really with them or if He'd abandoned everyone who had the great misfortune of calling Leadville home.

Ethan buried Clooney later that same day. Only Simms and Bingham and Julie were there to join him in seeing the gambler off. The Leadville preacher, they'd been told, wasn't feeling well and couldn't preside over the ceremony. It was Doc Bingham who stood at the foot of the fresh grave and read from the Bible, First Corinthians, Chapter Fifteen: " 'For since by man came death, by man came also the resurrection of the dead. For as in Adam all die, even so in Christ shall all be made alive. But every man in his own order: Christ, the firstfruits; afterward they that are Christ's at his coming. Then cometh the end, when he shall have delivered up the kingdom to God, even the Father; when he shall have put down all rule and all authority and power. For he must reign until he hath put all enemies under his feet. The last enemy that shall be destroyed is death." The physician then led them in the Lord's Prayer. Ethan realized that he had forgotten the words. When it was over he paid the gravediggers, just as he had paid a man to make Clooney's coffin, and another to burn the gambler's name and date of death into a wooden cross that was placed at the head of the grave. As they left the cemetery, Ethan wondered how many more graves would have to be dug in the weeks to come.

That night a heavy snow fell. The next morning Julie was vomiting and running a high fever.

She died three days later, in the small, one-room clapboard house they had occupied during their stay in Leadville. Doc Bingham spent as much time as he could by her side, but by now dozens of people had been stricken, and so for most of the time Ethan was left alone with her. Selfishly unwilling to share her last hours with anyone else, Ethan preferred it that way. He hoped, as the end drew near, that she would regain consciousness long enough for him to tell her how much she meant to him. The knowledge that he had not done that enough in years past filled him with remorse. But she didn't come to, and when he sensed that the time had come, and her breathing was shallow and ragged, he sat on the edge of the bed and kissed her gently on the lips and told her that he loved her, and as she breathed her last his tears fell on her gaunt white face.

Bingham returned early the next morning to find Ethan sitting in a chair in a corner of the room, leaning forward with his head hanging. The doctor moved quietly to the bedside and took Julie's fragile wrist between his fingers, thinking to feel for a pulse. But rigor had set in, and he knew there was no point in that. He looked across at Ethan, and saw that the latter had lifted his head and was staring at him as though he were a stranger.

"Get your hands off her," said Ethan.

There was something in Ethan's voice that sent a cold chill down Bingham's spine. It was like the growl of a rabid dog, filled with an unremitting madness and pain. The doctor let the hand drop and stepped away from the bed.

"Why don't you come with me?" asked Bingham, compassion overcoming fear. "You can stay at my place for a while. I'll . . . take care of everything."

"Go away."

"Payne, listen—"

He came out of the chair with a snarl not that different from a cornered animal's, and before Bingham could protect himself Ethan had him by the front of his coat and was shoving him backward across the puncheon floor, shoving him until he was out the door. Only then did Ethan let him go, slamming the door in his face.

Bingham went at once to the sheriff's office and told Simms what had happened.

"Well, that's just fine," muttered the lawman. "On a good day that man is as dangerous as a hole full of rattlers. And now he's gone crazy with grief."

"When a strong man finally breaks," said Bingham, "there's sometimes no putting him back together again. I've seen it happen before. I wouldn't be too surprised if he decided to kill himself."

"I'd hate to see that happen," said Simms, sincerely. "But it would be a long sight better than if he starts killing other folks."

"I don't think he'll do that, Sheriff. But we've got to bury Julie."

Simms heaved a deep sigh, thought longingly of the bottle of whiskey in his desk drawer, and then shrugged on his coat. He went to the gun rack and took down a double-barreled shotgun and loaded both barrels.

"What are you going to do with that?" asked the physician.

"Defend myself, if need be. I'll go try to reason with him. But I'm telling you right now that I don't think I'll do any good."

Simms approached the small house on the edge of town like he was walking into a cave where he knew a grizzly lived. When he knocked on the door he took the precaution of stepping to one side. There was no response from inside, so he knocked a second time.

"Payne? Are you in there?"

"Go away."

"I'm sorry about Julie, Payne. I truly am. But you got to let me in there."

"Get the hell away from my door."

"Damn it, Payne—"

The bullet punched a hole in the door's planking, and Simms flinched away from the spray of splinters. His anger surged—then ebbed as he noticed that the bullet hole was down near the floor. Ethan had shot low, so an ounce of lead in his leg would have been the worst that could have happened. The man wasn't crazy enough to be trying to kill him, and Simms took that to be a very good sign. Still, Simms hadn't lived this long by being careless. He catfooted across to the other side of the door.

"You missed, Payne."

"The next one won't."

"You've got to give her a Christian burial. You can't keep her in there, Payne. That's not her, anyway. She's gone . . . to a better place." Simms fell silent for a moment, hoping for a response, and getting none. His voice was softer when he spoke again. "I know how you feel, son. I lost the woman I loved many years ago. I can't honestly say I'm over the hurt, and God knows I didn't think I'd be able to survive it at the time. But I did. Life goes on and you've got to go with it, whether you want to or not. Sure, you could put a bullet in your own brainpan, I guess. Just ask yourself, though—is that what she'd want you to do? No, she'd want you to keep living. And you owe it to her to do what she'd want."

He stopped, listened again. A moment later the door creaked open a few inches. Simms pushed it open wider with the barrel of the shotgun, took a quick peek inside. Ethan was standing by the bed, his back to the door, looking down at Julie's body. The Colt was in his hand, held down by his side. Simms came up slowly and confiscated the pistol. Ethan didn't resist. At that point the sheriff decided it was safe to start breathing again. He, too, looked at Julie, and shook his head.

"There's just no way to figure out why these things happen," he said.

Ethan turned and walked out of the house. Simms covered Julie's face with a blanket and went out, too, to find Ethan sitting in the mud in front of the house, oblivious to the bitterly cold night air and the snow that was falling. Several men had ventured near, drawn by the sound of the gunshot. They stood off in the shadows, watching from a distance, too wary to come any closer. Simms called out to them.

"This is the sheriff. Two of you come here. I need your help."

They all hesitated.

"Goddammit," roared Simms. "Two of you get over here now or I'll throw the whole lot of you into jail."

Two men reluctantly responded. They walked wide around Ethan and followed Simms inside. At the sheriff's direction, they picked up the covered body and carried it out. This time Simms followed them. He paused to shed his jacket and drape it over Ethan's shoulders. He wanted to say something that would provide the man with comfort but couldn't think of anything, and with a shake of his head he walked on.

Later that night Ethan roused himself. The spectators were

gone. There was no one on the street. He got up and stumbled into the house. Removing the chimney from a kerosene lamp, he doused the bed where Julie had died and struck a sulfur match to life. The flames engulfed the bed, and in a matter of seconds were climbing the wall behind it. Ethan walked outside and down the street. In minutes the house was completely consumed by the fire. Belatedly, the alarm was raised, and the street was soon filled with running men. Ethan ignored the commotion. Reaching one of Leadville's saloons, he found the door locked, the establishment closed for the night. Without hesitation he kicked the door open and went around the bar and helped himself to a bottle of whiskey. Knuckling the sleep from his eyes, a man Ethan knew as the saloon proprietor came out of the back room, wearing a coat over his long johns. He saw the shattered door, Ethan leaning against the bar drinking straight from the bottle, and the men running in the street outside.

"What the hell?"

Ethan ignored him, too.

The saloonkeeper went to the door and stepped across the threshold, glancing down the street to see the flames licking at the base of a column of smoke that disappeared into the black winter sky. Then he went back inside, shut the door, and propped a chair against it to keep it closed since the latch was useless now. He turned to Ethan.

"What are you doing here?"

"I needed a drink."

The saloonkeeper sized up the intruder and decided the wisest course was caution. "We're, um, we're closed, you know."

"Not anymore."

The saloonkeeper nodded. "Well, if you don't mind, I'm going back to bed."

"Good idea."

The man returned to the back room. There he dressed hastily and slipped out the back way.

Two hours passed before Sheriff Simms slipped quietly into the saloon by the back door. By that time Ethan had

emptied two bottles of whiskey. He was sitting behind the
bar, so didn't see the lawman. But he heard the telltale creak
of a loose floorboard. He got up, but the room tilted madly,
and his vision was blurred. Simms moved swiftly, rushing
the bar, and slamming the barrel of the shotgun into the side
of Ethan's skull. Ethan crashed to the floor, out cold. Simms
breathed a heavy sigh of relief. Then he glanced at the bottles on the back bar, shrugged, and went around the mahogany
to select one. He took several long pulls from it before heav-
ing the unconscious man over his shoulder and heading out
into the street.

5

Ethan Payne spent the next seven weeks in the Leadville jail.

He didn't attend Julie's funeral. Sheriff Simms gave him the chance, wanting him to promise that he wouldn't make any trouble, and telling him that he'd have to wear shackles on his wrists. The lawman wasn't going to risk a man like Payne going loco and running loose. He explained to Ethan that it wasn't anything personal, but he had a responsibility to the people of Leadville. Ethan didn't respond. In fact, for the duration of his stay he said not a single word to Simms or anyone else. The sheriff took the silence to mean that he couldn't trust his prisoner to behave himself if he was let out. So he and Doc Bingham and the gravediggers were the only ones present when Julie was laid to rest. Simms knew that Julie had a couple of friends in town—there was that percentage girl and her daughter—but they had preceded her to the cemetery, victims of the typhoid epidemic. In fact, it seemed to the sheriff that every time he turned around there was another grim procession headed for the bone orchard. According to Bingham, thirty-four people perished in the first week, and fifty-nine in the second. Simms was never sure of the number of dead after that, because Bingham himself had died by that time.

The army did its share of killing. As the typhoid spread, more and more people came to the conclusion that everyone who stayed in Leadville was doomed. Simms had to admit that he even thought that way after a while. As a result, scarcely a day went by when at least one fool didn't try to slip through the army cordon. As far as Simms knew, no one made it. The soldiers would always return the dead men, leaving them in the street for someone else to bury. The Grim Reaper prowled at will through the streets of Leadville, and there was no escape.

For the first couple of weeks Simms did his best to keep the looting under control. When people lost hope, they also lost all respect for law and order. When a business owner died his store and everything it contained became a tempting target, and it quickly became impossible for Simms to prevent the looting. Besides, there really didn't seem to be much point in it. Most of the victims died without a last will and testament, and in most cases the sheriff had no idea if they had any next of kin.

The army had more luck protecting the prospectors' claims outside of Leadville. Colonel Bainbridge made every effort to stop claim-jumping. Simms found it incredible that some men would be so consumed by their lust for gold that they'd risk exposure to typhoid.

By the third week Simms had given up patrolling the town, and spent most of his time in the jail. Ethan was his only prisoner, and the sheriff would have liked it if the man in the strap-iron cell been inclined to talk, or play cards. But Ethan acted as though he wasn't even aware of the lawman's existence. He never responded when spoken to. He was lost in his own little world of grief and bitterness. Simms half-expected to come in one morning and find that Ethan had hanged himself, using the thin blanket on his bunk or a trouser leg. But that didn't happen.

So all Simms had left to do was while away the time at his desk, drinking whiskey. He made sure that he and Ethan ate only what he cooked himself on the potbelly stove. Beyond that it was just a matter of waiting for Death to come calling.

But it was Colonel Bainbridge who came calling instead, at the end of the sixth week, with word that, in his opinion, the epidemic had run its course. The gravediggers had been idle for seven days. They needed the rest, having dug one hundred and seventy-seven graves. Simms calculated that one out of every four inhabitants of Leadville had died. Bainbridge assured him that it could have been worse.

In the days to come, Leadville came to look very much like a ghost town. Once the army lifted the siege, many people wasted no time in leaving. Some had lost a loved one and could not bear to stay. Others feared the typhoid would return. Still others thought the town was jinxed. For a while the sheriff's main concern was arson—someone was burning down the buildings in which typhoid had claimed one or more lives. Thanks to a volunteer fire brigade, these fires did not result in a conflagration that could have consumed the entire town. And though Simms was never able to catch the man or men responsible, the arson soon came to an end.

It was in the seventh week of Ethan's incarceration that Sheriff Simms got the surprise of his life. When he brought supper to his prisoner, the latter spoke.

"When are you going to let me out of here?" asked Ethan.

"That depends on what your plans are."

"Plans?" Ethan shook his head. "I don't have any. What does it matter?"

"It matters," said Simms sternly. "I can't have you going around shooting people just because Julie died and you're angry at the whole world."

"Fine. I won't shoot anybody. Just let me out of here."

"On one condition."

"Okay."

"You leave Leadville. Today. And you don't come back. If I catch you in town after sundown I'll shoot you like I would a mad dog. It won't be a fair fight, either. Because I wouldn't stand a chance against you in a fair fight. No, I'll kill you any way I can. And I won't lose a wink of sleep over it, either."

"Fair enough," said Ethan. "There's nothing holding me here, anyway."

Simms went back into his office. He returned a few minutes

later with Ethan's gun-rig draped over a shoulder. All the
loops were empty, and Ethan figured the Colt in the holster
was empty, too. Simms was too old a hand to make foolish
mistakes.

The sheriff unlocked the cell door, tossed the rig to
Ethan, and stepped back, wary. He wasn't sure that Ethan
wouldn't hold his seven weeks of incarceration against him.
But Ethan made no hostile move. He strapped on the gunbelt
and didn't even check the Colt.

"Your horse is at the livery. If Peterson gives you any
trouble about paying the bill for it, just tell him to come to
me and I'll square things."

"Thanks."

Simms looked Ethan over. The man looked to have lost
twenty pounds. His gaunt cheeks were bearded now. And he
smelled bad.

"You look like hell," said the sheriff.

Ethan didn't say anything, and walked into the office,
with Simms following.

"Have any idea where you're going to go?" asked the
lawman. He had never particularly liked Ethan Payne, but he
was a compassionate man, and felt sorry for his former prisoner. He knew what Ethan was going through, as he'd been
through the same torment himself.

"No."

Simms nodded. Ethan's tone of voice made it plain that
he didn't care where he went. One place would be as bad, as
lonesome, as unrewarding as the next. In his many years
behind a badge Simms had seen men at the end of their rope.
Men who had come west seeking a new beginning, hoping
to make something of themselves, looking for a break or two
that they hadn't gotten back east. The West realized the
dreams of some men, and snubbed others. The latter usually
ended up dying violently, prodded by disappointment and
bitterness into lawless acts. Watching Ethan, Simms predicted that this would be Payne's fate as well.

"Wherever you end up," said the sheriff, "I hope it works
out for you."

"Thanks." It occurred to Ethan that maybe he'd made a mistake where the lawman was concerned. Simms had tried to befriend him, and he'd refused the proffer. Then he reminded himself that, in the past, his friends had either died or betrayed his trust. So a man was better off without friends. He hadn't made a mistake, after all.

He left the jail. The sun was shining, but it had no heat— there was snow on the ground and the cold north wind was, as usual, gusting down from the high reaches. The streets of Leadville were quiet; only a few civilians and an army detail were visible. Ethan walked to the nearby livery and retrieved his mountain mustang. The livery owner didn't give him any trouble.

Riding out of town, he considered swinging by the cemetery to pay his last respects to Julie. But he couldn't bring himself to do it. He didn't want to see her grave. He told himself that she wasn't there—that just the empty shell of what had been Julie Payne was buried there, and that Julie herself was gone. He'd heard people say that when loved ones died they weren't really gone, as long as you held them in your heart. Ethan had tried to hold Julie there, but he couldn't feel her presence. All he felt was an aching loneliness, and a weariness that made him indifferent to life and everything it might hold in store for him.

He headed north. There was no reason for it other than that he knew there were fewer settlements in that direction. Fewer people. He kept to the high country for the same reason. In his saddlebags were a dozen shells for his rifle, so he was able to hunt for food—only a rabbit and a marmot the first week, but then, luckily, a mule deer. He found a draw sheltered from the raw north wind and made a lean-to, and lost track of the time he spent just sitting there eating venison and drinking melted snow and watching the winter run its course through a seemingly endless succession of bitter gray days. He was in no hurry to move on. He had no specific destination in mind. His life had been boiled down to a very simple essence now; all he had to do was make it through a finite number of days—and nights, which were worse than the days—and then Death would come for him, just like it had come for Julie and Clooney and Doc Bingham. At least when that happened the pain and loneliness would go away. That was something to look forward to.

Later, thinking back to that time, Ethan would conclude that he spent more than six weeks up in the mountains, scarcely stirring except when it was necessary to go out and shoot something to eat. He did not venture far from the lean-to until there was visible evidence that winter was on the wane. The days were sunnier, and getting warmer, and the snow had not fallen for a fortnight. The streams, previously iced over, were running free again, tumbling vigorously down the rocky slopes, fed by the melting snow. And as the snow melted it exposed the new grass, while the trees, freed from winter's frigid grasp, began to bud. Ethan began to think about leaving. With spring would come more people into the high country, and he was not that far removed from Leadville. The typhoid epidemic would be old news by now, and it certainly would not be sufficient to keep the gold seekers away for long. But he wasn't truly motivated to make an effort until he heard, one morning, way off in the distance, the distinctive sound of an axe biting into timber. He never saw the person making that noise. He didn't need to. That same day he was mounted and headed north once more.

PART TWO

6

Two months later, Ethan Payne rode into the town of Medicine Bow in the Wyoming Territory. He was hungry, broke, and cold. A knifing winter wind made every bone in his body ache. Winter wasn't over at this latitude, not by a long shot. A heavy layer of snow carpeted the valley bracketed by the Laramie and Medicine Bow mountain ranges. Ethan had daubed tobacco juice under his eyes to prevent snow blindness. But there was nothing he could do about the knot in his belly or the pain in his joints.

Medicine Bow was a collection of a dozen clapboard buildings lining a muddy street—not much for looks, but it seemed like the next best thing to paradise to Ethan, who hadn't seen any sign of human habitation in days. Woodsmoke curled out of chimneys. Ethan was willing to trade his saddle for a few hours in a chair pulled as close to a roaring fire as he could get it.

Several horses stood with their rumps to the wind at a hitching post in front of a two-story structure at the edge of town. A creaking sign identified the establishment as a general store. Ethan dismounted and tied the mountain mustang to the post. He noticed that the other horses carried a shamrock brand.

A crackling fire in a cast iron stove had turned the store's interior toasty warm. A young man in cowboy garb was slumped in a barrel chair, whittling on a stick; he'd pulled off his boots and was thawing his feet, which were encased in socks much in need of darning. His saddle partner was tilting his lanky frame against the dry goods counter, talking to a white-bearded man in a canvas apron who stood on the other side of the counter, leaning with arms folded against back shelves packed with a great variety of merchandise. A black and white spaniel lay near the stove, snorting as it chewed methodically on a flea-infested foreleg. All three men and the dog stopped what they were doing to look at Ethan as he closed the door against the howling wind.

"Howdy," said Ethan, nearly gasping at the unaccustomed warmth.

"Howdy right back at you, stranger," said the white-bearded man cheerfully. "What can I do for you?"

"I'd just like to stand next to your stove for a minute."

"Help yourself."

"Cold as a witch's tit, ain't it?" asked the lanky range rider.

"Plenty cold enough for me," said Ethan.

"Just passing through?" queried the storekeeper.

"Guess so."

"Where you headed?"

Ethan shrugged indifferently. Where was he going? Nowhere in particular. "Just yondering," he replied. "If I'd been smart, I'd have headed south this time of year."

The cowboy in the chair leaned forward. "Don't I know you?"

Ethan gave the young man a closer look, but didn't recognize him. "I don't think so."

"Sure I do. You're Ethan Payne. A couple years back you rode into the K-Bar camp outside of Abilene and chewed the breeze with John McKittrick."

"You rode for McKittrick?"

The cowboy nodded. "After he sold that herd, I came up here. Slim, over yonder, had come up a couple years before with Seamus Blake. He and I go back a ways. He helped get me a job. So now I ride for the Shamrock brand, same as he does. Not that I had anything against Mr. McKittrick. Good man to work for. I just wanted to have a look at this north country. Long way from Texas, but otherwise it suits me fine."

"Ethan Payne," said the storekeeper. "Where have I heard that name?"

"He faced down a wild cowboy crowd all by his lonesome," said the cowboy in the chair. "They wanted to bust one of their own, Tell Jenkins, out of the Abilene jail. Jenkins was a Texan, and that counted for something, but when he killed Happy Jack Crawford he lost my vote. Suited me that McKittrick walked wide around that business."

"How come you ain't marshal in Abilene no more?" asked Slim.

"Personal reasons," replied Ethan. "It was time to move on."

"Time for us to move along, too," said Slim. "Billy, get your boots on and let's amble over to see if Rose is open for business."

When the Shamrock cowboys were gone, Ethan fired a questioning look at the storekeeper. "Who is Rose?"

The man chuckled. "Only whore within a hundred miles of here. You might say she's got a corner on the market. We had another one show up here about a year ago. She had a mind to move in on Rose's territory. That was the damnedest fight I ever saw, and I've seen plenty of dust-ups in my time." He shook his head, smiling at the memory. "Anyway, Rose got the best of her, and she hightailed it out of here."

Ethan didn't say anything. He pulled the chair recently vacated by the cowboy closer to the stove, pulled off his gloves, and held his hands close to the hot iron, hoping to soon get the feeling back in his fingers.

The shopkeeper wasn't deterred by his visitor's silence. "You a cowboy looking for work, by any chance?"

"I've been a lot of things, but never a cowboy."

"Too bad. We've got three spreads around Medicine Bow. There's Seamus Blake's Shamrock, Tom Chappell's ranch, and the Western Crown. All the cowboys who work for those outfits are in love with Rose Felder because there's no one else to fall in love with." He came around the counter and stuck out his hand. "My name's Brown. Chester Brown. I'm pleased to meet you, Mr. Payne."

"Likewise."

"If you're looking for a place to sleep and a good home-cooked meal, you might try the Sellers house at the other end of town."

"I don't have two bits to my name, Mr. Brown."

"I see." Brown pursed his lips. "Well, Martha Sellers is a kind-hearted woman. Her dining room's the only restaurant in Medicine Bow, and she has a couple of rooms she lets out. You see, her husband's away a lot. He's a mustanger. Catches wild horses, breaks 'em, and sells 'em to the army. He doesn't make a very good living at it, though, and Martha has to make a little extra on the side just to get by."

"Well, like I said—"

"I know. But she won't turn you away, mister, I can promise you that. With Frank gone all the time, she sometimes needs help around the house. If you're not too proud, maybe you could strike a deal with her."

"I'm too cold and hungry to be proud."

Brown nodded. "There you go." He gave Ethan a long look. "So you were a lawman in Abilene. That must have been pretty dangerous work at times."

Ethan wasn't inclined to talk about Abilene, or any other part of his past, for that matter. But the shopkeeper had shown him a kindness by suggesting he see Martha Sellers, so he decided it wouldn't kill him to respond. He figured Chester Brown was the kind of man who took delight in hearing a story.

"It had its moments," he replied.

"You really faced down an entire cow outfit all by yourself?"

"I didn't need any help. I just rigged the jail with dynamite. Those Texas boys had no choice but to back down when they found that out. Because I would have blown us all to kingdom come."

Chester Brown let out a low whistle. "Now that's what I call upping the ante. It takes a hard man to tame a trail town. Guess you must be pretty handy with that hogleg, then."

"I'm no gunslinger, if that's what you're worried about."

"Not worried," said Brown hastily. "No, sir. Not worried at all. So you don't have a place you call home?"

"No."

"I did my share of yondering when I was younger," said the shopkeeper. "I've been to San Francisco, Santa Fe, and New Orleans. Finally, though, I decided it was time to put down roots. So I found me a good woman and married her and . . ."

He saw the expression on Ethan's face and never finished the sentence.

"You want some coffee, Mr. Payne? If so, just help yourself to that pot on top of the stove. I made it this morning so it should be strong enough to suit you."

"Obliged." Ethan stood up, took one of several tin cups that hung on nails in the wall behind the stove, and poured himself some java. He drank it standing at the front window of the store, watching the one and only street in Medicine Bow. That put his back to Chester Brown. The shopkeeper knew he'd touched a raw nerve with his talk of being married to a good woman, so he took the hint and kept his mouth shut, busying himself with rearranging canned goods on a shelf.

Ethan stood at the window for such a long time that Chester Brown began to think that there was something wrong with him, and he began to worry. There was an aura around the stranger, an aura of death and misery, that was as cold as the winter wind howling down out of the high country. The shopkeeper could feel it now that the conversation had lapsed, and it made him uncomfortable. So he was very relieved when Ethan finished the coffee, which by now had cooled, placed the empty cup on the chair, and nodded at Brown.

"Thanks," he said.

"It was my pleasure," lied Chester Brown.

He'd never been so happy to see a person leave.

Ethan walked his horse to the other end of Medicine Bow's only street. The Sellers house was another two-story clapboard with a porch on three sides and a smokehouse and several sheds out back. The only tree for miles around, a big old elm, stood beside the house, its limbs weighed down with snow and ice. He tread carefully on the slick porch, avoiding several rotting planks, and knocked on the door.

The woman who answered was in her thirties, but hard years on the frontier had aged her, and she looked older than that. Her yellow hair, fast turning gray, was pulled back in a severe bun. The years had etched deep lines around her eyes and mouth. Once she had been a looker, but that had been long ago, in better days. Life's disappointments, coupled with the perils and hardships of life on the frontier, had taken their toll.

Ethan explained his situation. "I don't want charity, ma'am," he said. "I'll work for my room and board. And I won't stay long. Just a day or two."

"You're welcome, of course," said Martha Sellers, without hesitation. Like Chester Brown, she could sense the aura of danger and death around the stranger. But she had the capacity to look deeper. And she saw a fellow sufferer. "This weather's not fit for man nor beast. You can put your mare in the shed with my cow. Then come in and have something to eat."

"Obliged."

One of the sheds was divided into two stalls. A milch cow stood in one, and Ethan put his horse in the other, stripped it of his gear, and gave it some grain in a feedbag. He carried his possibles back to the house. Martha Sellers had some beef stew and cornbread waiting for him. Sitting at a kitchen table, he wolfed the fare down and drank a cup of steaming hot coffee. She left him alone to eat, and came back when he was done.

"Your room is ready," she told him. "Door on the left at the top of the stairs. Did you get enough to eat?"

"Yes, ma'am. Best meal I've had in a very long time."

She smiled. "Yes, I can tell by looking at you that you've missed a good many meals. The fare here is plain, but I can't afford better. Now and then the cowboys bring me a side of

beef. They come here to eat when they're in Medicine Bow."
She gave him an appraising look. "You're no cowboy, are
you, Mr. Payne? What do you do for a living?"

"Nothing. I'm just a drifter."

"You have no home?"

"I haven't had a place to call home for over twenty
years."

"I'm so sorry. Well, you make yourself at home under
this roof, you hear? I'm glad for the company."

"There must be some work I can do around the place."

"Tomorrow you can start on the porch. Someone's going
to break a leg if it isn't repaired. My husband is seldom
home, and when he is he isn't much for fixing things. The
sheds need some shoring up, too. And I'll be needing some
firewood soon. Lee Campbell hauls wood into town and
sells it. You have to go a ways from here to find timber. But
it would save me money if you could cut and haul some, so I
wouldn't have to pay Lee. I don't have a wagon, though, for
the hauling."

"That's no problem. I'll cut enough wood to last you the
rest of the winter."

Her smile was wistful. "We have real long winters up
here, Mr. Payne."

7

That night, Ethan slept better than he had in weeks, and awoke the next morning to the alluring aroma of bacon, eggs, and biscuits cooking. After breakfast he set right to work on the porch, tearing up the rotting boards and replacing them with rough-hewn planking that was stored in one of the sheds. This he trimmed and cut to fit and nailed into place. Not since his youth had he done such work. Back then, on the Illinois farm, he hadn't much cared for it, longing instead for fortune and adventure on the frontier. Now he found the work to his liking. Martha brought him coffee, surveyed his handiwork, and was pleased.

"I see you're handy with a hammer and saw," she said, by way of a compliment. "With that, too, I'll warrant." She glanced at the bulge of the holstered Remington under his coat.

"I've gotten into the habit of wearing it all the time. Sorry."

"Don't need to be. I'm used to having guns around. My father was an officer in the army. He was killed in the Mexican War. Battle of Buena Vista. My husband, Frank, used to scout for the cavalry. That's how we met, at Fort Leavenworth. That was right after I got the news about my father. Frank and I got married soon after."

"You must have been very young."

"Sixteen. Young and foolish, I suppose. That was my

mother's opinion, at least. She wanted me to come live with her back East. But I didn't want to." She looked out across the snow-covered plains. "Some folks complain about the loneliness of the prairie. But I know that you can be just as lonely surrounded by thousands of people. Cities don't suit me. They're too crowded, too mean, too ugly for my liking."

Ethan followed her gaze, then let his eyes pass over the plains to the craggy, cloud-wreathed mountains in the distance. He rolled a smoke. A gray overcast blotted out the sun, and it was bitterly cold. The ramshackle little town and the wind-swept vastness of the country made it seem somehow colder still.

"Even so," she said, "I get lonely out here sometimes, with Frank gone most of the time."

"No children?"

"Dead." She didn't elaborate, the subject was too painful. "Have you ever been married, Mr. Payne?"

He nodded, and the memory of Julie made him wince. "She died."

She touched his arm. "I'm so sorry. But you know, I've learned that it's much better to concentrate on the happy times we had when our loved ones were with us, rather than the sad times we've had since they left. Come inside and warm yourself. I'll fetch your dinner."

The next morning, taking an axe and some rope, he rode out of Medicine Bow. Martha Sellers had told him to ride due west about six miles. There he would find timber. He worked hard all day, pausing only once to eat the cold beef and biscuits she had prepared for him. Late that afternoon he felled several saplings and lashed them together with the rope, making a travois on which he piled and tied the firewood. He'd cut more than he could transport in one trip, and went back the following morning to get the rest. Rather than drag the first travois all the way back to the woods, he cut more saplings and was lashing them together to make a second travois when he heard cattle bawling. A lone rider pushing four steers checked his horse a hundred yards back in the trees and peered at Ethan. He sat his saddle for a moment, watching, and then spurred his horse onward to turn the cattle, who were heading straight for the spot where Ethan worked. This brought him close enough to Ethan to warrant an exchange of greetings. With the cattle turned, the man again checked his horse and nodded gravely.

"Mornin' to you."

The man's wariness in turn made Ethan cautious. He nodded back. "Morning." The rider had a dark beard, lank brown shoulder-length hair, and a prominent scar above his left eyebrow. He wore a ragged gray longcoat and Kossuth hat. Ethan thought he looked more like a road agent than a cowboy.

No other words passed between them. The man moved on in pursuit of the four steers.

Ethan had noticed that the cattle wore the Shamrock brand. But the man's horse was unbranded. Maybe that didn't mean anything. And even if it did, it was certainly none of his business.

When he got back to Medicine Bow early that afternoon, he found one of the cowboys he'd met at the general store a few days ago—the one called Slim—waiting for him in Martha Sellers' kitchen, nursing a cup of coffee.

"Mr. Payne," said the Shamrock hand, "my boss would like to talk to you."

"What about?"

"Can't rightly say."

But he knows, mused Ethan. "Look," he said, "I'm just passing through. I don't see that I've got any business with Seamus Blake."

"He wants to offer you a job, I reckon."

"I'm not a cowboy."

"I don't think that kind of job is what Mr. Blake has in mind. I can't say any more, except that he wants to see you." Slim glanced at Martha Sellers. "Generally, what the boss wants, he gets."

Ethan looked at Martha, too. She nodded.

"Okay," he said. Perhaps it was wiser not to offend a man like Blake. What could it hurt to hear what he had to say?

* * *

An hour's ride north of Medicine Bow, Ethan and Slim reached the top of a swell in the gently rolling plains and came within sight of a clapboard Victorian mansion standing alone in the middle of nowhere. It was the last thing Ethan had expected to see in this country, and he checked his horse to stare in surprise. Slim smiled knowingly.

"An eyeful, ain't it?"

"Seamus Blake lives there?"

Slim shook his head. "That's the Sweetwater Land & Cattle Company's social club."

"Say what?"

"Mr. Blake built it, along with Tom Chappell. They make up the Sweetwater Company. Neither one of them lives here. The Shamrock Ranch is about ten miles north of us, and Mr. Chappell's place is more than twenty miles to the east. Together they own just about all the land hereabouts."

"Then what's it for?" asked Ethan.

"The house yonder?" Slim shrugged. "Can't say as I'm real sure."

They rode down to the house. Two horses, one of them wearing the Shamrock brand, were tethered to iron tie rails in front of the porch. Hitching their own ponies, Ethan and Slim were met at the door by a broad-beamed matron with iron-gray hair and a ready smile. Slim introduced her as Mrs. Riegel. The cowboy explained that she and her husband, German immigrants, stayed at the social club and maintained the place.

"Vill you come in, please?" She gestured for Ethan to enter, and he stepped over the threshold into a wide entrance hall adorned with gilt-framed mirrors, potted plants, and ornate mahogany furniture. Through a door to his right he glimpsed a long, gleaming dining table supported by three pedestals and encircled by more than two dozen upholstered chairs. A crystal chandelier hung from the ceiling, and the walls were covered with Japanese paper.

After Mrs. Riegel had relieved him of hat and coat, Ethan

was ushered through a pair of doors on his left, into a spacious parlor. Plush blue and yellow rugs covered the hardwood floor. A fire crackled cheerily in a huge fireplace decorated with blue and yellow tiles. Velveteen draperies covered the windows. A grand piano stood in one corner of the room. The furniture was the most splendid Ethan had ever seen. He couldn't even imagine how much it had cost to furnish this house with so many fine pieces. The cost of transporting it all undoubtedly had been more money than he would see in a lifetime.

Slim did not follow him into the parlor. Mrs. Riegel softly shut the door behind him. There were two other men in the room. One was pouring himself a drink from one of an array of decanters on a sideboard. The other was sprawled on a mohair sofa big enough to accommodate six people with room to spare. This one leaped to his feet and strode toward Ethan, while the other man turned from the sideboard with drink in hand.

"I'm Tom Chappell," said the man who approached Ethan with a big smile and hand outstretched. He was burly and weathered, with a broad, sun-darkened face. "Welcome, Mr. Payne. Mighty glad you could come."

"Seemed like the thing to do."

"Sure it did. That ugly Irishman yonder, presiding over the liquid refreshments, is Seamus Blake."

"Drink, Mr. Payne?" queried Blake, a solid, ruddy-faced individual. His brogue was scarcely noticeable. He wore a tweed jacket and buckram trousers stuffed into tall riding boots. "Name your poison. Rye, bourbon, gin? We've also got Napoleon brandy, English ale, a selection of wines. Claret, burgundy, or port?"

"Bourbon will do."

"Have a seat, Mr. Payne," said Chappell, and escorted him to a chair. As he waited for his drink, Ethan glanced at the reading material on a nearby table. *Harper's,* the *New York Tribune,* the *Atlantic Monthly,* all of fairly recent vintage. It couldn't have been easy, he mused, to get these publications out here on the Wyoming frontier, hundreds of miles from the nearest town of any consequence, on anything like a timely basis.

Blake delivered the drink to Ethan and took another chair, while Chappell resumed his place on the sofa. The latter was smiling amiably, but Blake was very serious. He peered at Ethan as though he could see right through to his soul.

"You must be wondering why we asked you here today," said Blake. "But first, perhaps you'd like to know a little bit about us.

"Tom and I believe that, in time, Wyoming Territory will dominate the cattle industry. That's why we both set up shop here. We moved lock, stock, and barrel from Texas several years ago. Our spreads together cover nearly five hundred square miles. We've got maybe twenty-five, thirty thousand head of cattle. Federal land laws do not provide for the needs of cattlemen like us, Mr. Payne. So what we do is control the public domain. We exercise range rights by filing preemption claims on the water sources."

"Without access to water the land is worthless," said Chappell. "It's all perfectly legal."

"Isn't there another spread hereabouts?" asked Ethan.

Blake nodded. "The Western Crown. Owned by British investors. In the last ten years or so an epidemic of anthrax has caused beef prices to soar in Britain. A royal commission concluded that the average profit of an American cattleman is thirty-three percent a year. I think that's a little high, but the British money men listened, and decided to buy into the market."

"Western Crown beef are shipped by rail to Chicago," said Chappell, "then up the Great Lakes and the St. Lawrence and across the Atlantic."

"They transport cattle from Wyoming Territory to Great Britain?" asked Ethan. He'd had no idea that such an enterprise had been undertaken.

"They make two or three times the profit per head that we do selling to eastern slaughterhouses," said Blake, sourly.

"Is the Western Crown part of the Sweetwater Land & Cattle Company?"

"No, but there'll be other cattlemen moving in soon," replied Blake.

Ethan sipped his bourbon, thinking ahead. "And when they do, you'll get them to join the company, which will become a power to be reckoned with in the Territory."

"You've got to plan for the future," said Blake. "Before long, once the Indian problem is taken care of, the homesteaders will start moving in."

"But we'll be in control," said Chappell confidently. He glanced over at Blake, and in that glance Ethan could detect subordination. Blake and Chappell were both cattle barons, and they were both partners in the Sweetwater Cattle Company, but clearly Seamus Blake was the senior partner, to whom Tom Chappell deferred.

"At the moment, however," said Blake, "homesteaders aren't the problem. Rustlers are. We've got a plague of night riders running irons in this valley. They're selling hundreds of our beeves to army quartermasters to feed the garrisons of the Bozeman Trail forts."

"Then why don't you go to the law?"

Blake and Chappell exchanged glances. The latter looked amused. Blake's expression was still grave, and Ethan had a hunch that this was a man who found nothing particularly amusing.

"There's a federal marshal," said Blake, causticly. "I've never seen him. We make our own law up here. Which is why we want to hire you, Mr. Payne."

"Hire me? For what?"

"Range detective for the Sweetwater Company."

"Why me?"

"Who better to get the job done? You were once a troubleshooter for the Overland Mail, weren't you? And then you did a stint as town marshal of Abilene, Texas. You've got the qualifications."

In other words, mused Ethan, *I have a reputation as a killer of men and that's just what these two are looking for.*

"You're just the man we've been looking for," said Chappell.

"You showing up in Medicine Bow like you did, that was a Godsend."

"Or just luck." Whether that would be good luck or bad, Ethan wasn't quite sure.

"I don't believe in luck," said Blake briskly. "Your reputation precedes you. When the word gets out that Ethan Payne is working for the Sweetwater Land & Cattle Company, I expect half the rustlers will haul freight."

"What about the other half?"

"They'll be your responsibility."

Ethan finished his bourbon. Chappell got up, took Ethan's glass to the sideboard, and refilled it.

"I think I might have seen one of your rustlers this morning," said Ethan.

Blake leaned forward. "Where?"

"The woods west of Medicine Bow. A man was pushing four head of Shamrock cattle. He was headed south. Somehow I don't think he was on your payroll, Mr. Blake."

"Bastards are bold as brass," said Chappell angrily, handing Ethan his second shot and sprawling into his chair with a disgusted sigh.

"Four steers, you say?" asked Blake. "Damn it all."

Ethan wondered why a man who owned tens of thousands of cattle would be so upset by the loss of four head, or even four hundred. Blake seemed to read his mind.

"Right now it's just an annoyance, but if something isn't done we'll soon have an epidemic on our hands. Word gets around. We've got maybe ten rustlers in the valley this year. Next year it might be fifty. And make no mistake, Mr. Payne. These are dangerous and desperate characters. They killed one of my line riders a few months ago. Ordinary cowboys are no match for such men. We need a professional man-hunter. So what do you say?"

"How much does this job pay?"

"Two hundred dollars a month. If you have to kill a man, we'll pay you an extra hundred dollars. Bring him in belly down over his saddle and I'll pay you, no questions asked."

It was good money, twice what Ethan had made in monthly wages as Abilene's peace officer.

"We're not saying you're a bounty hunter, or anything like that," Chappell hastened to add.

"Certainly not," concurred Blake. "But you may have to shoot one or two of the sons of bitches. That will probably do the trick. I figure the rest would make for the tall timber after that. And if you put your life on the line for my benefit, I think I owe you a bonus, that's all."

"You gentlemen have a high opinion of me," said Ethan. "Maybe too high. Maybe you don't know why I got fired by Ben Holladay. Or why I'm no longer marshal of Abilene. Maybe you should know these things before you put your trust in me."

"The kind of man you are is not all that important," replied Blake bluntly. "Fact is, your reputation is what I'm buying. That, and your expertise with that Colt revolver you're packing. I'm not looking for a saint, and I don't care if you're a sinner."

Ethan nodded. "I'll want a day or two to think it over."

That wasn't what Blake wanted to hear. "That's not satisfactory," he replied, exasperated. "I want to have your answer now, if you don't mind."

Ethan knew it wasn't really a request. He mulled over the offer. Two hundred dollars a month was a lot of money, especially when you were stone broke. The job wasn't altogether unattractive. He would work alone, and he'd be his own boss, with no one looking over his shoulder, the way the town fathers had in Abilene, or Holladay and his division agents had done on the Overland. The bad part of it was that he might be put in a position where he would have to kill someone. Blake and Chappell thought he was a cold-blooded killer. That was his reputation. But reputations were often built on myth, not fact. In all his years as badge toter and troubleshooter he'd only killed ten men, all of them in self defense. But then maybe these cattle barons were right— maybe once word got out that he was working for the Sweetwater Company most of the rustlers would clear out.

Besides, he felt as though he had the experience to handle any potentially lethal situation in such a way that killing wouldn't be called for.

And if he didn't take the offer—what were his prospects? He could stay with Martha Sellers for a while, doing odd jobs around her place, but sooner rather than later he would have to move on, because the time would come when he'd have done everything she needed a handyman to do, and he wasn't so bad off that he'd take charity in the form of free room and board. And when he left Medicine Bow, where would he go? His pockets would be as empty as they were now.

"Okay," he said. "I'll give it a try. One thing, though. I need to meet all your hands. I want to know them by sight, in case they cross my path out there in the big lonesome."

"Good idea. We'll take a further precaution. Tom and I will have every man who rides for us wear a red bandanna around his arm."

"That might work for a while, until the rustlers get wind of it. Then every pilgrim in Wyoming will be wearing a red bandanna. Best way is for me to know their faces. Unless you think one or two of them might be in business for themselves."

Blake's eyes were as cold as the wind humming against the windows. "I sure as hell hope not." He glanced at Tom Chappell, who shook his head. "If that turns out to be the case, though," added Blake, "the bonus goes up to two hundred."

"Any ideas where I might start looking?"

"We think there's only one outfit," said Chappell. "But we're not absolutely sure. And we have no idea where their base camp might be. Sorry. This is a mighty big country."

"You might want to take a long look at Frank Sellers," suggested Blake.

"Seamus, there's no proof," protested Chappell.

"Martha Sellers's husband?" asked Ethan. "I heard he was a mustanger."

"I've heard a lot of things about Frank Sellers," said Blake sourly, "and none of them are good."

Ethan grimaced, and finished off his second shot of

bourbon. It figured that Fate would throw him a joker like that. Such was usually the case—just when he began to think he was starting to get ahead, things would turn sour. He liked Martha Sellers, so he hoped that Blake's suspicions about her husband were unfounded. But the way his luck had been running, it probably wouldn't play out that way. He had an urge to back out of the deal; all of a sudden he had this feeling that if he stayed, and went to work for these men, that he'd regret it the rest of his days. But two hundred dollars a month . . . he had so many regrets, what was one more?

"All right," he said. "I'll take care of your problem, no matter who it is."

8

Blake and Chappell told Ethan that they would make the social club of the Sweetwater Land & Cattle Company available to him as a base of operations. The Riegels, the club's immigrant German steward and cook, would be at his disposal. The arrangement held no appeal for Ethan.

"If it's all the same to you," he told them, "I'll stay in Medicine Bow for a few days, at least. I'm boarding with Martha Sellers. If your hunch is right about her husband, that puts me in a good position to smoke out the truth."

"The people in town must have seen you leave with one of my hands," Blake reminded him.

"That can be explained away."

Blake shrugged. It was apparent that he didn't really care how Ethan went about doing the job, just as long as he got it done.

"When you're ready to head out after the night riders, swing by my place first," he told Ethan. "I'll make sure you have all the supplies you need."

Ethan said he would do that. Blake paid him a month's wages in advance. It was more money than Ethan had seen all at once in a very long time. He peeled off a few banknotes and handed the rest back to the Scotsman.

"Hold on to this for me. I'll pick it up when I need it."

They shook hands, and a moment later Ethan was riding

away from the big Victorian house. He made the return trip alone; Slim stayed behind.

He wasn't sure that staying at the Sellers place was the right thing to do. If indeed there proved to be any substance to Blake's suspicions regarding her husband, he'd be imposing on her hospitality and worse. On the other hand, he figured he might learn more about the rustling operation if folks hereabouts didn't know he was employed by the Sweetwater Company. He wasn't sure how long he could keep that a secret, but if he abruptly left the Sellers house after being seen riding away with one of Blake's cowhands, he doubted it would be a secret for very long.

He arrived back in Medicine Bow after dark. Martha Sellers had already had her supper, but she'd kept the stew and biscuits warm, and insisted that he sit down at the kitchen table and eat before he turned in. She sat across from him, knitting by the light of a kerosene lamp. He watched her nimble, work-callused fingers while he ate. She glanced at him a time or two, and he could sense that she was curious about his day. But she had been on the frontier too long to let her curiosity get the better of her, and she didn't ask him. Ethan had hoped she would; he'd already planned out the lie he would tell. As things stood, he had to broach the subject himself.

"What do you think of Seamus Blake?" he asked, after he'd finished eating and was nursing a cup of strong fresh coffee.

"I don't think about him much at all, frankly," she said, with an edge to her voice that told him otherwise. "Why do you ask?"

"He offered me a job. I met that cowboy, Slim, the day I rode in here. He mentioned me to his boss, who sent him back to fetch me."

"I wouldn't think Mr. Blake would have to go to all that trouble to hire an extra hand. Most men who pass through here looking for work find their way to the Shamrock ranch without having to be summoned."

He smiled. "He'd heard of me. Wanted to hire me to ride the line. Said there was some rustling trouble lately."

She put down her work and folded her hands together on the table in front of her and looked him squarely in the eye. "Heard of you? Why would he have heard of you, Mr. Payne?"

"I used to work for the Overland as a troubleshooter. And I wore a badge in Abilene for a while, too. I guess I have something of a reputation following me around."

"I see. So Mr. Seamus Blake wanted a hired gun."

"That's right."

"And you said?"

"No thanks."

"How come? Don't you want a job?"

"Not that kind. Not anymore."

She nodded. "Good for you. Those who live by the gun die by it. So tell me. How did you wind up being an Overland troubleshooter?"

"It's a long story."

Martha Sellers rose and went to the stove to fetch the coffee pot. She refilled Ethan's cup and poured herself one. Then she sat down again.

"I have plenty of time," she said.

"Well, I'm not really sure where to begin."

"Begin at the beginning."

"I was born in Illinois. My mother died when I was young. It broke my father's heart, and he turned to drink. Then a friend of mine talked me into going to California with him. They'd found gold in the American River just the year before."

She nodded. "I was at Fort Leavenworth at the time of the gold rush. I saw many a gold hunter pass through on his way to California."

"I swore that after I struck it rich I'd go back to Illinois. You see, there was . . . there was a girl there. . . . "

Seeing him falter, she gently spurred him on. "And what was her name?"

"Lilah. Lilah Webster. We were going to get married. It just seemed like we were meant to be together. We always had been, ever since we were small. She said she didn't mind being a farmer's wife. But I minded. I wanted to be able to afford to give her nice things. To be rich enough so she didn't have to worry about making ends meet, or having to work just to keep food on the table. The way my mother had worked, and worried. That's why I went to California. Almost didn't make it. Ran into some trouble on a Mississippi riverboat. Then more trouble when we crossed the isthmus to the Pacific. But we finally made it, my friend and I. But we didn't strike it rich. I went to work for a mining outfit. My friend fell in with a bunch of road agents."

"Did you ever see him again?"

Ethan smiled ruefully. "I'm afraid so. He and his saddle partners were holding up the gold shipments the company I worked for was sending to San Francisco. They put me in charge of getting one of the shipments through. That's when we ran into each other again."

"Did you get the gold through?"

"Yes." Ethan paused, his melancholy thoughts drifting to Gil Stark, and he wondered what had become of his friend. One of the few real friends he'd ever had. Odds were that Gil had never stopped following the outlaw trail, which meant that in all likelihood he was dead by now. Just like everybody else Ethan had cared about.

"Then what happened?" asked Martha softly.

"The Overland heard about me, offered me a job. And I took it. I worked for them for several years. All in all, it wasn't a bad job. But I managed to muddy up my own water. Her name was Julie Cathcott. She was married to a man who operated one of the Overland stations. He was no-account, and one day he just up and left her. That's when I took up with her." He shook his head. "I often wonder how different everything might have turned out if I'd resisted the urge."

"Yes, well," said Martha, sipping her java, "thinking too much along those lines can drive a person crazy."

"Of course Cathcott came back one day. And when he found out about Julie and me, he tried to shoot me. I killed him. If I'd killed him because he was stealing from the company, the Overland wouldn't have cared. But I was the thief, in a way. And it just didn't sit well with Mr. Holladay, or the division agent. So they cut me loose. And I started drifting then."

"And ended up in Abilene."

"That's right. Just in time to see a cowboy by the name of Tell Jenkins gun down the town marshal in cold blood. I got the drop on Jenkins and put him in jail where he belonged. The town fathers hired me to wear the badge."

"Why did you do that? Step into that kind of trouble, I mean. Most men would have minded their own business."

Ethan smiled. "I'm not really sure. Anyway, there for a while I just tried to keep the lid on the town. And then Julie showed up again. She was in a bad way, and I figured it was mostly my fault. We got married. Don't get me wrong— I didn't marry her because I felt sorry for her, or felt guilty about what I'd done."

"Of course not," said Martha, ambiguously.

"Then some men came gunning for me. They'd been hired by a man I'd met many years earlier, on that riverboat I mentioned. He'd been a thief back then, and I'd helped catch him, and he held a grudge. The town fathers decided I was a liability. There was a good bit of gunplay, and since it didn't have anything to do with the cattle trade they weren't happy about it. To make a long story short, Julie and I pulled out of Abilene about two years ago. We ended up in a Colorado gold camp. And that's where she died. Of typhoid."

"And you wish you'd died there, too."

He looked at her, sitting there calm and composed, with that direct gaze, not judging him, and he was surprised at how easy it was for him to talk to her about these things. He'd never talked to anyone so frankly about his past.

"Yes, I did wish that. But I didn't die. And here I am." My next stop on the road to hell, he thought, bitterly.

They were silent a moment, drinking their coffee. Then she asked, "Whatever happened to the girl in Illinois?"

"The last I heard, she got married. I didn't go back because I hadn't struck it rich. Sounds stupid, now."

"Pride is an awfully powerful emotion. You thought you were a failure, and you didn't want to risk seeing in her eyes that she thought so, too."

"I guess that's true," admitted Ethan. "But I know now I wouldn't have seen that. Maybe I knew that a long time ago. My father had failed at living, you know, and I guess I just couldn't go home having done the same."

Martha nodded, smiling gently. Then she did something that surprised him—she reached across the table and put her hand over his.

"Don't give up hope. We get second chances. Even when we don't think we deserve them."

She got up and went to the stove and poured herself another cup of coffee. Ethan was moved, and didn't know what to say, so he kept silent.

"You asked me earlier what I thought of Seamus Blake," she said. "I think he's a greedy, ruthless man who, if he has his way, will own everything in this territory. He thinks it all belongs to him—the grass, the water, the animals, the people. Even the sky, I suppose, has his brand on it. Frank has had a run-in with his hands a time or two, chasing mustangs on what Blake claims to be Shamrock land. According to high-and-mighty Mr. Blake, even the wild horses that wander onto *his* land belong to him. Of course he doesn't actually hold title to the land. No, he only owns the water. But out here, whoever controls the water controls everything else. I'm glad you decided not to work for him. He probably offered you a lot of money, and perhaps you were tempted to take it. But believe me, Mr. Payne, when I tell you that you'd have lived to regret it had you decided to ride for the Shamrock brand."

She put down her cup and retrieved her knitting and thanked him for sharing his story with her. Then she left him there, and he listened to her weary tread on the stairs as she headed for her bedroom. *You'd have lived to regret it.* Yes, he thought, that was probably true.

9

The next day he continued to work around Martha Sellers's place as though nothing had happened the day before. His room here was small and Spartanly furnished, but it suited him much better than the Sweetwater mansion. That kind of luxury was alien to him, and he knew he would have felt uncomfortable there. It struck him as comical—an incongruous Victorian manor, maintained by a German couple who could barely speak English, stocked with French cognac and adorned with Japanese wallpaper, and all that out in the middle of the Wyoming Territory, a hundred miles from nowhere. He wondered why Seamus Blake had had it built. The Irishman didn't strike Ethan as the sort who would be obsessed with the trappings of wealth. No, it was power that Blake wanted. Maybe he thought it was important to the acquisition and maintenance of that power to impress the common folk.

Ethan had slept little the night of his conversation with Martha Sellers, troubled by second thoughts about taking the job as the Sweetwater Company's regulator. He knew it mostly had to do with the possibility that her husband might be one of the rustlers. But he decided to stick it out for a while. If he quit and moved on—and he would have to move on after backing out on Seamus Blake—then the cattlemen would just find some other hired gun to do their dirty work for them. Ethan had already made up his mind that if, in fact,

Frank Sellers was running irons, he would not kill the man, even though that was what Blake and Chappell would expect him to do. He wasn't sure how he would get around it, but he'd have to find a way. No matter what, he wouldn't leave Martha Sellers a widow.

Not that he intended to stay long. His mind was already made up on that score. A month or two, and then he would move on, and this time he'd at least have some money in his pocket. He'd still be a drifter, but at least he wouldn't be a penniless one. He couldn't drum up much enthusiasm for this job. It occurred to him that maybe he was past the point of being enthusiastic about much of anything. And he was a little tired of working for men like Seamus Blake. The Irishman was cut from the same cloth as Ben Holladay and Abilene honchos Colonel Ransom and Bill Langford. They had all come west to get rich—and they'd succeeded. Why, he wondered, did men like that succeed while he had failed? It seemed that all he was good for was to deal with anybody who jeopardized the profit margin of such men. He wasn't anything but a hired killer, cloaked in whatever authority money could buy.

He realized now what a fool he had been as a young man, scorning the farmer's life his father had led. As least a homesteader worked for himself, profiting from the sweat of his own brow and answering to no one, so long as he could pay the bank mortgage on time. Ethan had come west seeking his fortune, too blind to see that his fortune, and his future, already lay within his grasp. He had given up the farm and Lilah Webster—and for what? The phantoms of a foolish dream.

Still, he had a job to do, whether he was enthusiastic about it or not, and despite the fact that he had no idea where to start. To allay any suspicions the people of Medicine Bow—and, in particular, Martha Sellers—might have about his connection with the Sweetwater Company, he would linger in town for a couple of days. But eventually he would have to ride out to the Shamrock Ranch and met all of Seamus Blake's hands, then do the same thing with Tom Chappell's outfit. Next he'd have to made the rounds of the line shacks. That might take weeks, and it didn't strike him as a pleasant job, either, considering the weather.

As it turned out, though, he didn't have to wait long. At the end of each day he would head for Medicine Bow's one and only saloon for a drink. One evening, while he nursed a whiskey at the mahogany, he was approached by a grizzled cowboy named Williams, who introduced himself as one of the Shamrock's line riders.

"The boss said I was to come to town and talk to you," said Williams. "Told me not to go near the Sellers place, though. I been waitin' here for hours, hopin' you'd show up." He flashed a toothless grin. "But I ain't complainin', mind you. They don't water down their whiskey here."

Ethan nodded. Williams looked like he'd be an expert on such matters. "Why did Blake send you?"

"I seen sign of cattle being moved into The Breaks," said Williams. "That's some rough country due west of here. Most of the time it was just a few head. Never more than twenty. Now and again, in the middle of the night, if the wind was right, I could hear steers bawlin'. So they were movin' 'em at night."

"Did you ever follow that sign, to see where it led?"

"I did, once. But it goes way back up into The Breaks. Mr. Blake don't pay me enough to get myself kilt. So I didn't stray too far from home, if you know what I mean. The Breaks—that there's some mean country."

"You told Blake about this."

Williams nodded. "Sure I did. A week or so later, he was up at the line shack with a dozen men. We covered this whole area, looking for fresh sign. Funny thing about it is, we didn't find anymore. Whatever was going on, it just stopped. I reckon maybe having half the Shamrock crew prowling around in those parts put a stop to it."

Or, mused Ethan, the rustlers have a source of information among Blake's crew.

"How long ago did this happen?" he asked the waddy.

"Two months back, I guess. Just before the first snow."

"Nothing since?"

"Not a damned thing. But if them rustlers have got their-selves a base camp, my bet is it's somewhere in The Breaks. That's where I'd hang out if I was on the wrong side of the hangman's noose. A thousand good hiding places, and plenty of spots for a nice little bushwhacking, in case anybody is fool enough to come in there lookin' for you."

Ethan sighed. It figured that sooner or later he would have to head into The Breaks and risk a bushwhacking if he planned to produce any results for Blake.

"How many cattle wear the Shamrock brand?" he asked, motioning for the bartender to fill the cowboy's glass.

"Obliged," said Williams, pleased by Ethan's generosity. He downed the shot in one gulp and gasped, an expression of pure delight on his weathered face. "I don't rightly know the answer to your question, mister. Thousands."

"And how many cattle have been rustled?"

Williams shrugged. "I dunno about that, either."

"But as to the sign, the most you think the rustlers ever got off with was about twenty."

Williams peered at him suspiciously. "Just what are you trying to get at, anyway?"

"Just trying to figure out what kind of operation I'm up against. Sounds like a pretty small one."

"It don't matter to Mr. Blake that it's small, if it is. Two summers ago he caught some folk who'd killed one of his steers. They were farmin' folk, on their way to Oregon in a covered wagon, and they'd gotten separated from the others they were traveling with. The man told Mr. Blake that his wife had been sick, and his children had gone several days without any food, so when he'd seen the steer he'd shot it for meat."

Ethan had a feeling he knew how this story was going to end—and that he wasn't going to like it.

"Anyways," said Williams, looking morosely at his empty glass, "Mr. Blake heard him out without saying a word. If he was mad he didn't show it. And when the man was done, Mr. Blake, he just matter-of-fact like told the boys who were with him to shoot the man. They did, too. You do what Mr. Blake tells you if you know what's good for you."

"What happened to the woman and children?"

"Mr. Blake apologized to the widow for what he'd done, but told her it was necessary. It was the law of the open range, he said. He had some of the prime cuts of beef taken out of that steer and given to the woman. Then he had his boys escort her and her kids and the wagon until they were able to rejoin the folks they'd been traveling with."

Ethan bought the cowboy another shot, and thought that Seamus Blake sounded like the most cold-blooded man he'd ever known.

He learned from Williams that the line shack was the better part of a day's ride from Medicine Bow, and informed the Shamrock hand that he intended to ride out there the following day. Williams said he would stay the night in Medicine Bow and ride with him. That, he added with a crooked grin, would give him an opportunity to pay Rose a visit.

Ethan was up well before dawn, and slipped out of the Sellers house before Martha had awakened. He didn't want to have to lie about where he was going. It would be time enough to lie when he got back.

He and Williams made the uneventful ride out to the line shack. The sun was out, the wind had died down, and the day seemed to be a tad bit warmer than usual. Ethan shared the line shack with the old cowboy that night. Williams told him a few tales about his younger days, when he'd first come west with the American Fur Company to trap beaver, and how he'd tangled with Blackfoot Indians and spent one winter playing house with a pretty Absaroka gal. He played the harmonica and shared his beans and redeye with his guest. The next morning, they saddled up and rode west so that Williams could introduce him to The Breaks.

The country looked every bit as rough and dangerous as Ethan had been led to believe—a hundred square miles of rocky canyons and steep, inaccessible ridges cloaked with timber. From his vantage point atop a high, windswept table of land, Ethan could tell that Williams hadn't been exaggerating about The Breaks. They *did* offer any outlaw a thousand good hiding places, and as many good spots for a bushwhacking. He could understand why the Shamrock hand had been leery about venturing down there alone.

"I hope you ain't plannin' to ride down in there," said Williams. "If you are, you'd best tell me how to get in touch with your next of kin."

"I don't need a last will and testament," replied Ethan wryly. "I've got no family or friends. But I think I should go take a closer look."

"You ain't gonna ask me to go with you, are you?"

Ethan suppressed a smile. "If I did, would you?"

Williams rubbed his stubbled chin. "Well, I like you and all, Payne, but it would take an act of Congress—or an order from Mr. Blake—before I sashayed down into that country."

"Don't worry about it. I wasn't going to ask. I'll be back in a day or two."

"Maybe," said Williams, dubiously. He reached behind him and took a spyglass from the blanket roll tied to the back of his saddle. "Here. You might need this."

Ethan thanked him, and promised to return it in good condition. He could tell that the old cowboy wasn't expecting to see it—or him—again.

He returned to the line shack two days later. Williams was surprised to see him.

"You see anything?" asked the waddy.

"I saw some critters, but not the two-legged kind. Strikes me as odd, too. You're right—that's perfect country for night riders."

"Maybe you just missed 'em."

"I don't think so. I don't think the men I'm looking for are down there. Maybe they used to be. But not anymore."

"You don't? How come?"

"I think you scared them off, Will. I think they moved their base camp. And I'm pretty sure your boss doesn't believe they're around here anymore, either."

"What makes you say that?"

"He didn't bother to tell me about The Breaks. Which tells me he didn't think it was worth checking out. Besides, I think I saw one of the rustlers near Medicine Bow a few days ago. He was pushing four Shamrock steers—and he was heading south. Not in this direction."

Williams pushed his hat back and scratched his head in puzzlement. "South of Medicine Bow, you say? That's Western Crown range."

Ethan spent another night at the line shack listening to Williams talk fondly of past adventures. The next morning he thanked the old waddy and rode out still in possession of the spyglass, which Williams insisted he keep. Now, he thought, was as good a time as any to pay his visit to the Shamrock ranch and acquaint himself with Blake's other employees.

He arrived at the ranch—a sprawl of buildings alongside a creek winding its way through a narrow valley—early that same afternoon. There was a commotion in some horse pens behind the main house—it looked to be horse-breaking time. As he neared the house a young woman emerged onto the wide veranda. She was dressed for riding, and the jodhpurs she wore accentuated the flare of her hips below a narrow waist. There was a riding crop in her hand, and she wore calfskin gloves. She was pretty, with big brown eyes, a seductive mouth, and long chestnut-brown tresses. There was nothing demure about the way she looked Ethan over. Her gaze was bold and inquisitive.

"Are you looking for work?" she asked.

"No, I already have a job. I'm looking for Seamus Blake."

She gave a sideways nod, indicating the pens where the noise was coming from. "He's doing what he does best."

"What's that?"

"Breaking things," she replied. "I'm Kathleen, his daughter. Who are you?"

"Ethan Payne."

Recognition flashed in her eyes. "You're the new regulator.

He's talked about you. He said you were a dangerous man."
She cocked her head to one side and smiled. "Are you as
dangerous as they say?"

"I never have been as dangerous as they say."

A man came around the side of the house, leading two
horses. He was clad in cowboy garb, but he was obviously a
full-blooded Indian. Inscrutable, he looked at Ethan, and
then at Kathleen, and finally beyond them both. Ethan followed the direction of his gaze and saw that Seamus Blake,
covered with mud, was heading their way.

"Payne," he said, with a nod. "Did Williams come to see
you?"

"He did."

"Found anything yet?"

"Not yet. I came to meet your hands."

"Right." Peeling rawhide gloves off his hand, Blake
turned his attention to his daughter, and scowled. "Where
are you going?"

She uttered an exaggerated sigh, slapping the riding
crop into the palm of a gloved hand. "I'm going for a ride,
Father."

"I don't like it when you ride out alone."

"I'm not going out alone. I never do. The Indian is coming with me. You trust him to keep me safe, don't you?"

Blake looked at the Indian, and Ethan thought his features were as inscrutable as those of the other man.

"I suppose," he said. "But don't be gone long."

"Yes, Father."

Ethan thought there was more rebelliousness than obedi-
ence in Kathleen's tone, but to his surprise Seamus Blake
said nothing more on the subject, simply watched his daughter climb onto the back of one of the horses that the Indian
had brought. Before the Indian could mount up she was on
her way, urging the horse into a gallop with a liberal use of
the crop.

Blake looked with exasperation at Ethan, who could
sense that the cattleman didn't appreciate the fact that his

daughter's hardheadedness—and his inability to do anything about it—had been witnessed by a stranger.

"Where have you been?" he asked curtly. "My boys tell me you haven't been seen in Medicine Bow the last few days."

"You've got your boys spying on me, Mr. Blake?"

"Not exactly. But I like to know everything that goes on around here. Hardly a day goes by there isn't at least one Shamrock cowboy in Medicine Bow, and sometimes they drop by the Sellers house for a good home-cooked meal. She's glad to take their money, and I make sure they always pay."

"I've been in The Breaks."

"Because Williams thinks the rustlers are operating out of there."

"But they're not."

"You're sure about that."

"Aren't you?"

"I was pretty sure," admitted Blake. "But it was a good idea for you to check it out, all the same. Now what?"

"I'm going to do some looking around in the area where I saw that rider pushing four of your cattle. When I told Williams about it, he said that sounded like Western Crown range."

"Really." Blake's face was again an unreadable mask. "Well, come on. Most of the boys are over here."

He started walking back to the breaking pens. Ethan dismounted and followed him.

After getting a good look at the Shamrock cowboys—and letting them get a good look at him—Ethan rode back to Medicine Bow. He arrived a little after dark. Martha Sellers promptly answered his knock on the door.

"Ethan!" she exclaimed, with a smile. "Where have you been? I was starting to worry about you."

"I was lucky at poker a couple nights back. Collected some IOUs from a Shamrock line rider. I went out to collect my money."

"Well, I've got supper on the table. Come on in."

Once across the threshold, Ethan said, "If you don't mind, I'll go to my room and get a clean shirt on. I've been in the saddle for a long spell."

"Of course. But don't take too long. I want you to meet someone." Martha Sellers was beaming. "My husband, Frank. He just rode in a couple of hours ago."

10

Martha's husband wasn't too happy about having company, and was begrudging in his cordiality when his wife introduced Ethan. Ethan couldn't be sure—perhaps it was only his imagination—but he got the impression that Frank Sellers already knew who he was and what he was doing for Seamus Blake. That hardly seemed possible, and Ethan would have been willing to mark it down to paranoia on his part, but for the fact that Sellers kept eyeing him suspiciously.

He was a brawny, rough-cut man with a square jaw, steely eyes, and a nose that looked like it had been broken more than once. Here, decided Ethan, glancing at the scarred knuckles of Sellers' big hands, was a man it wouldn't do to tangle with in straight-up fisticuffs.

As they ate, Sellers seemed intent on saying as little as possible in front of the stranger at his dinner table. Martha, on the other hand, was interested in knowing what her husband had been doing in the weeks since they had last seen each other, and she was so persistent in her questioning that Sellers had to divulge some information.

He told her that he and his outfit had gone all the way down the North Fork of the Platte to the mouth of the Encampment River, in the valley that lay between the Sierra Madre to the west and the Medicine Bow Range to the east. They'd managed to round up nine mustangs—one stallion, the rest mares. It was getting harder and harder to find wild horses in this country, he complained.

"Where's your outfit?" asked Ethan, as though out of idle curiosity.

Sellers scowled at him. He clearly wanted to tell Ethan to mind his own business, but he couldn't be rude in the presence of his wife, especially since Ethan had given him no cause to be.

"We've got a camp about twenty-five miles southwest of here. We handle the horses for a spell before selling them to the army green-broke. Get more money for them that way."

Ethan nodded. "I've heard there's been some rustling going on in these parts. In your line of work you have to cover a lot of ground. Have you seen anything suspicious?"

"Why are you interested in rustlers?"

Ethan shrugged. "Just curious."

"Seamus Blake tried to hire him as a regulator," said Martha.

"Is that right," said Sellers.

"But he turned Blake down," she continued, with a smile aimed in Ethan's direction. "Honestly, I don't know how they're going to find a few rustlers in this great big country."

"Oh, they'll be found, eventually," predicted Ethan.

"What makes you think so?" asked Sellers.

"They've been having it all their own way for a while now. When that happens, men tend to get a little careless. So far, from what I've been told, they've just been taking a few head of cattle. But they'll also get greedy, since it's been so easy for them. Sooner or later they'll get in a real bind."

Sellers had a mouthful of steak and potatoes. He glared at Ethan while he chewed, swallowed, and then sneered, "You know, even if I had seen something I sure wouldn't be saying anything about it to anybody. Far as I'm concerned, whoever's running irons on Seamus Blake and that Chappell feller can keep doing it until Judgment Day. I'm certainly not going to help that son of a bitch Blake out."

"Frank!" exclaimed Martha. "I apologize for my husband's rudeness, Mr. Payne."

"Don't," snapped Sellers.

"Mr. Payne is our guest. You could at least try to be civil."

"I got a right to like who I please. And I don't like this feller. Not one bit. He's a hired gun. And I wouldn't be surprised if he really is working for Blake."

"He isn't. But even if he was, I'd still let him in the door," replied Martha, provoked. "The two Shamrock cowboys who sat at this very table last night work for Mr. Blake. Whoever Mr. Payne is, and whatever he does for a living, he's paying good money to eat at our table, just like they do. And since you never bring any money home with you, I have to make do as best I can."

Sellers just stared at her.

"I'd have thought you'd make decent money selling mustangs to the army," remarked Ethan. "They're always in need of remounts."

"Like I said, wild horses are hard to find, and harder to catch."

"Have you had any luck in The Breaks? That looks like prime mustang country to me."

Sellers nodded. "There are some wild ones in there, true enough."

"Some folks think that's where the rustlers are holed up."

"Could be. Somebody took a potshot at me down in The Breaks not too long ago."

"Frank!" gasped Martha. "You didn't mention anything about that to me."

Sellers shrugged. "Not important. As you can see, the bastard missed."

"When did this happen?" asked Ethan.

"Not more than a fortnight ago."

"No idea who it was?"

"Couldn't find a trace. Maybe it was one of the boys Blake and his crew are hunting."

"Maybe so," said Ethan. "Except that the rustlers aren't in The Breaks anymore. Haven't been for months, far as I can tell."

That caught Sellers off guard, as Ethan had intended it to.

"How do you know?" queried the mustanger.

Ethan shrugged. "I was up that way just yesterday." He glanced at Martha, flashing a disarming smile. "That Shamrock waddy that wrote those IOUs lives in a line shack on the edge of The Breaks. I rode through there a bit, just to take a look around. In fact, if I had to guess about where to find those night riders, I'd say they were operating on Western Crown range. Just a hunch." He said it with just the trace of a sly smile, trying to convey that he was going on much more than that.

He left it at that, and after coffee and apple pie, took his leave, with a mention to Martha that he intended to pay his usual nightly visit to the saloon. Leading his horse, he walked all the way to the watering hole but instead of going inside, he slipped into the black shadows of an adjacent alley. Then he circled around until he found another alley between two buildings across from the Sellers house. Sitting with his back to a wall, he pulled his coat collar up around his ears, tugged his hat brim down low over his face, and tried to ignore the bitter cold while keeping an eye on the house across the street.

He was beginning to think that Seamus Blake had been right about Frank Sellers. There was no solid evidence to connect Sellers with the rustlers, but Ethan wasn't convinced that the mustanger—if indeed that was Sellers' true vocation—had been shot at by a drygulcher down in The Breaks. It was possible that Sellers had made that up on the spur of the moment in hopes of laying a false trail for Ethan, a trail that would lead into The Breaks, and away from the rustlers.

Of course there was a possibility that he was altogether wrong about Sellers. But he had tried to leave the impression that he knew a lot more about the rustling operation than was actually the case. If he'd guessed right, and the night riders were operating on Western Crown range, then maybe— just maybe—Sellers would want to warn them. Assuming he was involved. It was a long shot, a real fishing expedition, but Ethan was obliged to grasp at straws.

Before long, the lights in the Sellers house were extinguished. Ethan sighed and tried to get some sleep. That was no easy task. A Wyoming winter's night could freeze a man's ears off. Ethan was glad Blake had paid him a month's wages in advance. With the portion that he had taken he'd purchased a good heavy longcoat from the Medicine Bow mercantile, along with a pair of gloves and some new flannel under riggings.

He slept in fits and starts, dozing off only to be awakened by the violent shivering of his body. By the end of the long night he had decided he would never be warm again. To make matters worse, a light snow had begun to fall.

Then a door slammed, and he saw Frank Sellers walking from the back corner of the house to the shed where his horse was keeping Martha's milch cow company. A few minutes later he was riding south out of town.

Ethan realized this was proof of nothing. The early morning departure of Frank Sellers might have absolutely no connection with the rustling ring Ethan was trying to crush. Still, Ethan felt a stir of anticipation as he mounted up and followed the mustanger.

Trailing Sellers without being seen wasn't difficult. Ethan tried to stay at least a half mile back. The mustanger's horse left clear sign in the snow, and as long as it didn't become a blizzard Ethan had no trouble keeping the trail. Now and then he checked his horse and scanned the country up ahead with the long glass that Williams had given him until he spotted the dark speck that was Sellers and his horse through a veil of falling snow. Ethan doubted that Sellers could see him with the naked eye, should the mustanger check his back trail.

Sellers rode due south from Medicine Bow for two hours. At a frozen creek he turned east to follow the stream's course for several miles. This brought him to a collection of buildings and corrals that Ethan assumed had to be the ranch headquarters of the Western Crown.

This was a development Ethan wasn't prepared for. He'd expected Sellers to lead him to the rustlers' hideout, not to the British-owned cattle concern. It seemed he'd wasted his time, after all. So he *had* misjudged Frank Sellers. Maybe the mustanger had struck a deal with the Western Crown to provide the ranch with horses. Or was hoping to strike such a deal.

Though his hopes were dashed, Ethan settled down on a low rise north of the creek across from the ranch buildings and watched Sellers through the long glass. The mustanger was greeted at the door to the main house by a tall, fair-haired man. They shook hands and went inside.

With a sigh, Ethan lowered the long glass. He was beginning to feel like a damned fool, lying here belly-down in the snow, freezing his butt off, apparently on a wild goose chase. *I might as well go back to Medicine Bow,* he thought, thaw out by the Sellers fireplace, eat breakfast at the Sellers table, and try to come up with a whole new approach.

At that moment the door to the main house opened and a man emerged. It wasn't Sellers, or the fair-haired character, either. The man seemed to be in a big hurry as he walked with long strides to the nearby barn. Ethan raised the long glass to get a better look at him.

No. It couldn't be.

The man disappeared into the barn. When he came out again he was mounted. He rode west, along the creek. This time Ethan got a good look at his face. There could be no mistake.

The man was Gil Stark.

11

Back in Roan's Prairie, Illinois, Gil Stark had been Ethan Payne's one and only friend. Though Ethan had been a farmer's son, and Gil lived in town—his father was a store-keeper—they'd been just about as inseparable as circumstances would allow. They were a study in contrast, too. Gil had been the big talker, brash and bold and full of wild stories, and seemingly born with an innate ability to make mischief. Ethan, on the other hand, had been quiet and reserved, shy around strangers. Gil was the type who thrived on being the center of attention, while Ethan had tried to remain as invisible as possible. And Gil was better looking than he was—tall, broad shouldered, and full of confident swagger, constantly flashing the crooked buccaneer's smile that told anyone he met that here was a young fellow who knew how to get what he wanted from the world.

Looking back now, Ethan knew that his shyness had a lot to do with the fact that he'd been embarrassed by his father, and his father's circumstances. Abner Payne had been a failure at farming even before his wife's death and his subsequent dependence on strong spirits. The Paynes might not have been the poorest family in the county, but they were close to it. Just about the only thing Ethan had felt he could do better than Gil was fight. He'd had plenty of practice; on the rare occasions when he got to go to school, the other boys were prone to chiding him mercilessly about the condition of

his clothes and the fact that he didn't often wear shoes and
usually smelled of the barnyard. Ethan had fought them, and
won. He'd even fought Gil Stark—even the best of friends
occasionally had a falling out—and always prevailed.

It was Gil who'd come up with the idea that they should
run away to California and strike it rich. He'd grown tired of
being a clerk in his father's store. And Ethan had become
weary of trying to keep the farm going while his father lay
all day in a drunken stupor. The only thing that had held
Ethan back was his love for Lilah Webster. But Gil had
finally persuaded him that if he really wanted to do right by
Lilah he would go west to find the mother lode. That way,
when he came back for her, Ethan would have more to offer
than a rundown farm on a marginal piece of land.

Ethan vividly recalled Lilah's words when he'd told her
of his plans. *I do not think you're a fool, Ethan. I think Gil
Stark is a fool, though. In fact, I always have thought so.
And he's always getting you into trouble. But nothing to
match this.* And she'd told him that it didn't matter to her
that he wasn't rich; she loved him for who he was. Of course
he hadn't believed any of it. That had been the biggest mistake of his life, a life filled with the taking of wrong turns.
Hardly a day went by now that he didn't wish he'd said no
to Gil and stayed in Roan's Prairie and married Lilah. He
might not have had much in the way of material things, but
he'd have had her undying love, and that would have been
all he'd needed to be happy. It was a shame that you had to
grow old before you were wise enough to make the right
decisions.

Gil had betrayed his friendship on more than one occasion since. On the first leg of the long journey to California,
aboard the Mississippi riverboat *Drusilla*, Gil had taken up
with Ash Marston, a thief who had tried to rob the well-to-
do passengers. Gil had been in on the scheme with him.
Working as a steward aboard the *Drusilla*, Gil had access
to the staterooms and was able to serve as Marston's scout,
identifying the valuables that the thief would purloin. They
had planned to leave the boat together in the dark of

night—but Ethan had stopped them. He'd apprehended Marston, and let Gil go. It wasn't the last time he would cover for his friend.

In California they had gone their separate ways. Ethan had met Ellen Addison, the pretty and vivacious daughter of a British engineer who was going to work for one of the big mining operations in the Sierra Nevada Mountains. Ellen had convinced him to go to work for the same outfit, so that they could be together. But Gil had been determined to prospect for gold, as they'd originally planned. *I know you think you've lost a friend,* Ellen had told him. *But believe me, you're better off going your own way.* At the time, Ethan had thought he would likely never see Gil Stark again. In retrospect, he might have wished that had been the case. Because, like so many gold seekers, Gil had failed to find his mother lode, and he'd fallen in with some bad characters, a gang of outlaws who, as chance would have it, had preyed on the gold shipments of the company Ethan worked for. And they'd come after a shipment Ethan had been put in charge of. Gil had saved his life then, and Ethan had repaid the favor. He'd gotten the gold back and killed most of the road agents in the process—the launching of his reputation as a hired gun to be reckoned with—but he'd once more let Gil off scot-free.

He'd expected never to see Gil again. How many coincidences did a man have to endure in a single lifetime? But they'd met once more, back in the days when Ethan had been a troubleshooter for the Overland Mail, and Gil Stark had, as was his habit, fallen in with some bad characters. He'd been a member of a gang of road agents holding up Overland stages and robbing the passengers. And during one holdup they'd shot and killed a man. Ethan had tracked them down. Killed one, captured the rest. And again he'd cut Gil loose. *I figured you would look the other way again,* Gil had told him. And that was exactly what he'd done, for old times' sake, and because while he'd known then, for certain, that his friend would come to a bad end, he had not wanted it to be at his hand.

And that was the last he'd seen of Gil Stark.

Until today.

It was enough to leave him dazed, in wonder at the whimsical nature of a Fate that would conspire to cross his path with Gil's once more, in this time and in this place, so far removed in both space and time from that remote hut in the foothills of the Sierra Nevada where last they'd met so many years ago. Ethan had no doubt that it was a coincidence that would cost him dearly. Coincidences involving Gil Stark always did.

Ethan followed his old friend in the same manner he had used to trail Frank Sellers to the Western Crown ranch headquarters. As the day grew old, the snow fell more heavily, and that worked to Ethan's advantage. Since there was no telling what Gil Stark was doing up here in the Wyoming Territory, Ethan tried not to distract himself with idle speculation. Still, the most obvious answer was that Stark worked for the Western Crown. But Ethan had trouble buying into that. Gil Stark had never been one for making an honest living. Unless he was a drastically changed man, he wouldn't stoop to the hard life of a cowboy for a paltry thirty dollars a month and board. Fruitless months of panning for gold in the California fields had cured him of any romantic notions about what honest labor could do for a man.

Stark led him west for more than an hour, straight to a timbered coulee where a log cabin stood nestled in the evergreens. A corral behind the cabin held a dozen horses. Woodsmoke curled from the cabin's rock chimney. A man came out of the cabin with a repeating rifle cradled in his arms as Stark rode up. Utilizing the long glass from a hundred yards away, Ethan could tell that the man knew Stark. The rifleman called back into the cabin as Stark dismounted, and two more characters emerged. One of them was the bearded, scar-faced man Ethan had seen with the four Shamrock steers a few weeks ago. Stark and the three men went inside.

Climbing stiffly out of the saddle, Ethan tethered his horse to the low-lying limb of a spruce tree and checked his canteen. The water within was frozen, so he searched his saddlebags for a bottle of whiskey he'd bought at the Medicine Bow saloon some days earlier. A few sips of the liquid brave maker warmed him and smoothed his nerves. An arm draped over his saddle, he peered at the distant cabin and tried to put all the pieces together.

Little doubt remained that the men Stark had come to see were the night riders he was looking for. The rustling ring's base of operations had been moved, as Ethan had suspected, from The Breaks onto Western Crown range after Blake and his Shamrock cowboys had scoured the former in search of it. Now, Frank Sellers had come to warn them that Seamus Blake's new range detective was hot on their trail. What had thrown Ethan was that Sellers had conveyed this news through the Western Crown. Could it be that the British cattle combine was actively participating in the rustling of cattle bearing the brands of the Sweetwater Land & Cattle Company?

The owners of the Western Crown were British investors; the closest they had come to a cow was the prime cut served them in the plush dining rooms of their London gentleman's clubs. No, it seemed more likely that the man they had hired to manage the ranch was the one involved, leaving his overseas employers blissfully unaware of his criminal sideline. The extent to which the Western Crown manager was involved remained to be seen.

One other consideration merited serious thought. When Seamus Blake learned that the Western Crown was harboring the rustlers who had become the bane of his existence, all hell would break loose. Ethan figured a range war was imminent.

But tomorrow's range war was of much less importance to Ethan than the decision he had to make right here and now about Gil Stark.

For such a big country, this was still an awfully small world. No matter how far he ran, Ethan knew now that there was to be no escape from his past. First Julie had shown up in Abilene. And Ash Marston had reappeared, too, hiring gunslingers to wreak his vengeance on Ethan. Now here was Gil Stark, in Wyoming of all places.

I'm going to let you go, he'd told Gil, back in that hut in California, the day he'd abetted his friend's escape from the hangman's noose. *But I don't ever want to run into you again.* And then again, in Arizona, when he'd let Gil go free rather than see him hang for crimes committed against the Overland, *Saving your worthless hide again. But this is the last time, you hear? Get going, and don't stop until you're one step beyond as far away from me as you can get.* Ethan vividly remembered those parting words to Gil Stark.

I owe you, Gil had said.

I won't collect, because I don't plan to ever see your face again.

He'd sure been wrong about that. Obviously he had no say in his own fate. So what was he going to do with Gil Stark on this go round? How many times was he going to look the other way? He'd betrayed the trust of the Eldorado Mining Company and the Overland Mail by letting Gil go on two occasions in the past. Why would this time be any different? Especially since he was working for a man who was, in some respects, a worse character than Gil Stark had ever been.

It didn't take Ethan long to make up his mind.

He drew his Henry repeater from its saddle boot and levered a round into the breech.

His horse whickered, its ears swiveling. This was the first warning, and it came too late. Ethan whirled as Frank Sellers, who had been trying to Indian up behind him, charged forward. The burly mustanger plowed into Ethan, driving him into the horse; the horse shied away and the two men fell, grappling, in the snow. Ethan hurled a fist that connected with Sellers' jaw, but the mustanger shook it off and returned the favor. He was quick and strong and overpowered Ethan, pummeling his face with iron fists until Ethan lost consciousness.

12

Frank Sellers announced his arrival at the cabin by hurling Ethan's body through the door. Gil Stark was sitting at a trestle table with the three men he had come to see. They were talking business over cups of hot coffee. All but Stark jumped up and clawed for their sideguns. Framed in the doorway, Sellers leered at them.

"You boys are a sorry excuse for owlhoots," declared the mustanger. He tossed Ethan's Henry rifle to Ames, while keeping the Colt revolver he had confiscated under his belt. "How come you ain't got no lookout posted?"

Gil Stark looked down at the unconscious man sprawled on the puncheon floor, and strove mightily to prevent his expression from betraying him.

"What are you doing here, Frank?" he asked.

"Looking out for my own interests. You lit out so fast I didn't get a chance to remind you about that money you owe me. You know, my share of the sale of the last bunch delivered to Fort Marcy."

"You'll get your share. Or I should say, Rose will get it."

Sellers' expression darkened. "How I spend my money is none of your affair, Stark."

"Just seems like to me a man ought to provide for his wife, instead of the local whore. I'm talking financially and in other ways, too."

"Why don't you keep your nose out of my business,

Stark? Besides, Rose and me are gonna go off together."

"Really?" Stark could not refrain from smirking at that bit of news. "When? How much money do you have to show her before she'll consent to leave with you?"

"Damn you, Stark. I want my share now. Seems to me this operation is going to hell in a handbasket." None too gently, he prodded Ethan with the toe of his mule ear boot. "Weren't for me, this pilgrim would have got the drop on you boys. I reckon the whole lot of you will be dancing at the end of Shamrock rope before too much longer. But not me. I aim to get while the gettin's good. And I'm taking Rose with me."

"So that's the famous Ethan Payne," said one of the rustlers, a young man named Calkin. "He don't look so tough. You done a number on his face, Frank." He giggled.

Stark glanced at Calkin with poorly concealed pity. The boy was just a hair shy of being a certifiable idiot. As for the other two, Ames had a short temper and drank too much, and was capable of dazzling explosions of violence, while the half-breed who called himself Charley Young made Stark uneasy with his brooding silences and shifty eyes. He never knew what Young was thinking. The man didn't open up to anyone. That made him doubly dangerous because you didn't know what to expect of him.

"Yeah, well, I'm gonna do worse," vowed Sellers. He looked long and hard at Stark. "You know this son of a bitch?"

"What makes you think I might?"

"Oh, I don't know. The look on your face when his name was mentioned."

"I've heard of him," said Gil casually, thinking that maybe he was starting to slip in his old age. There had been a time when he could have pulled the wool over even the sharpest eye.

"They say he's kilt fifty men," said Calkin.

"His killin' days are over." Sellers drew his pistol. "I think I'll just put a bullet in his brainpan and call it a day."

"Wait a minute," said Stark.

"We got to kill him," growled Ames, tugging fiercely on his beard.

"Not yet. We need to find out how much Seamus Blake knows about our operation. If he knows about Lansing, there'll be a range war, and we'll be out of business."

Ames just grunted. He was perfectly willing to let Gil Stark do the thinking for this outfit, but he didn't cotton to the idea of letting Seamus Blake's range detective live one minute longer. Especially a man as dangerous as the legendary Ethan Payne.

"It was a fool's game to bring Lansing into this in the first place," declared Sellers.

"We had to leave The Breaks," said Stark. "The Shamrock outfit would have cornered us in there sooner or later. I knew Lansing would listen to a proposition. The Western Crown owners were the real fools to hire Lansing as their manager. Sure, he knows cattle ranching. When I met him down Texas way, he was straw boss on the Spur Ranch, and when he was through he'd culled over a thousand steers and put his own brand on them and nobody was the wiser."

"Sure, he's a slick operator," allowed Sellers. "Which is why you can't trust him."

"Did I say I trusted him? I don't. Any more than I trust you, Frank."

Sellers grinned. "Well, now, that's right smart of you."

Stark went to the stove to refill his tin cup with strong java and shook his head. "I wouldn't be calling other people fools," he said. "You've got a home and a good wife, and you're putting it all at risk by helping us steal cows from Blake and Chappell. And for what? A buck-a-poke prostitute who has never loved anybody, including herself."

"Mind your own business," snapped Sellers. "It ain't just the money. Lord knows there ain't much of that, what with us having to give Lansing an equal share just so's he'll leave us alone and keep his mouth shut. And it ain't Rose. Not really. I know she don't love me. What do I care? This love business is for poets and fools. Martha loves me, and look where it's got her. No, I don't care what Rose thinks of me, long as she lays back and spreads her legs when I want her to. And when I get my share of the proceeds, that's exactly what she'll do."

"If it's not about the money, then what *is* it about?"

"I like seeing Seamus Blake squirm. That bastard treats me like old dirt. He thinks he's so almighty better than me. I tried to get a job on the Shamrock as a wrangler a few years ago, when times were hard. But he wouldn't hire me. Said I was a no-account and couldn't be trusted."

Stark nodded. Which just proved that, if nothing else, Seamus Blake was a very good judge of character.

With a groan, Ethan moved. He wasn't conscious, but he was on the way there. Sellers didn't wait, lifting him off the floor and slamming him down across the table and then backhanding him so hard that blood sprayed from Ethan's mouth. Some of the blood got on Ames, who was standing nearby.

"Dammit, Frank, watch what you're doing!" shouted Ames, wiping the specks of blood from his cheek.

Sellers laughed. "This is gonna be a real messy business, Ames. If you ain't got the stomach for it, you'd better step outside." He glanced at Stark. "You want him to talk, is that it, partner?"

Stark just stared at the mustanger. What he wanted was to keep Ethan Payne alive. He just didn't know how he was going to accomplish that. He needed time to think, to come up with a scheme. But Ethan had run out of time.

"Ames, you and Calkin go out and have a look around. He might not have come alone."

"He was alone," said Sellers. "I tracked him while he was trackin' you. Ain't nobody riding with him."

Stark pinned Ames with a hard gaze. "I said go have a look."

Traipsing around in the snow and the bitter cold wasn't a prospect to please Ames, but he could see the sense of it. Maybe Sellers was mistaken. Maybe there *were* others out there. Being careful beat getting hanged any day of the week. He didn't mind riding with Gil Stark because Gil was a man who always took precautions. That was why he'd lasted so long on the outlaw trail, where life expectancy was more often measured in months rather than years. Ames was somewhat new to the life of a long rider. Like so many others he'd come west for a fresh start after the war was over and the South lost, and after getting out of a prison camp he'd gone home to Alabama to find his wife run off with a carpetbagger and his farm sold to some freed slaves. He'd tried his hand at a lot of things—swamping out a saloon, hunting buffalo, even cowpunching. But nothing had worked out for him, so he'd decided to try an easier way of making some money. He'd started off by robbing a general store, and made off with thirty dollars and some change. After a few more small-time robberies he'd been caught and thrown into a Laramie jail, and it was there that he'd met the half-breed, Charley Young. They'd busted out and later met up with Calkin and Gil Stark, and then things had started improving. The four of them had held up a few stages over in Montana before the law started making it too hot for them there. Now they were running irons, and the payoff was fair. The army was paying top dollar for beef, and didn't ask any questions. Ames figured that as long as he stuck with Gil Stark he'd be okay. Maybe he wouldn't get rich, but he wouldn't likely swing from a rope, either.

"Come on, boy," he growled at Calkin.

They put on their hats and coats, took up their rifles, and went outside.

Ethan was coming to, his eyes flickering open, and Sellers planted the barrel of his pistol against Ethan's forehead.

"You've got a choice, Payne. You tell us what we want to know and I'll put you out of your misery nice and quick-like. If you go mule-headed stubborn, I'll let the breed there skin you alive. I hear he's a real master at it. Had a lot of practice."

Ethan kicked Sellers as hard as he could right between the legs. The mustanger let out a wheezing howl of anguish and doubled over. Stark expected the pistol in his hand to go off, but it didn't. Sellers grabbed the edge of the table as he sank to his knees, turning pale. Ethan was rolling off the table, but he was groggy, and moving too slow, giving the half-breed time to react. Charley Young rose, pistol in hand, thumbing the hammer back, drawing a bead, and Stark realized that Young wasn't going to fool around—he fully intended to gun Ethan Payne down. That was Charley's way; he wasn't one to believe in half measures.

Stark drew his own pistol and fired.

The bullet caught the half-breed in the chest and knocked him backward into the fireplace. He twitched for a second or two, and the stench of burning hair and flesh filled the cabin.

Before Frank Sellers could make his move, Stark's pistol barked again. This time it was the mustanger's blood that splattered all over the table. He knelt there, beside the table, a stunned look on his face—and a black bullethole right between his eyes. He was dead before he toppled over sideways.

Swaying on uncertain legs, Ethan looked at Frank Sellers' corpse and then at Gil Stark.

"I owed you one, remember?" asked Stark, and tossed his gun to Ethan, who caught it clumsily.

When Ames and Calkin burst through a door an instant later, Ethan swung the pistol in their direction, and they froze.

"Shed all the hardware, boys," said Ethan, "and have a seat."

13

He took them all back to Medicine Bow, the living as well as the dead. Frank Sellers and the half-breed made the trip draped over their saddles. Ames, Calkin, and Gil Stark had their hands tied behind their backs. Ethan strung their horses together on a rope and put the ponies of the two dead men at the end of the procession. He left all the weapons except his own at the cabin, freed the rest of the ponies in the corral, and then headed home, towing the rustling ring along behind. There were only a few hours of daylight left, but he didn't want to linger at the cabin. These men had at least one partner-in-crime—the man named Lansing. And there might be a few more in on the rustling racket. Ethan wasn't going to take any more chances than he had to, and his hands were full with three prisoners.

No words were spoken. There were some questions Ethan wanted to ask Gil Stark, but now was neither the time nor the place. Far as Ames and Calkin knew, Ethan had somehow gotten his hands on Stark's gun and killed Sellers and Charley Young. Gil made no effort to correct this faulty assumption, and neither did Ethan.

They were still well shy of Medicine Bow when night fell, and Ethan made camp. He built a fire—the night was too cold to go without one. Then he lashed Ames and Calkin to a pair of tree trunks before using a pocketknife to cut the rope that bound Gil's wrists together.

"Hey, what's going on?" asked Calkin. "You lettin' us go, mister?"

"Not likely," said Ethan.

Calkin was scared—scared enough to forget about his pride. "Please, mister. I don't want to hang. It was just a few scrawny cows, that's all. We were just trying to make enough money to live off of."

"There are other ways to make a living," said Ethan.

"I'm begging you, mister. . . ."

"Don't beg, kid," growled Ames.

"But I don't want to die, damn it!" Calkin was on the verge of tears.

"We don't get to pick when we die, boy," said Ames gruffly. "All we can do is make sure we die game. So stop whimperin' like a sick pup or I'll kick your teeth in."

Calkin shut up.

Ethan kept his Henry repeater trained on Gil, who had been rubbing his wrists and listening to this exchange with a bemused expression on his face.

"We're going to need a lot more firewood," said Ethan, "and you're going to collect it. Don't try anything, or I'll shoot you."

Gil looked at the rifle, then at Ethan, and decided that his old friend meant what he said. He nodded, and led the way into the dark timber nearby, picking up a likely looking stick here and another one there as he went along. When they were well out of earshot and sight of Ames and Calkin, and only just able to catch a flicker of the distant campfire, Gil stopped and turned and flashed that crooked buccaneer's smile. Ethan couldn't see it very well—it was a clear night and an early moon, but they were in the trees, and there was a lot of night shadow.

"I always had this hunch," said Gil, "that we'd meet again."

"I wish you'd been wrong."

"Yeah, me, too. Damn, Ethan, why did you have to show up here? I had a good business going there for a while."

"Stealing from the likes of Seamus Blake and partnering

up with someone like Frank Sellers? You call that a good business? I call it a fool's play."

Gil Stark shrugged. "Blake has—I don't know—eight, ten thousand head of cattle. Hell, he doesn't even know how many wear the Shamrock brand. We haven't taken more than a few hundred all told. The army is paying ten dollars a head for beef."

"Split what—six ways?" Ethan shook his head. "Those are small pickings, especially to die for."

Gil Stark was quiet for a moment, staring at his friend in the darkness. "Am I going to die, Ethan?" he asked, finally.

"You think I should let you go, like the last time? And the time before? Because you saved my life back there?"

"Well, I did do that, didn't I? But no. That was a debt I owed. You could say that squared things between us. So you don't owe me anything."

"That's right," said Ethan curtly. But he knew it was a lie. Knew that he *was* going to feel as though he owed Gil. He cursed his luck, wishing, almost, that Gil hadn't gunned down the breed and saved his life. Because this was a decision he absolutely did not want to have to make. Not again.

"You could say I got away from you in the dark," said Gil. "But to be honest, I'd rather you took me in and cut the kid loose instead. He's not a bad kid. Just a little slow. And because of that, people have taken advantage of him his whole life. He's never gotten a fair break, far as I can tell. This'll scare the outlaw right out of him. He's only eighteen, Ethan, and eighteen is way too young to hang."

"Well, why don't I just cut you all loose," said Ethan dryly.

"You've got Sellers and Charley Young. It's not like you haven't done something to earn your pay. You *are* working for Blake, right?"

"Yeah. But this isn't about Blake, or the cattle. It's about me, Gil. It's about doing something I said I'd do, for once. To hold up my end of the bargain. If I don't do that, then what damned good am I?"

Gil thought it over, and nodded. "No, you're right. You've

got a job to do, and you should do it. Won't be your fault if we hang. If it wasn't you it would have been somebody else, I guess."

Ethan muttered a string of heartfelt curses under his breath. "Start finding some firewood, Gil," he said, "and keep your mouth shut. I just don't want to hear it."

That night Ethan cooked some beans and brewed some coffee and made sure that all three of his prisoners had an opportunity to fill their bellies. He untied one at a time and kept a gun on them until they'd finished eating; then he'd tie that one up again and untie the next. Ames ate well; he'd been around too long to let anything interfere with his appetite, and Gil ate a little, too. Calkin tried to, but he couldn't keep it down; he had a few spoonfuls of beans and then promptly threw them back up again.

"I'm sorry," he said, with a mortified glance at Ethan. He said it again, this time looking at Ames.

"Don't worry about it, kid," said Ames, sympathetically.

Ethan got each of them a blanket. Ames seemed to fall right to sleep. Calkin was wide-eyed. Ethan was pretty sure all the kid could think about was what it would feel like to be hanged by the neck until dead, and felt sorry for him. Gil didn't sleep, either.

"I wonder whatever happened to our folks," he said, suddenly, after a long stretch of silence during which he and Ethan and Calkin watched the fire and listened to the whisper of the wind in the treetops. "You know, I once wrote a letter to my father back in Roan's Prairie. Never got a letter back. Maybe he wrote one and I just didn't get it. I haven't stuck in one place long enough to get regular mail." He flashed that crooked grin again, and just as quickly it faded away. "But to tell you the truth, I kinda doubt he even bothered to write."

"I ain't never learnt to write," lamented Calkin.

Gil looked at the kid and didn't say anything.

"Or it could be he never got your letter," said Ethan.

"No, I reckon he got it. My leaving the way I did must have nearly killed him. He wanted me to follow in his footsteps. To be just like him. A shopkeeper. To wear an apron and have my nose stuck in ledgers my whole life." Gil snorted, shook his head. "I wasn't cut out for that. I've got no regrets. I'm glad we left Roan's Prairie. Hasn't turned out exactly the way we planned it, but still, all in all I'd have to say it was a long sight better than what would have happened had we stayed."

"Speak for yourself," said Ethan.

Gil's eyes widened. "Oh. I forgot about her. Lilah Webster, wasn't it? Ever hear from her again, after the letter I gave you?"

Ethan shook his head. During his stint as road agent preying on the Overland stagecoaches, Gil had intercepted a letter that Lilah had written; he'd read it, kept it, and handed it over to Ethan when he'd been captured. Ethan no longer had the letter; he'd fed it to a fire somewhere on the trail to Abilene. But every word of it was etched in his memory. *You will be even more surprised to learn that I am getting married. His name is Stephen, and he is the son of the man for whom my father works. He loves me madly, and I love him. He treats me like a princess, in fact I sometimes think he treats me better than I deserve. Both my mother and father like him very much. I should add that my mother had often encouraged me to find someone else. She insisted that you were not coming back. I would always defend you, and sometimes we would get into these horrible rows. Please don't be angry with her. She is concerned only with my welfare, and carries no ill will toward you. And, as it happens, she was right and I was wrong. Oh, Ethan, I wish things had turned out differently for us. I still think of you often, and care for you, and I hope you know that you will always be in my heart.*

"I guess you could say I'm to blame," murmured Gil, reading Ethan's expression and realizing that the old memories could still hurt. "I'm the one who talked you into going."

"We've been over this before," said Ethan, wearily. "You didn't twist my arm. It was my choice. I just made the wrong one."

Gil shook his head. "I'm sorry, but I just can't see you as a farmer, spending your years behind a mule and a plow."

"And I wish I couldn't see you hanging from a gallows," said Ethan curtly.

Gil lowered his gaze, a half-smile frozen on his angular face.

It was Calkin who broke the silence this time. The kid had been staring back at forth at Ethan and Gil while they conversed. And now, with a tone of puzzlement, he said, "So . . . you two know each other?"

Gil looked at the kid and had to laugh. "Nothing gets by you, now does it, Calkin?" He glanced at Ethan. "Maybe you should go back. Maybe she isn't married anymore."

"There is no going back," said Ethan woodenly. Wishing to terminate the conversation, he lay down, pulling the thin wool blanket over him. Though he couldn't sleep, he pretended to, just to shut Gil up. But he was awake when, some time later, Calkin whispered to Gil.

"How come he's takin' you in, if you two are friends? Why don't he let you go?"

"He's just doing what's right, kid. That's why he's a better man than either one of us."

Ethan pounded on the door to the general store until Chester Brown came down from his living quarters, located on the second floor of the clapboard building. It was nearly dawn. They'd broken camp two hours ago; Ethan had wanted to arrive in Medicine Bow before the whole town had awakened.

"I need your help, Mr. Brown."

The storekeeper raised the lantern he was carrying in order to throw more light on the street, and he stared with sleep-heavy eyes at Ethan's prisoners. "Who are these yahoos?"

"The rustlers."

Suddenly the storekeeper's eyes widened. "Isn't that Frank Sellers' horse?"

Ethan nodded, and he watched realization dawn on Brown's face. The storekeeper stepped out into the street and went to Sellers' horse and peered at the face of the dead man belly-down over the saddle.

"Oh, Lord," he breathed. "Poor Martha." He turned back to Ethan. "He was in on it?"

"Afraid so."

"You look like you've been beat half to death, Mr. Payne."

"It could have been worse. I'm getting old; I let Sellers sneak up behind me. Like I said, Mr. Brown, I could use your help."

"How so?"

"I need a place to keep these prisoners."

"Keep them? I assumed you'd just hand them over to Seamus Blake."

Ethan shook his head. "They're going to get a fair trial."

Chester Brown stared. "You must be joking."

"No, sir."

"Seamus Blake is the law around here. I'd have thought you knew that by now."

"This is a territory of the United States, isn't it? That means you're bound to have marshals and judges."

Chester Brown took Ethan's arm. "Look here, son. I admire what you're trying to do. You and I both know Blake will hang these men five minutes after he gets his hands on them. But if you butt heads with him you'll lose. He's not a man to cross. Might be you'll wind up dancing on the end of a rope yourself. Take my advice. Hand these men over to Blake and ride away and don't look back, or think twice."

"I can't do that."

Chester Brown stepped back, as though he had just learned that Ethan was the carrier of a fatal and highly contagious disease.

"I can't help you, son. If I go against Blake, at the very least I'll lose my business. Maybe you don't know the way things are around here—"

"I know," said Ethan. "Thanks all the same."

He mounted up and rode down the street to the Sellers house, hauling his prisoners and the dead men along with him.

When Martha opened the door, Ethan said, "I've got some bad news, ma'am." He'd spent hours trying to figure out a good way to break the news to her. But there *was* no good way.

She looked past him, and recognized her husband's horse, too. Without a word she went to see for herself, clutching her flannel wrapper tightly at the throat. Ethan lingered on the porch, his heart twisting as he watched a sob wrack her frail body. But that was the only sound Martha Sellers made. She was made of stern stuff. Ethan forced himself to approach her. She looked at him, her eyes wet with tears, but her voice was remarkably steady.

"Was he . . . was he stealing cattle?"

"Yes, ma'am. He was part of the operation."

"Did you kill him?"

"No."

"That was my doing," said Gil, still sitting on his horse, hands tied behind his back. "I shot your husband, ma'am."

She stared at him. "I don't think I know you."

"Gil Stark's the name, ma'am. I'm sorry, but I had to do it."

"He did it to save my life," explained Ethan. "Frank was trying to kill me."

Martha shook her head. "I don't understand. Why would a rustler want to save your life?"

"Ethan and I go back a long ways."

"And yet," she said, studying Ethan closely, "you still brought him in."

"Yes, ma'am."

She drew a long, ragged breath. "I don't understand. But I understand this." She reached out and with a trembling hand touched the cold stiff corpse that had once been Frank Sellers. "I had a feeling he was involved. He hated Seamus Blake, you see. At least I didn't have to see him hanged."

"I want to turn these men over to the law, not to Blake. Will you help me?"

She gave him a long look, weighing the consequences, and Ethan braced himself for another refusal.

"Seamus Blake will kill you if he has to. But then you know that, don't you."

"They're going to get a fair trial."

She nodded, then looked at her husband again, and at the house, and Ethan knew that she would agree to help him, because she was realizing that she had nothing left to lose. Unlike Chester Brown, and probably everyone else in Medicine Bow, who were too afraid to stand up to Seamus Blake.

14

Ethan put his prisoners in a stone smokehouse behind the Sellers home. Martha provided them with some blankets and a lantern, and Ethan cut the hard twist that bound their wrists together. The door was made of square-cut timbers strengthened with strap iron, and was secured by a stout crossbar sliding into iron fittings. Designed to keep varmints out, Ethan was confident it would serve to keep the two-legged variety in. There was no window, no other way out. They had no tools with which to try to chip through the thick walls of stone or to dig in the frozen hardpack.

He carried Frank Sellers into the house. Martha directed him to lay the dead man on a horsehair sofa in the downstairs parlor. Gil's head shot had made a mess of the mustanger's face, and Martha found it impossible to maintain her composure. She sank into a chair, buried her face in her hands, and wept inconsolably. Ethan sought in vain for words of comfort. Martha Sellers was a good woman, and Ethan thought it was a damned shame that she had loved a man like Frank. Even though she'd known what kind of man he was, and had all along feared he would come to a bad end, she had cared for him. Her situation was uncannily similar to the one Julie Cathcott had found herself in at Wolftrap Station. Similar, too, mused Ethan bitterly, to Lilah Webster's situation, because Lilah had loved a man who'd turned out to be a no-account, and had almost let that love ruin her life.

Unable to stand by and bear witness to Martha's grief, Ethan went outside. He took the horses around to the lee-ward side of the house and unsaddled them. Charley Young's frozen corpse was left on the ground, covered with saddle blankets. Then Ethan went around to the back door stoop and sat down, a blanket over his shoulders. From this vantage point he could keep an eye on the smokehouse. Not that there was much chance, yet, that Seaṁus Blake knew what had happened and where Ethan was keeping the rustlers. But you never knew. And he didn't feel comfortable in the house.

He was prepared to spend his third night in a row out of doors, but later Martha found him, insisted he come inside, and made him some fresh coffee and warmed some beef stew. Although he told her he wasn't hungry, he wolfed down the stew and drank several cups of coffee. Soon he could scarcely keep his eyes open—the warmth emitted by the stoked kitchen stove and a full belly conspired against him.

"Go upstairs and get some sleep," she told him. "Nothing will happen tonight."

He shook his head. "I need to keep an eye on things. Besides, the horses need some feed, and my prisoners need something to eat."

"Fine. We'll take care of the horses and the prisoners, but then I want you to get some sleep."

Ethan shook his head. She amazed him. Her husband had been killed and he'd had a hand in it and yet, instead of being consumed with her own grief she was concerned about his welfare.

"Sooner rather than later Blake'll find out I'm back."

"Of course. But you're doing the right thing, and I'm willing to help you."

"Even though your husband's dead because of me."

"He's dead because he was doing wrong."

Ethan shook his head. "You'll do, Mrs. Sellers. You'll do."

In spite of everything, she gave him a little smile. "Thank you. And so will you, Mr. Payne. You'll do what I tell you. Don't worry, I'll wake you if anything happens."

Ethan told her it was a deal.

In spite of the danger he was in, Ethan slept like a baby, awakening with the dawn to the smell of breakfast cooking. Again he marveled at Martha's inner strength. Though Frank Sellers' corpse lay in the parlor, she was still thinking of others, cooking for the man who bore at least some measure of responsibility for the death of her husband, and for his prisoners, as well.

Over breakfast, at her insistence, he told her what had happened, providing the unvarnished truth—hesitating only when it came to the part where Frank Sellers died. But Martha insisted, and he provided her with the details. She maintained her composure; he could see that it required a great effort on her part to do so. Then she asked him to tell her about his friendship with Gil Stark. He didn't want to have to rehash the whole sorry history of his connection with Gil. Too many memories lay in wait for him down that road. But because she had asked, he obliged. He figured if she could stand hearing about how her husband had died he could bear the other. When he was done she was silent a moment, seeming lost in thought.

"Isn't it funny," she murmured.

"What?" he asked, surprised. He didn't see anything at all funny about the narrative he had just concluded.

"Life."

"Maybe. But you won't catch me laughing."

"We might have a day or two's grace," she said, "before Seamus Blake finds out what's going on."

Ethan nodded. "Until a Shamrock cowboy comes into town. I need to get word to Fort Laramie, to the U.S. marshal."

"There is no telegraph line within two hundred miles, I'm afraid. The sutler at Fort Laramie runs a freight line, and tries to send a wagon out this way once a month with mail and supplies. This time of year, though, that wagon might not show up for months."

"Then I might be better off taking my prisoners straight to Fort Laramie."

"That's a difficult journey. And the weather is worsening. Another norther is about to blow through. Perhaps the last one of the year. At least we can hope so. But if it catches you on the trail you might not make it at all."

Ethan smiled. "I seem to have a knack for boxing myself in, don't I?"

After he had eaten, he and Martha carried several plates of food out to the smokehouse. Setting the plates he had on the ground, he removed the crossbar and pulled the heavy door open, his Colt revolver drawn.

"I'll let you out one at a time to stretch your legs and have a bite to eat," he told the three men huddled inside, blinking at the sudden brightness pouring through the open door to illuminate the interior of the smokehouse. "You first," he said, using his pistol to indicate he meant Gil Stark.

Stark came out of the smokehouse. Ethan shut and barred the door and nodded at the plate on the ground. "Pick it up and walk to the house."

Stark did as he was told. Sitting on the steps leading up to the back door, he began to shovel the food into his mouth, using his fingers. Ethan watched him in silence as Martha went to the shed to check on the horses. When every bit of food was gone, Stark took a look around. The wind was kicking up flurries of snow, and a gray cataract of clouds blotted out the weak winter sun.

"Looks bad," he remarked. "We're liable to freeze to death in there." He pointed with his chin at the smokehouse.

"Well, we wouldn't want that. I'll round up some blankets."

"Seems to me you're taking a big risk, going up against Seamus Blake, if he's as hard an hombre as they say he is."

"He is. And maybe I am."

"So why don't you just hand us over to him and save yourself the trouble. We're going to hang anyway."

"That's right. But not by his hand."

Gil shook his head. "You always have to do things the hard way. Or I should say the *right* way. Same thing, I guess, most of the time."

"How would you know?"

Gil laughed.

"Why did you do it, Gil?"

"Like I said, I owed you. You saved my hide, and I returned the favor. That's all. Now we're even."

"That's not what I meant. You had the gun. I didn't. You could have gotten away."

A bleakness deepened the lines at the corners of Stark's mouth. "You got the makings, Ethan?"

Ethan reached into his coat pocket, pulled out his tobacco pouch, and handed it over. Stark took out one of the papers, poured the tobacco, and built a smoke.

"Let's say I'm tired of running," he said, finally. "Leave it at that."

Ethan took a strike-anywhere, flicked the match to life with a thumbnail; Stark cupped the match with his hands and lit the quirly, savoring the first long draw.

"You're not making sense," said Ethan. "You know you're bound to hang."

"Damn it, Ethan, I'm tired of running. I'm tired of being partnered up with the likes of Ames and Calkin. I mean, I'm going to meet a bad end sooner or later. There's no way out once you've done what I've done. It just gets worse. And you reach a point where you don't care anymore. Where you'd just as soon finish it. Maybe what those Chinese say is true. Maybe when you die you start all over in another life. They say the key to happiness in learning from your mistakes in past lives. If I do get a second chance, I'll walk the straight and narrow, for certain."

"You figure you're better than men like Ames and Calkin?"

"No, I'm not. Could be that I'm worse, when you get right down to it. At least worse than a kid like Calkin, who, if you ask me, didn't have a choice. He was forced into a life of crime. Me, I had a choice. I wanted to strike it rich, and it looked like turning outlaw was an easy way to do that. Certainly easier than playing by the rules. You're living proof of that. You always tried to play by the rules, Ethan. And where did it get you?"

"With that kind of attitude I don't think you'll fare much better in the next life."

Stark smiled. "I've still got a little time left to mend my ways. I'm not trying to put you in a bad spot, Ethan. Like I said, we're even. I don't expect any favors. I didn't figure you were going to let me go this time, but I wasn't going to stand by and watch that bastard Sellers kill you. And he would have, too."

"I know."

Stark shook his head, glancing toward the shed. "I just don't understand how it is that a man like Sellers can warrant a good woman like that one. I sometimes think that if I'd ever met a good woman she might have set me straight."

"I doubt it would have done any good."

"Yeah, you're probably right. Some men are just born to hang, aren't they?" Stark took one last drag off the cigarette and flicked it into the snow piled up against the back of the house. "You know, even if you were of a mind to give me a horse and tell me to ride out, I wouldn't do it."

"I wasn't going to make that kind of offer."

"Good. Well, I'm done here. It's the others' turn. Their food's getting cold." He stood up, stretched. In spite of his assurances that he had no desire to escape his destiny, Ethan took a cautious couple of steps back and kept the Colt trained on him. Stark saw this, and his smile was rueful. "You just don't trust me, do you?"

"Do I have reason to?"

"No, I reckon not. We sure made a mess of things, didn't we, partner?"

Ethan didn't reply.

"We were gonna strike it rich. Now look at us. We sure got dealt a couple of bum hands."

"We dealt the cards to ourselves."

"Guess you're right. Ethan, I wish like hell you'd do me one more favor. I wish you'd go home."

"I don't have a home."

"Yes, you do. You know what I mean. Go home. Get out of this damned country before it kills you. Mend your fences and start all over. You've got a chance. That's more than I've got."

Ethan laughed. "What chance? Seamus Blake is going to kill us both before the week is out."

"That's what I've been trying to tell you. Forget about me and Ames and Calkin. Frankly, I don't care who's on the other end of the rope. But you don't have to be here. Why don't you get on a horse and ride? You don't have a damned thing to prove."

"That's where you're wrong," said Ethan grimly, "I'm tired of running, too. I'm tired of men like Blake, who make their own law and ride roughshod over everybody who gets in the way of their making a profit."

Stark chuckled. "You're just jealous, my friend, because he struck it rich out here and you didn't."

"Shut up and get back inside," said Ethan, motioning toward the smokehouse with the Colt. "You talk too much, Gil. You always did."

15

The snow came, wrapping the house in a cocoon of white, and the howling wind beat against the windows. Ethan didn't think it could get any colder than it had already been, but he was proved wrong. The temperature plummeted. He'd taken three blankets out to the smokehouse, but at Martha's behest he brought his prisoners inside. It occurred to him that freezing to death might be a more merciful way for them to go than dancing at the end of a rope, but he didn't try to make that argument. The fact was that if they froze to death in the smokehouse his whole reason for crossing Seamus Blake would die with them.

He whiled away the time thinking about what Gil Stark had told him. Whether the rustlers were hanged from the nearest tree by Blake and his cowboys, or from a gallows after being sentenced in a duly constituted court of law might seem like hair-splitting to Gil, and certainly not worth getting killed over. But to Ethan there was a huge difference. As an Overland troubleshooter he'd let a two-bit road agent named Wesley Grome hang for a crime he didn't commit. Sure, Grome had committed many other crimes, but that wasn't the point. And as the town marshal of Abilene he'd faced down an entire Texas outfit not for the purpose of upholding the law, but in order to secure his own future.

Gil had said Ethan had always tried to do the right thing, always played by the rules. But that wasn't true. Giving Gil

Stark the opportunity to ride out and escape justice years ago at Rattlesnake Springs wasn't exactly playing by the rules. If his sole purpose had been to see justice done, Stark would have paid the piper back then. But Gil had saved Ethan's life. That counted for something. Or so Ethan had told himself at the time. But if it had counted for something on that occasion, why didn't it count for something now? Wasn't it a little late to start worrying about doing the right thing? And was it worth seeing his old friend die just for the sake of proving something to himself?

When he brought the three outlaws into the house, Ethan tied them up. With their hands and feet bound, the three night riders were placed back to back, sitting on the floor in the front room, where a fire was blazing in the hearth, and then tied together with more rope. The Colt in hand, Ethan sat in a chair nearby and kept an eye on them. The youth, Calkin, stared at Ethan with the same fear in his eyes that had been there from the start. But Ames had had a change of attitude. He glowered at both Ethan and Stark with murder in his eyes.

"You sold us down the river, didn't you, you son of a bitch?" he asked Stark, finally. "I know what happened back there. I've heard enough to know you shot Frank Sellers."

"Sorry." Stark didn't sound at all contrite. "Ethan and I go back a long ways."

"If I get out of this, Stark, you're a dead man."

Stark laughed. "Ames, we're all going to be wearing wings and playing harps pretty soon, so don't work yourself into a lather."

"You killed the breed, too, I guess."

"That's right. But I know you don't care about that. You never liked Charley."

"I never liked Frank, either. That's not the point. Point is, if you'd let Frank do what he wanted, we wouldn't be in this mess. I figure to hang, but you never know. Long as you're sucking air you've got a chance. If somehow I live through it, I'll deal with both of you. But you're first, Stark. I don't cotton to turncoats."

Stark didn't appear very concerned.

Later, Martha Sellers made a fresh pot of coffee and brought Ethan a cup. She wanted to give some to the prisoners, too, but Ethan wouldn't let her. She took another chair in the room and began knitting. After a while, Ethan stood up and crossed the room. It was then that he noticed that from where she was sitting one could glance across the front hall into the parlor, where her husband lay, his body covered with a blanket.

"Hopefully this storm won't last," she said. "When it's over, I'll bury him."

"We'll leave as soon as the weather clears," he told her. "With any luck we'll be long gone before Seamus Blake finds out what happened." He tried to sound like he believed things would work out that way.

She nodded and kept her attention fixed on her knitting, and did not look up at him or at the body in the other room.

"How will it go for you when Blake finds out your husband was part of the gang that was stealing his cattle?"

"It won't matter. Nothing will happen to me. To tell you the truth, I think Seamus Blake has always had a hankering for me."

Ethan was stunned.

"He's a widower, you know," she continued. "His feelings for me are not exactly a secret. That's another reason for the bad blood between him and Frank. Maybe the main reason."

"Well, I'll be damned."

"So you see," she said, forcing a smile, "I'll be just fine. Seamus Blake is used to getting what he wants. Now that I'm a widow, well . . . you understand."

"Yes, I think I do. But don't you have something to say about it?"

"Do I?"

He glanced at the corpse of Frank Sellers. "I'll help you bury him when the storm lets up."

"When the storm lets up, you better leave as quickly as possible."

"You could leave, too. That is, if you didn't . . ."

This time she did look up at him, a bemused expression on her face. "If I didn't what? Want to share a bed with Seamus Blake? This is my home, Ethan. Has been for many years. This is where my memories reside. I don't want to leave it. I won't be forced to. I don't want to share Blake's bed. Don't worry, I can hold him off for quite a long time. My husband has died. There has to be a proper mourning period. And then he'll have to start courting me. By that time I might be dead. Or he might be."

"I see," said Ethan. He didn't know what to say to all of that, so he returned to his chair and resumed his vigil.

The hours weighed heavily on them all. There was nothing to do but wait out the bad weather. Gil Stark asked Martha if she had some writing material. He told her he wanted to write a letter. Ethan nodded that it was okay, and she provided Gil with ink, pen, and paper. Ethan untied his hands.

"I think it's about time I write to my folks," said Gil pensively. " 'Course, I'm not sure if they're still in Roan's Prairie. Hell, I'm not even sure if they're still alive. But, just in case they are . . ."

It took him a long time to finish the letter. Sometimes he would just sit there and stare for a long time at the window, where the snow whirled in the gusting wind that made the panes of glass shudder. Ethan could well imagine how difficult the task was for Gil. He'd had trouble writing the occasional—and long overdue—letter to Lilah.

The words obviously weren't coming easy. At one point he laughed, embarrassed, and confessed to Martha that he'd never actually written a letter before. He didn't have to point out that he would never write one as important. It took him hours. Several times he seemed compelled to turn and look over his shoulder, across the hall into the parlor at Frank Sellers; Ethan figured the corpse was serving as a vivid reminder to Gil of his own sordid past, a life of wrong turns and missed chances and sudden violence, a life he was trying to put into words in a kind of last will and testament.

More a confession than a testament, really, and if it was a will, all he had to leave behind were his regrets.

When, finally, he was finished, he folded the single sheet of paper and slipped it into an envelope and addressed it. Then he looked at Ethan, almost apologetically.

"I'd ask you to make sure this got where it needs to go. But I'm not too sure you'll live much longer than I will." He glanced at Martha Sellers, who was still knitting. "I know I've got no right to ask anything of you, ma'am. Not after what I've done. But I was wondering . . ."

"Of course I will," she said. She rose, set aside the knitting, and approached him. Ethan watched, alert for any trouble, aware that Gil's hands were untied, and feeling almost guilty for suspecting that Stark might try something at a time like this. She read the front of the envelope. "I'll make sure it gets there."

"Like I said, I just hope they're still there."

"I hope so, too."

Not for the first time, Ethan marveled at the qualities of Martha Sellers. There weren't many women who would be genuinely concerned about the affairs of the man who had killed her husband.

Ethan tied Gil's hands behind his back again.

Later that day the wind and snow subsided, and when the sun finally set they could watch its flaming orange death behind tattered shreds of purple clouds over the distant mountains. Ethan told Gil Stark they would leave in the morning—right after Frank Sellers had been buried. Stark clearly didn't think wasting time, especially to bury Sellers, was the smart thing to do, but he raised no objections. He knew Ethan well enough to know that argument was pointless.

Ethan intended to stand guard all night. But once again Martha intervened, concerned for his well-being. She insisted that she would take a four-hour shift herself. He had reservations, wondering if she could be counted on to keep the three prisoners under control. But she reminded him that she'd spent most of her adult life on the frontier, and was perfectly capable of looking after what needed looking after. Ethan was persuaded. She hadn't let him down so far, and he didn't think she would this time, either. He took the first four-hour shift, and spent it trying to figure out why he trusted Gil. Gil and Ames went to sleep; Calkin was still too anxious to get much shut-eye. When Ethan's shift was done, Martha came downstairs to relieve him. She was carrying a ten-gauge double-barreled shotgun, and the way she handled it revealed to him at once that she'd used it before and wouldn't hesitate to do so again. He went up to bed and lay down with his Colt under the pillow and fell immediately into a deep sleep.

He woke to discover that Martha had spent the night preparing her husband—cleaning him up as best she could and dressing the corpse in a clean white linen shirt and a somewhat threadbare suit of brown broadcloth. Ethan wondered if Martha had ever really loved her husband. She had married the mustanger because she was alone in the world. She was estranged from her mother back east, and her father was dead and buried somewhere in Mexico. From what little Ethan knew of Sellers, he couldn't imagine the man had been a very good husband. But Martha remained a dutiful wife to the end. And regardless of whether she loved him or not, she had grown accustomed to his being with her, and missed him now that he was gone. Ethan knew from experience how powerful loneliness was as a motivator. It could make a person spend years with someone he or she didn't really love, and no matter how bad it became, the alternative always seemed worse.

She wanted him to leave as soon as the blizzard had passed—not out of concern for herself, or what might happen to her when Seamus Blake learned that she had become Ethan's accomplice in an attempt to thwart his will, but rather for Ethan's sake. And there was more to it. Though she hadn't come right out and said it, he sensed that the thought of Blake being denied the pleasure of hanging the men who had been stealing his cattle—a pleasure the cattle king evidently thought was a God-given right—gave her immense satisfaction. Clearly she didn't care for Blake any more than Ethan did. But that wouldn't stop her from tolerating his advances; Martha Sellers had experience in being the object of desire for the wrong kind of man.

Ethan refused to leave, though, until Frank Sellers was in the ground. He felt an obligation to see the task done, to be with Martha when she laid her husband to rest, and besides, he argued, who else was going to dig the grave in the frozen ground? For all her wiry strength and endurance, she couldn't do it.

She wanted the grave to be beneath the old elm tree beside the house, and after temporarily depositing his three prisoners in the stone smokehouse again, Ethan ventured out with pick and shovel and attacked the frozen ground and nearly killed himself in the process. But he got the job done, and he and Martha carried the corpse, now wrapped tightly in blankets tied with rope, and placed it in the ground. He stood by while she read from the Bible, and when she was finished she looked up at him and nodded, indicating that he could go ahead and start filling the grave. But he was staring off into the distance, and when she looked north she saw what he had seen—dark specks of mounted men moving across the virgin snow.

"Dear God," she murmured, because even though the riders were much too far away to identify, she knew somehow, as did he, that their horses wore the Shamrock brand.

"Maybe you'd better go," he told her. He put down the shovel and picked up the Henry repeating rifle, which was leaning against the trunk of the old elm. It was too late for him to make a run for it, but there was no point in Martha getting caught in a lead-slinging contest. "Go stay with Chester Brown or somebody until it's over."

"This is my house," she said firmly, and that was that. Ethan realized there was nothing to be gained by arguing with her.

He retrieved Stark and the other two night riders from the smokehouse, marching them back into the main house. Once they were inside, Ethan informed them that the Shamrock outfit was on its way.

"How the hell did they find out so quick?" wondered Stark.

"Like everything else, this town and the people in it belong to Seamus Blake," replied Ethan. Glancing apologetically at Martha, he amended his remark. "Almost all the people. Someone managed to get word to Blake in spite of the blizzard, I reckon."

"Oh God," said Calkin. "We're gonna die. Please, you gotta let us go! I don't want to die!"

With his hands still tied behind his back, Ames shifted his considerable weight sideways and drove a shoulder into the trembling Calkin. The kid, outweighed by at least fifty pounds, went down. He hit the floor hard. Lying on his side, he pulled his knees up, trying to curl into a ball, sniveling inconsolably. Ames looked down at him with pure disgust.

"I guess it's askin' too much for a wet-behind-the-ears kid to die like a man," he growled. He looked at Ethan. "He's right about one thing. You should let us go. Give us back our weapons. That way we can at least go down fighting."

Ethan shook his head. "Not a chance. You'd wind up killing a few of those Shamrock cowboys, and I don't want that on my conscience."

"Well, it's good to know our deaths won't bother your conscience none," said Ames dryly.

"Yours won't," said Ethan curtly.

In just a matter of minutes the riders had arrived. Ethan took full advantage of the time. He made his prisoners sit in the middle of the floor and, using a short length of rope, lashed together the bindings around their wrists. Neither Ames nor Gil Stark said anything more, and all Calkin could do was blubber.

They listened to the thunder of iron-shod horses on the hardpack all around the house, and then Blake's stentorian voice: "Ethan Payne! I want a word with you."

"He's not a man to be trusted," warned Martha. "Don't go out there."

Ethan ignored her advice. Carrying the Henry repeater, he stepped out onto the porch. Blake and five riders sat their horses in front of the house. Slim and Billy, the pair Ethan had met at the general store on his arrival in Medicine Bow, were among the cowboys who had accompanied Blake. Ethan was sure he had seen more men than this from a distance, and figured at least a half dozen more Shamrock hands were watching the sides and rear of the house.

"I've come for the rustlers," said Blake. He nodded at the open grave under the elm tree. "Was Frank Sellers in on it?"

"Yes, he was."

"I never trusted that man," said Blake. "And I never understood what Martha saw in him, either."

"So is the manager of the Western Crown, a fellow name of Lansing. He took his cut for letting the gang operate on his range after you flushed them out of The Breaks."

Blake bit down hard on his anger. "I shouldn't be surprised. I'll deal with Lansing later. How many men did you bring in?"

"Three."

"How many did you kill besides Sellers?"

Ethan wasn't going to waste his time trying to explain why he hadn't been the one to shoot Frank Sellers. "One other. A half-breed by the name of Charley Young."

Blake nodded. "I'm impressed, Payne. You've done fine work, and in much less time than I expected it to take you. I'd like to keep you on for a while, just in case we have any more problems. And I'll pay you a bonus of one thousand dollars for handling this situation so quickly. Now, just hand your three prisoners over to me."

Ethan saw that Slim had a rope with a noose already made, which he was shaking loose from a saddle tie. "You can put that away," he said. "There won't be any lynchings today."

Slim froze, looked at Ethan in surprise, then at his boss, waiting for orders.

Blake's eyes narrowed into bleak slits of steel. "You work for me, remember, Payne? I'm the law around here and I'll decide who hangs and when."

"No, you won't. And you're not the law. You just think you are. I'm turning my prisoners over to the real law."

"Jesus Christ," muttered Billy.

Ethan smiled coldly at the cowboy. "Remind you of Abilene, does it? History repeats itself. Only this time you didn't steer clear. You'll wish you had, though."

"Mr. Blake, maybe—"

"Shut your trap, Billy. He's just one man. Forget his reputation. Probably nothing but a pack of lies anyway. Hand those men over to me, Payne. I won't tell you again."

"Don't do this, Seamus," said Martha Sellers as she emerged from the house to stand beside Ethan, pulling a shawl tighter around her shoulders against the cold. "You know they'll hang. You don't have to be the one to do it. Leave it to the law."

In spite of the tenseness of the situation, Blake remembered himself and swept the hat from his head. "Good morning, Martha. I'm sorry about Frank. But I hope you understand that he brought it on himself."

"Thank you," said Martha tersely. "And yes, I understand that. I also know that you're a very important and powerful man. But it's not your place to be judge, jury, and executioner for the men inside."

Blake's gaze grew steely again, but he kept his tone civil. "Yes, it is. Out here a man has to make his own law and keep it, because there's no one else who will. I do not relish the responsibility, but I accept it."

"You don't relish it? I wonder about that."

"You misjudge me, Martha. And I've misjudged you, apparently. I always thought you were a level-headed and practical woman. So I'm surprised that you would stand in my way, knowing how dangerous such foolishness can be."

"Well, well," she said, with a faint smile. "That sounds very much like a threat."

"You would do better if you didn't try to tell me how to conduct my business."

"I forbid you to take those men out of my house by force."

"Martha, don't do this. It's none of your affair."

"I'm making it my affair."

Blake drew a long breath and flexed his shoulders. Giving Ethan a close appraisal, he made up his mind. Ethan knew what he was going to say even before he said it. Seamus Blake was the kind of man who, once a decision had been made, would see a thing through to the bitter end, and no matter what stood in his way.

"Martha," he said curtly, "Billy here will take you down to Chester's place. I don't want you to get hurt."

"Do as he says," said Ethan.

Martha almost refused. But she studied Ethan's face a moment, and then Blake's. She nodded.

"Don't forget about that letter," said Ethan.

"I'll see to it," she promised.

Billy dismounted, helped Martha into his saddle and, a look of vast relief on his face, led the horse down the street into Medicine Bow.

Blake brandished a stem-winder. "You've got two minutes to bring those men out to me, Payne. Then I'm coming in to get them."

Ethan went inside and shut the door.

16

He walked back into the room where Stark and the others were sitting on the floor, bound back to back.

"Looks like the end of the road, Ethan," remarked Gil. He sounded very calm.

"We're not finished yet."

"For what it's worth, I'm sorry I got you into this. Sorry about everything."

"You didn't get me into this, Gil. I managed to do that all by myself."

"No, I mean everything. Wasn't for me and my grand ideas you'd still be back in Illinois, where you belong, married to Lilah. You'd probably even have a passel of kids by now."

Ethan just shook his head. That was the last thing he wanted to think about at a time like this. "Don't go getting sentimental on me, Gil. It doesn't suit you."

"I'm saying this one more time, old friend. Turn us over to Blake. All three of us. That way you might just get out of this in one piece."

"Forget it. Besides, none of this is really about you or Blake."

"I know, I know. It's all about you doing what you think is right."

"For a change." Ethan bent down and used his pocket-knife to cut the rope that tied the three men together. His thoughts were of Blake and the Shamrock riders. The two minutes were nearly up. What would they do? And whatever they did do, how was he, one man, supposed to stop them? He'd hoped they would back down, that his reputation might have served a useful purpose for a change and given them second thoughts about trying him. He should have known that a man like Seamus Blake would not back down. There wasn't much left to do now but die. Like Blake, he wasn't about to back down.

As soon as the blade of his knife had cut through the rope binding the trio together, Calkin struck. Shouting like a crazy man, he swung his legs, bound together at the ankles, knocking Ethan off balance. Ethan sprawled sideways, letting go of the knife and clawing for the pistol in his holster. But Ames was quick to get into the act; the big man drove the heels of his boots into Ethan's face. Ethan experienced a painful explosion of bright light. Ames struck again, and this time Ethan had the sensation of falling, which a part of his mind told him was ridiculous, since he was already on the floor. But he kept falling, falling, falling into a bottomless black pit.

He came to seconds later—and froze when he felt the barrel of his Colt revolver pressed hard against the side of his head. It was Gil Stark. He was untied now, and he knelt beside Ethan, shaking his head regretfully. "You were always too hardheaded for your own good, old friend."

Nearby, Ames was using the pocketknife to cut the ropes binding Calkin's hands and feet together. When he was done, Ames confiscated Ethan's rifle, which was leaning against a chair.

"Hey, what about me?" whined Calkin.

"What about you?" asked Ames.

"You got a gun and so does Gil. But I don't."

"You're breaking my heart." Ames looked at Stark. "So what do we do now?"

"We're gonna make a run for it."

"Are you loco? We don't stand a chance out there. I say we fort up in here and try to fight 'em off. We kill enough of them cowpushers they'll turn tail."

Stark stood up, backed away from Ethan, and turned the Colt on Ames.

"You've got a choice. You can go out there with that rifle and die fighting, or you can go out unarmed. But you're going out."

Ames gave him a long, dark look. "I know what you're doing. We don't stand a chance either way. In here or out there makes no difference. But out there he's not a part of it." He nodded at Ethan. Then he shrugged. "Well, it beats having my neck stretched."

"Sure, it does," said Stark.

Calkin was white as a sheet. "W-what about me? D-don't I get a gun?"

"Sorry," said Stark. He didn't sound sincere. "Maybe you can get away while Ames and I keep them busy."

"I d-don't want to die," whined Calkin. His knees were about to give out on him.

Ames laughed at him. "Then you should have stayed home and gotten a job as a store clerk or sumpin', boy."

"Tie him up," Stark told Calkin. "And do it fast."

"Payne!"

It was Seamus Blake, calling into the house. "Your time is up! Hand those men over or we're coming in to get 'em!"

Calkin took the ropes that had once bound him and tied Ethan's hands behind his back.

"Don't do this, Gil," said Ethan. "You don't stand a chance."

"None of us do—except for you. Let's just say this is my doing something right for a change. My way of paying you back."

Calkin was finished tying Ethan's ankles together. Stark nodded to Ames. "Show them what you're made of," he said, dryly.

"Go to hell, Stark." But Ames was grinning.

"After you."

Ames grabbed Calkin and hauled him out of the room into the front hall. Stark followed them.

"Gil . . ."

Gil Stark glanced back at Ethan, and that crooked buccaneer's smile that was usually on his face wasn't there this time. He looked as serious as Ethan had ever seen him. He gave a little shake of the head, walked back to Ethan, and said, "I'm sorry, but maybe it's best this way," and before Ethan could figure out what he meant, the butt of the Colt came down on his skull and he was out cold.

They exploded out the front door, Ames going first, and shoving Calkin out ahead of him. Stark was right behind them, and when Ames moved left, he stepped to the right. Some of the cowboys already had their guns ready—a few with rifles, the rest with the six-shooters—and as soon as they saw the trio emerging, a couple of them fired. Ames got off two shots, winging a Shamrock cowboy and knocking him out of the saddle, and killing a second cowboy's horse. Then he took a bullet in the groin and another in the chest and went down. Before he could lever another round into the breach of the Henry repeater, several more bullets struck him, and he let go of the rifle. Stark grabbed the boy and yanked him to the corner of the house. A mounted cowboy took a shot at Stark and missed by inches, the bullet plowing into the clapboard behind Stark's head. Stark returned fire, and the cowboy, crying out in pain, toppled from his horse.

Towing Calkin, Stark moved to the corner. He didn't really think they had a chance of reaching the shed where the horses were being kept, sheltered from the elements. But trying for them made more sense than just standing on the front porch trading lead with a half dozen Shamrock riders. Most of Blake's men were shooting, but all save one or two were still aboard their ponies, which were moving around in the street, unnerved by all the gunplay. That threw off the cowboys' aim. Stark wondered just how long he'd stay lucky. An instant later he got his answer. A bullet smashed into his leg as he went around the corner of the house, and he dropped to one knee, gasping. Calkin took one in the head and died instantly. A second bullet hit Stark high in the shoulder and slammed him against the house.

He raised the Remington. Three of Blake's men fired simultaneously from their pivoting ponies. Stark slid sideways down the wall, leaving a smear of bright red on the weathered clapboard, convulsed once, watched the white snow turn gray, and died.

Ames was still alive, writhing on the blood-splattered porch, laboring to drag one more breath into his bullet-torn lungs. The cowboy whose horse the bearded rustler had killed walked up, put his gun to Ames' head, and pulled the trigger.

"That was the best pony in my string, you sorry son of a bitch," he muttered angrily. Turning away, he took two steps, dropped to his hands and knees, and puked his guts out. Wiping his mouth with a sleeve, he looked up to see Seamus Blake, still aboard his horse with a smoking pistol in his hand, frowning at him.

"We got 'em, Boss," said Slim, coming around the corner of the house, having just checked Stark to make sure he was finished.

Blake looked bleakly at the dead. "Get the ropes and hang 'em from that tree yonder." He nodded at the old elm that stood alongside the Sellers house.

"But they're all dead, Mr. Blake."

"I want to see them hanged," barked Blake, perturbed. "And by God I will. Now do what I tell you."

With a sour expression on his face, Slim went to his horse, held by one of his cowboy colleagues, and retrieved his rope. Blake dismounted, motioned for several of his men to accompany him, and crossed the porch to enter the house.

When Ethan came to, he was lying on his back on the floor in Martha Sellers' parlor, looking up into the faces of Seamus Blake and several of his Shamrock cowboys. His face was wet and cold—Slim held a wooden bucket by its bale in one hand and had a white-knuckled grip on his pistol in the other. Ethan blinked water out of his eyes. They'd roused him with a dose of well water.

For a moment he couldn't remember much of anything. He knew where he was, but what he didn't know was how he'd ended up on the floor trussed up like a Christmas turkey. Where was Gil and the other two rustlers?

Looking close, he saw the fear in the cowboys' eyes. They were afraid of him. He found that funny, considering his situation. The holster on his hip was empty, Ames had taken his Henry repeater, and even his pocketknife was gone. They could see he was not only unarmed but tied up, as helpless as a baby. Still, they were wary.

"Cut him loose," said Blake.

One of the cowboys advanced, making sure he didn't put himself between Ethan and the other cowboys' line of fire. Using a knife taken from inside a boot, he slashed the ropes that bound Ethan's hands and feet together, then backed away.

"Get on your feet, Mr. Payne," said Blake.

Ethan tried to oblige, but his vision blurred and the room seemed to spin madly. He touched the side of his head and his fingers came away sticky with blood, and suddenly he remembered how he had gotten on the floor of Martha's parlor. Gil Stark had pistol-whipped him. He and his partners in crime had gotten the jump on him, taken his weapons, and . . . Peering at Blake and the cowboys, Ethan put two and two together. He could smell powder smoke on these men. There had been some gunplay.

The only thing that got him on his feet was stubborn pride. Gritting his teeth, he fought through the pain and the nausea, and struggled to stand. Swaying, he focused on Blake, hating the man more than he had ever hated anyone in his life—except maybe himself.

Because he knew Gil Stark was dead.

"Looks like things didn't work out the way you wanted," said Blake, a sneer in his voice.

"Where are my prisoners?"

Blake made a curt gesture. "Come on. I'll show you."

They walked out onto the porch, followed by the Shamrock cowboys, and Ethan saw the bodies twisting slowly on the ropes from the limbs of the old elm tree. He could tell that all three men had been shot to pieces. He felt like throwing up, but once again pride kept him together. He stared at Gil Stark's corpse, not wanting to believe his eyes. Even though he'd known, from the moment he'd seen Gil down on the Western Crown, that Stark was going to end up this way, and he'd tried to prepare himself, he just didn't want to accept the truth. He'd known Gil his whole life; they had shared so many adventures. So many dreams of the future. Gil had been such a big part of his life, in both good ways and bad, that now that he wasn't here anymore it was as though Ethan had lost a part of himself.

"That's what happens to men who cross me," said Blake.

Ethan whirled and drove a fist into the cattle king's face. He didn't even think about how dangerous it was, with trigger-happy cowboys all around. Blake was caught completely by surprise. Slim and the other cowboys had their charcoal burners drawn, and several more Shamrock hands sat their horses in the vicinity of the tree. Blake hadn't expected Ethan to try anything with so many guns turned on him. The blow rocked him back on his heels, but he didn't fall. Seamus Blake was a tough customer, a plainsman, and he knew how to take a punch.

The cowboys on the porch surged forward, thumbing back the hammers on their sixguns. Ethan turned on them, snarling like a wolf caught in the steel jaws of a trap.

"Go ahead," he rasped. "Kill me, damn you."

"No!" Blake wiped blood from a cut lip. Shaking with fury, he glared at Ethan. "No, I'm not going to make it that easy for you. Get another rope."

Ethan made a snap decision. He knew Blake was serious. Even though he wasn't a rustler, the cattleman wouldn't hesitate to lynch him. But Ethan wasn't going to let the bastard stretch his neck. Turning his attention to the pair of cowboys on the porch, he decided to make a move at Slim, who was standing nearest. He would try to wrestle Slim's pistol away from him. Not that he had a chance in hell of succeeding. But he wasn't going down without a fight. And he wasn't all that keen on the idea of staying alive anyway.

So this is it, he thought. This is where it ends.

That suited him just fine. What did he have to lose?

"Seamus Blake!"

It was Martha Sellers, marching down the street, and being chased by the cowboy named Billy, who looked thoroughly flustered. His job had been to keep Martha at Chester Brown's general store until the killing was done, and in this he had failed. There was no way to stop Martha Sellers short of manhandling her, and Billy wasn't about to grapple with a lady, even though by not doing so he had let Seamus Blake down. That was something a Shamrock employee did at his peril. The black cloud of fury on Seamus Blake's face made Billy regret ever having left Texas.

Martha had seen Ethan strike Blake, and the way the cowboys on the porch raised their charcoal burners. She was surprised that Ethan was still alive, and she wanted to keep him that way.

"Go back to Chester's store, Martha," barked Blake. "I'll send for you when—"

"Don't be telling me what to do," she snapped right back at him. "You don't own me, Seamus Blake. This is my house, and I'll have no more killing." Reaching the porch, she inserted herself between Ethan and the Shamrock cowboys.

"Better stand aside, ma'am," said Ethan.

"You hush." Glancing bleakly at the men hanging from the elm tree, she turned angrily on Blake. "How dare you! I want those men cut down and given a Christian burial."

"What?" Blake was outraged. "My God, woman! You expect my men to go to the trouble of digging graves for scum like that?"

"I most certainly do."

"Not a chance," growled Blake.

"Then get off my property."

Blake stared at her. "Frank's dead. You ought to give some thought to your situation."

She was furious. "I said git! This instant!"

Blake glowered past her at Ethan. "I've still got some unfinished business with you, Payne."

"You're right about that," said Ethan.

"Shut up, the both of you," snapped Martha.

The Shamrock boss was fuming, but he did as he was told. Ethan watched in pure astonishment as Blake went to his horse, mounted up and, with one last long look at Martha, rode away, followed by his cowboys. Two of the range riders discarded Ethan's rifle and sixgun in the snow near the porch steps.

Ethan could scarcely believe he was still alive. But then, it did make sense to him that Seamus Blake would back down from Martha Sellers. She was probably the only person in the whole territory whom the cattle king would allow to give him orders, and talk to him the way she had. He wanted something from her, and as long as he thought there was a chance of getting it, he would give her plenty of leeway.

Martha turned to Ethan. "Best come inside and let me take a look at that scalp of yours. You've got a nasty cut."

"I'm okay. Gil knocked me out, made a break for it with the other two. He knew he didn't have a chance, but he was trying to save my hide."

"And you jumped right back into the fire, didn't you? I'm so sorry about your friend. And he turned out to be a good friend, still, didn't he? But it's not like you didn't see this coming. You knew what kind of man Seamus Blake is."

"I didn't think he'd back down from you."

Martha looked off in the direction Blake had gone. "I wasn't too sure, either," she confessed. "He wanted no lead-slinging while I was in the way."

"I'll bury Gil and the others," said Ethan.

"No, you won't. You'll come inside and let me see to that nasty cut on your head. Then we'll bury the dead. And after we're finished, you are going to get on your horse and ride out of here, Mr. Payne. Put as many miles between you and Seamus Blake as you can."

"You heard Blake. There's unfinished business between us."

"Why are men such damned fools!"

Her vehemence startled him. It startled her, too. There was a momentary silence, into which the only sound intruding was the creak of rope pulled taut by the dead weight of the three corpses dangling from the elm tree. It was a sound that grated on Ethan's nerves.

"Gil was my friend," he said, realizing that wasn't much of an answer, yet not knowing exactly how to say what was on his mind, and why he was committed to a reckoning with Seamus Blake, a reckoning that even he didn't think he would survive.

"Yes, and he did everything in his power to keep you from getting yourself killed. And if you do what you're set on doing, that will count for nothing. If you want to do something for your friend, ride out of Medicine Bow and put all of this behind you. Live and let live."

Ethan nodded. He knew that it was a rule that she herself lived by; that was evident by the way she had treated him and Gil, knowing that they'd both figured into the killing of her husband.

She put a hand on his arm, and her voice was gentle now. "You're *trying* to get yourself killed. Don't you think I can see that? That's why you decided to cross Seamus Blake even though your friend was going to end up the way he did whether you won or lost, and now that you've lost you're still dead set on provoking Blake, or one of his cowboys, into killing you. I don't know the whole story about what has happened to you in the past, but you've told me enough so that I have a pretty good notion of how you see things. You've had some bad luck, and most of it you didn't bring on yourself. As far as I'm concerned, that just means you're due some *good* luck for a change. You really ought to try to stay alive long enough to find out what that good luck brings you."

Ethan just nodded, and let her lead him inside. He'd made up his mind that the only way to keep Martha Sellers out of danger was to let her think she'd persuaded him. He'd let her patch him up, and let her think he was riding out of Medicine Bow, just as she'd suggested.

And then he was going to finish his business with Seamus Blake.

17

He spent the next several days prowling around the Shamrock house, like an old loafer wolf warily circling its dangerous prey, knowing that it had to pick the right moment to close in because otherwise *it* would become the hunted. He used the spyglass that the line rider named Williams had given him, keeping his distance, and watching the comings and goings. The weather helped him; although it didn't snow anymore the sky remained overcast, reducing visibility. He used the contours of the snow-covered plains, never skylining himself, and keeping when possible in the timber that dotted the open countryside.

There was very little doubt in his mind that Seamus Blake would send some of his cowboys to Medicine Bow for the express purpose of finding out what he was up to. Ethan hoped that they would get around to questioning Martha Sellers as to his whereabouts. She would tell them that he had gone away, that she had persuaded him to put what had happened behind him, to go and never look back. And he also hoped that the cowboys—and Blake—would believe that he had done so. Perhaps maybe then Blake and his hands would let their guard down just a little, thinking that the rustling problem had been taken care of, and that Ethan— a man with a reputation as a gunslinger—had decided not to take issue with them. And if that happened, sooner or later he would find his opening, and get close enough to the cattle king for the reckoning.

And as far as Martha knew, he had put aside his desire for vengeance and ridden away. He hated to lie to her, after everything she had done to help him, but it was the only way to keep her out of whatever trouble would arise. Even though she was opposed to the idea of seeking revenge, he was sure she would have been compelled to help him, and that would have put her in jeopardy. Ethan figured there was a limit to the tolerance Seamus Blake would show her. The last thing Ethan wanted was for Martha to be hurt, especially on his account. She had been put through enough.

At night he would find a place deep in the timber—a different place every night—and dig an outlaw oven, a hole a couple of feet deep in the snow, in which he would build his fire. Then he would tie one of his blankets—Martha had made sure he didn't leave without several—to four trees a few feet above the firehole. That not only reflected some of the warmth back to him when he huddled beneath the blanket covering, but also diffused the smoke and prevented the firelight from playing in the trees overhead. When he was finished cooking up some coffee and beans to go with the biscuits Martha had given him, he would cover the fire with dirt and snow, lay his blankets out over it, and try to sleep, helped by the little warmth emanating from the buried embers. In the morning he would rise before the sun and do his best to erase any trace of his camp before continuing his surveillance.

After four days of it he was beginning to think he'd have to go in after Blake. Not once in all that time did the cattle king leave the vicinity of the ranchhouse. Ethan saw him twice, once on the porch of the house and another time at the corrals. But he never strayed farther afield. Cowboys came and went, and so did Blake's daughter, Kathleen, on two of the four days, riding out with her Indian bodyguard. But not Blake. Ethan judged his chances of actually getting close enough to Blake to kill the man if he had to venture closer to the ranchhouse and decided they were somewhere between slim and none. Yet he couldn't keep prowling around without getting caught. That was bound to happen. So he had to do something. He had to make *something* happen.

He had no definite plan in mind when, on the third occasion that she left the ranch, he followed Kathleen Blake and the Indian. They rode east for two hours, and by the end of it Ethan counted himself lucky that he hadn't been spotted, because even at a distance he could tell that both the Indian and the woman were alertly watching their backtrail. That piqued his interest. They came eventually to a log cabin built in a small valley alongside a frozen creek. Woodsmoke curled from the cabin's chimney. A single horse, saddled, stood in the small adjacent corral. Ethan found a good vantage point about five hundred yards away and, leaving his horse out of sight in a hollow, he climbed to the rim and used the spyglass to get a closer look. A man emerged from the cabin as Kathleen and the Indian were dismounting. Ethan recognized him instantly.

It was Tom Chappell.

He watched as Kathleen melted into his arms. They kissed passionately, and then he led her inside and closed the door. The Indian took his horse and the woman's to the corral. Then he returned to the cabin's porch and sat against the wall and began to smoke a pipe.

Ethan lowered the spyglass. It was obvious what was happening here. Kathleen Blake was carrying on a romance with Chappell, Blake's partner in the Sweetwater Company—a romance that Seamus Blake did not know about.

A plan sprang immediately to mind. It was a desperate plan, and he could think of a dozen ways it could go wrong, but then he was a desperate man. He had to act soon, and it didn't look as though a better opportunity would present itself.

Like the Indian on the cabin's porch, he settled down to wait.

About an hour later Chappell and Kathleen emerged. The Indian got up and went to the corral and brought back his horse and the girl's. Ethan didn't wait to see more. He went down the slope to his mustang, climbed into the saddle, and rode back toward the Shamrock ranch. He was working on the assumption that Kathleen and her escort would return the way they'd come. This was a trip they'd probably made numerous times before, and being creatures of habit, they would not deviate from the usual route unless they had to. Holding to that assumption, Ethan pressed ahead of them and reached some woods through which they had passed on their way to the rendezvous with Chappell. He waited in a thick set of conifers, keeping an eye out for their approach.

He didn't have long to wait. As he'd expected, they were passing through the woods in the same spot as earlier, along a game trail winding through the trees. It was a route that took them within a few yards of his hiding place. They were not as watchful on the return trip, and Ethan knew why— they no longer had to fear that Blake or one of the Shamrock cowboys would follow them to Kathleen's secret assignation. For that reason Ethan remained undetected until they had passed his location and he urged the mustang through the trees and down onto the trail behind them. The Indian heard him first and turned quickly, his hand falling to the butt of the pistol on his hip. But then he saw the Colt in Ethan's hand, and wisely decided not to draw his gun. He murmured something that Ethan couldn't make out to the girl, who turned to look at Ethan as well. She was startled, but recovered quickly.

"Mr. Payne," she said, her voice calm. "They said you had moved on."

"Not yet, Miss Blake."

"You can put the gun away. The Indian won't shoot unless I tell him to."

"Sorry, but I'm not going to take that chance."

"What do you want?"

"You're going to have to come with me." As he said it, Ethan kept his eyes on the Indian. He figured if the man was going to react violently, it would be at this moment, when he learned Ethan's intentions. His job, after all, was to protect Kathleen, and he wouldn't be doing his job if he simply stood by and did nothing while Ethan stole her.

Kathleen must have been thinking the same thing. "Don't," she said, softly but firmly, to the Indian.

"Throw down the iron," said Ethan.

The Indian hesitated. He thought about making a play, but he knew as well as Ethan did that he would die if he did, and he came to the rational conclusion that he would not do Kathleen Blake much good if he got himself killed. So he took the gun slowly from its holster and dropped it on the trail.

"Now you can go," said Ethan. "Tell Seamus Blake I've got his daughter. He'll hear from me. And if he sends his men after me, and they catch up, I'll make sure she dies before I do."

He intended to do no such thing, but tried to sound ruthless enough to convince the Indian that the opposite was true. The Indian's features were a stoic mask now, and Ethan couldn't tell if he'd succeeded.

"Go ahead," said Kathleen. "Do as he says."

The Indian nodded, and Ethan got the impression that he would not have been able to leave had she not given him the okay to do so.

As he rode on down the trail, Kathleen turned her attention back to Ethan. "You *will* die for this, you know." It wasn't conveyed as a threat, but rather as a statement of fact.

"Probably," he said.

She tilted her head slightly to one side, reading him. "But you don't care about that, do you?"

"Not really."

"That makes you an even more dangerous man than you already were."

He admired her coolness. He figured most young women in her situation would have panicked and done something foolish, or broken down. But she apparently wasn't most young women. And the fact that she kept her wits about her made him even more wary.

"Please don't try anything," he said.

"What could I do?" she asked, feigning helplessness.

"You could try to ride away. And if you do I'll shoot the

horse right out from under you. And if you try to *run* away, I'll shoot you."

It didn't work on her. She smiled faintly, still reading him. "I really don't think you'd shoot me, Mr. Payne. But don't worry. I won't try anything. You don't want me anyway, do you? It's my father you're after."

She was too smart, thought Ethan. And the smarter she was the bigger threat she became. He almost wished she'd indulge in a little hysteria.

Bringing his horse alongside hers, he tied her hands behind her back. Then he dismounted and tied her ankles to the stirrups. She watched him, not saying a word, and with a somewhat amused expression on her face. She didn't seem the least bit worried, or afraid of him. It was as though she already knew that there was nothing he could do to her that she couldn't survive. She was either terribly naive, he thought, or extremely brave. Ethan didn't think she was naive.

Once he had her securely trussed, he took up the reins to her horse and led her westward.

He headed for The Breaks. During his ride through that country he'd seen dozens of likely hiding places; it was the best country in the area if you were on the run. They reached their destination by nightfall—a high ledge of rock with a shallow cave nearby, and a sweetwater spring at the foot of a steep but negotiable slope. The only approach was by a narrow canyon, and from the ledge a man could command that approach.

Although it was a safe bet that Seamus Blake had every available Shamrock hand in the saddle and on the search, and that Ethan was the most wanted man in the territory at the moment, he built a fire. There was plenty of deadwood available.

"That can be seen for miles," remarked Kathleen, as he built the fire into a roaring blaze that exceeded what was necessary for warmth.

"It doesn't matter." He put some coffee on to boil.

"Because you think you're safe as long as you have me. That he won't risk my getting shot."

"Am I wrong?" he asked.

Kathleen shrugged, an ironic smile tugging at the corner of her mouth. "I suppose not. It isn't that he loves me. I don't think my father loves anyone but himself, and anything besides power. But he made my mother a promise on the day she died. A promise that he would make sure nothing happened to me. So it just wouldn't do for me to get killed."

"Well, that's what I'm counting on. Sorry, nothing personal. But you turned out to be Seamus Blake's Achilles' heel."

He offered her some beans and biscuits, and she accepted, eating the food with relish. Ethan watched her, wondering about her history. She was well educated, possibly the product of a finishing school. She *looked* very small and delicate, and he was sure that if the situation demanded it, she could play quite the lady. But at the core Kathleen Blake was a woman of the West. Like Martha Sellers, she was tough, and a survivor. She wasn't going to let a little thing like being abducted ruin her appetite, and if she was afraid, she didn't show it.

"I know why you're doing this," she said a little while later, when they'd finished eating and he'd given her a cup of coffee. "But you should have known better than to try to cross my father. He always wins."

"Then you're taking a pretty big chance yourself."

"You mean with Tom Chappell."

"Or maybe I should say it's Chappell who's taking the big chance. What would your father do if he found out?"

"Oh, he'd kill Tom, with his own two hands. Or try to."

"But your father always wins, remember?"

"Yes, that's right." She sipped her coffee. A blanket was draped over her shoulders against the chill of the night. The weather had cleared, and the sky was filled with stars. Way off in the distance a coyote was yapping at the pale yellow moon.

"Then Chappell must love you very much, to take such a risk," said Ethan.

"Yes, he does." It was said matter-of-factly, without a trace of arrogance, but that, he thought, was in itself arrogant.

"I take it you don't have any brothers."

She told him that she'd had a brother, but that he had died in childhood. Then she gave him a sly look. "I know what you're getting at. You're wondering, since I'm my father's only heir, if Tom is just *saying* that he loves me."

"You're a smart woman. I'm sure that possibility occurred to you a long time ago."

Kathleen laughed. It started out a soft laugh, but then grew louder, out of control. She laughed so hard it brought tears to her eyes. The sound echoed down the canyon, black with night shadow. Ethan just sipped his coffee and watched her, his features betraying nothing.

"Oh," she sobbed, gasping for breath. "I'm so . . . I'm so sorry. It's just . . . funny. Terribly funny, that's all."

"What's funny?"

"The idea that Tom . . ." She wiped a tear from her cheek. ". . . that he would pretend to love me so that he could inherit the Shamrock Ranch."

"Why is that? Doesn't he have the ambition? Or do you think it's impossible for anyone to pretend to love you?"

"Oh, no. I'm sure a man could just pretend. But a woman knows when a man is in love with her. And Tom is in love with me. He's so in love with me, in fact, that he has offered to sell his ranch and run away with me. So, yes, he is an ambitious man. And his ambition is to spend the rest of his days—and nights—with me."

Ethan shrugged. He had no stake in any of this, but he was mildly curious about the subterfuge involved in Kathleen's assignations with Tom Chappell.

"I don't understand," he confessed. "Why keep it a secret? Why doesn't Chappell simply court you openly? Surely your father wouldn't object. Seems like he'd be all for you marrying a man like that."

"My father doesn't want any man courting me," said Kathleen, fiercely. "Like you, he assumes any man who did would be after his ranch."

"I see. Well, now it makes more sense. Why you were sneaking around behind your father's back. But if you loved Chappell, why didn't you take him up on his offer to elope?"

She didn't answer at once. Finishing off her coffee, she put down the cup and pulled the blanket closer around her before lying down, her saddle for a pillow. She stared at him for a moment, her eyes bright with reflected firelight. Then she raised the blanket that covered her, invitingly.

"Don't you want to?" she asked, barely above a whisper.

Ethan was speechless, caught completely by surprise.

"It's very cold," she said, affecting a little girl's voice. "It won't hurt anything. Nobody will ever know. Why shouldn't we?"

"No thanks," he said gruffly, thinking he would be safer sharing a blanket with a rattlesnake.

"Suit yourself." She lowered the blanket and closed her eyes and pretended—or so he assumed—to go to sleep.

It occurred to Ethan that he now had another answer—the answer to a question he hadn't asked. Tom Chappell's love for her was probably genuine, especially if he was willing to give up everything just to have her as his bride. But one thing was certain: Kathleen Blake wasn't in love with him. Ethan couldn't imagine that she would offer herself to him so casually if she'd really been in love with another man.

18

Ethan was already up and had a small morning fire going when Kathleen awoke. Shivering from the bitter cold, she wrapped the blanket tightly around her and left the darkness of the cave to join him on the ledge. She was glad to see that the sky remained clear. The sun threw the sharp edges and earthy colors of the canyons and ridges of The Breaks into sharp relief. She stood for a moment at the mouth of the cave and gazed at the panorama and realized that she'd never before recognized how beautiful this country could be.

Sitting on his heels near the fire, with a pot of coffee balanced on the flat rocks he'd used to encircle the small, crackling blaze, Ethan looked up at her, then followed her gaze.

"I wouldn't stand there like that," he remarked casually.

"Why not?"

"You don't see them?"

"See whom?"

Whom. She was well educated, mused Ethan. And she could ride and probably shoot as well as or better than most cowboys. It was a shame, he thought, that she was such a vixen. She didn't love Tom Chappell. She was seeing him, sleeping with him—using him. But for what? Just to satisfy her desires? Any thirty-dollar-a-month cowboy could do that. Ethan had a hunch that Kathleen was playing a dangerous game of her own.

"The Shamrock boys."

Kathleen took another look, only this time it wasn't at the scenery. Try as she might, though, she couldn't see anyone, and wondered if her kidnapper was pulling her leg.

"I don't see anything," she said suspiciously. "Are you sure there's someone out there?"

"I'm sure."

"And how can you be sure that they're Shamrock men?"

"Just guessing."

"Then why are you out here making coffee? Aren't you afraid they'll shoot?"

"I'd be interested to know if they will."

She thought that one over, and decided to err on the side of caution. She sat down, cross-legged, near the fire, next to him, scanning the canyon and the slopes and the ridges for some sign of the men he said were there.

"That's right," she said. "You want them to find us. You're betting that they've got orders not to shoot, for fear of hitting me. But if they do shoot, then that means we're both as good as dead."

"Pretty much." He poured her a cup of strong, steaming hot coffee. She wrapped her hands around the cup and held it close to her face, more for the warmth that the coffee provided than anything else. She noticed that his hand was very steady as he poured. If he was the least bit afraid, he didn't show it.

"You intrigue me, Mr. Payne," she said. "You're not scared of dying. In fact, I'd dare say you're more afraid of living."

He sipped his own coffee. It scalded his tongue. His narrowed brown eyes scanned the steep slope below the ledge. Then, suddenly, he put down the cup and picked up his rifle and, coming up on one knee, brought the rifle to shoulder in a swift, sure motion and fired without taking time—or so it seemed to Kathleen—to even aim.

The bullet ricocheted off stone, and the gunshot echoed down the canyon. An instant later there was a shout of alarm from down below.

"Don't shoot, Payne!"

"Show yourself!" Ethan called down.

Kathleen was on her feet again, and she could see beyond Ethan to the slope below, to the place among the boulders where a man appeared, holding both hands high. She recognized him. It was Slim.

"I just come to talk," said Slim.

"Then you're close enough for that."

"Miss Blake, are you okay?"

She called out an assurance that she was.

"There's no way out, Payne," said Slim. "You're surrounded. There are five more with me."

That came as no surprise to Ethan. He'd known there were several men closing in under cover of the pre-dawn darkness. He'd heard them—the whicker of a horse, the trickle of rocks tumbling down a slope caused by a carelessly placed foot, the clatter of metal—probably a rifle—against stone.

Six Shamrock men, but Seamus Blake wasn't one of them. Ethan was sure of that. Because if Blake was here he would be the one talking. He wouldn't hide in the rocks and let Slim do his talking for him.

"Go tell Blake my business is with him. If he wants his daughter back, he better come here himself."

"We could pick you off right now, Payne, and take Miss Blake home. Be reasonable. Throw down your guns. Give yourself up."

Ethan had to smile at that. He could well imagine what his fate would be if he did as Slim suggested.

"You better make the first shot count," he called back to the Shamrock cowboy. "Because if you don't, I'll kill her."

He glanced over his shoulder at Kathleen as he said it, and saw her look him square in the eye, unafraid, and shake her head. She didn't believe him. But that didn't matter, as long as Slim believed.

"Okay, Payne," called Slim. "Have it your way."

"Ride back and tell Blake to come here," said Ethan, a warning in his voice. "Don't make me wait too long."

Slim disappeared back into the rocks. Ethan watched for a moment, then set the rifle down and picked up his cup of coffee and took another sip. The brew had cooled off considerably.

Kathleen sat back down. She was still shivering, Ethan noticed, and added another piece of wood to the fire. It was a small gesture of kindness that did not escape her notice. She smiled at him, and this time it was a genuine smile.

"You're right," he said, "I wouldn't kill you. Even if you tried to run."

He wasn't sure why he felt compelled to make that admission.

"I know."

"But I will kill your father, if I get half a chance."

"I know that, too," said Kathleen Blake, and drank her coffee.

It was the middle of the afternoon before Seamus Blake arrived. Ethan saw him coming down the canyon, followed by a half dozen riders. He used the long glass and was surprised to see that one of the men with Blake was Tom Chappell. He handed the glass to Kathleen.

"You might want to see this," he said.

She looked through the glass. He watched her face intently. She displayed no emotion.

"It was the Indian," she said.

"What?"

She handed him the glass. "The Indian. He works for Tom. My father doesn't know that. Father thinks he hired the Indian away from Tom, but it was Tom's idea for the Indian to get on the Shamrock payroll. That was years ago. Tom pays him, too. Not that he would have to. The Indian is loyal to Tom, and keeps him informed of everything my father does. So you see, the Indian must have gone back to the cabin and told Tom what had happened. And Tom, being the foolish romantic that he is, has come to rescue me."

Her tone was derisive, and Ethan was certain then that he'd been correct in his assumption that she didn't love Chappell.

"Yes, the Indian went back to tell Tom first," she continued, "because he wasn't sure that my father wouldn't kill him for failing to protect me."

Blake and the other riders checked their horses in the canyon bottom directly below the ledge. Using the long glass, Ethan watched Slim emerge from the rocks and speak to Blake. He turned and pointed toward the ledge. Blake looked up. The distance was too great, even with the long glass, to read the cattle king's expression, but Ethan had a pretty good idea what it would be. It would be the same expression that had been on Blake's face when he'd ordered his cowboys to string up the corpses of Gil Stark and Calkin and Ames in Medicine Bow.

The riders dismounted. Blake started toward the slope, but Tom Chappell grabbed his arm. They spoke for a moment. Blake jerked his arm free, and when he proceeded to climb, Chappell climbed with him. So did Slim. The other cowboys remained with the horses.

Ethan turned to Kathleen. "You'd better get to the back of the cave. Keep your head down."

"There won't be any shooting if I'm standing right beside you."

"Just do what I tell you," he rasped.

She looked at him, considered arguing the point, then went back into the cave.

Ethan drew his Colt revolver, aimed it at the sky, and pulled the trigger.

At the sound of the gunshot Blake and Chappell and Slim all ducked, instinctively seeking cover.

"That's far enough," shouted Ethan.

Blake was the first to show himself. "Where's my daughter?"

"She's here. Safe and sound."

"Let her go, Payne, or by God, I'll—"

"I'll let her go. She can ride away. With your men. But you'll stay, Blake. It'll be just you and me."

"Let her go."

"I want your word first. I want you to say it, in front of all
these men. That you'll stay and finish the business we have.
One on one."

Blake hesitated. Ethan knew that the cattle king understood the stakes involved. If he gave his word, and then went
back on it, his reputation would be ruined. People would
talk behind his back, calling him a coward. His authority
would be undermined. Ethan had him over a barrel. But
what choice did he have? If he didn't agree, he would be
risking his daughter's life. Kathleen Blake knew that Ethan
Payne was not a threat to her, but her father couldn't know
that. He thought Payne was a killer. He believed everything
he'd heard; had bought into the Ethan Payne reputation,
lock, stock, and barrel. That was why he'd hired Ethan in the
first place. Which meant he had to know, too, that if he stood
mano-a-mano against Ethan, he wouldn't stand much of a
chance. Ethan felt a moment of pure elation. He had the bastard right where he wanted him. He was making Seamus
Blake sweat. He was already paying for what he'd done
back in Medicine Bow, and he wasn't even dead yet. . . .

Blake turned his back on Ethan and spoke to Slim, making a curt, angry gesture. Ethan couldn't hear the words, but
Slim's body language told him plenty; the Shamrock cowboy was startled. He actually took a step back from Blake.
Than the cattle king grabbed him by the front of the shirt,
yelled at him, pushed him away in disgust.

"Kill the son of a bitch!"

It was Blake, shouting at his men—and Ethan threw himself to the ground as rifles spoke from several places on the
slope below. The men in the canyon bottom drew their guns
and sought cover. With hot lead screaming through the air
around him and whining off the rocky ledge, Ethan's elation
vanished, replaced by disbelief and defeatism.

The ruthless bastard had decided to sacrifice his own
daughter's life rather than risk his own.

19

Then the anger came, surging through Ethan, blinding him to the risks as he pushed himself up and, on one knee, brought the rifle to his shoulder and began to return fire, as fast as he could work the repeating rifle's action. He fired at the powder smoke that marked the positions of the Shamrock guns, and had he given it any thought he would have realized that his chances of actually hitting a target were very slim. But he wasn't thinking, simply reacting, fighting back. It was instinctive, not a conscious decision.

When his rifle was empty, Ethan didn't hesitate; he turned and ducked into the cave. Some of the Shamrock men had stopped shooting and ducked for cover, but there were still plenty of bullets flying around inside the cave. Kathleen Blake was in the very back, her body curled up into a tight ball, and Ethan threw himself over her, trying to shield her. In that instant he experienced a keen regret for having exposed her to this kind of danger, and a fierce determination to keep her alive. He hadn't expected her to be in harm's way, not really. But that was because he had misjudged Seamus Blake. He'd known Blake was a ruthless man, a man capable of coldhearted cruelty. But he hadn't expected the Irishman to be a coward.

And then, abruptly, the shooting tapered off. Ethan checked Kathleen and was relieved to find that she was unharmed. He checked himself next, and was equally amazed that he hadn't even been nicked. Men were shouting down in the canyon. He couldn't make out what was being said. But *something* had happened. The Shamrock men seemed to have forgotten all about them.

Kathleen tried to rise, but Ethan pushed her back down. He kept an eye on the mouth of the cave, the Colt revolver in his hand, the hammer back. The first man to appear was going to get a bullet between the eyes—Ethan wasn't going to waste time identifying him. But no one appeared. A few minutes later—it felt like an eternity—he heard the thunder of horses on the run. Was the Shamrock crew leaving? Ethan considered the possibility and rejected it. There was no reason, as far as he could tell, for them to pull up stakes and withdraw. Maybe it was a trick. Yes, that was it. Had to be. They were trying to make him believe they were pulling out. And when he showed himself the ones who'd been left behind would fill him full of holes. So he resisted the urge to leave the cave, remained crouched in the darkness, ready to shoot, keeping one hand on Kathleen's shoulder to keep her down. He figured if he waited long enough the Shamrock men would grow tired of waiting and send at least one person up to the cave to see if he and Kathleen were still alive.

"Let me up," whispered Kathleen.

"Stay down."

"They're gone," she said. "Let me up." She pushed his hand away, sat up. "Something's happened. They rode away."

"It's a trick."

She didn't say anything for a moment, and Ethan thought she was going to take his word for it, accept the fact that he had more experience in such matters. But a few minutes later she shook her head and stood up.

"No. They're gone." She stood up and moved toward the mouth of the cave as though drawn by some irresistible intuition that was telling her she needed to see what was outside. Ethan followed her, expecting guns to speak as soon as they showed themselves, preparing himself to bring her down with a flying tackle when the bullets began to fly again. But there wasn't any guntalk when they emerged from the cave. The canyon was embraced by an eerie silence.

They climbed down the slope, and when they reached the general location where Ethan had last seen Seamus Blake, they found her father, sprawled on his back at the base of a large boulder, staring with sightless eyes at the sun, the front of his shirt dark with blood. Ethan noted that his pistol was still holstered. By the look of things, Blake had been shot in the back; the bullet had exited out of his chest. He had probably died in a matter of seconds.

About ten feet away lay another corpse, this one with much of the head blown away, and Ethan wouldn't have been able to identify him except for the clothes that he wore. He'd seen Tom Chappell twice in the past twenty-four hours, and on both occasions the cattleman had been wearing a distinctive brown cowhide coat. There was a gun in Chappell's lifeless hand. He'd been hit half a dozen times at least. But it was undoubtedly the head shot that had proved fatal.

Ethan glanced at Kathleen, curious to see her reaction to Chappell's death. She appeared regretful, but not exactly grief-stricken.

"The poor romantic fool," she said. "I was wondering if he would ever have the nerve to stand up to my father. I guess I know the answer now."

"I don't know about standing up," remarked Ethan. "Your father was shot in the back."

There was no sound, no warning of any kind, except for Ethan's instincts. He suddenly realized they weren't alone, and whirled, the Colt still in hand, to see Slim emerging from the rocks, holding his hands up high.

"For God's sake, don't shoot," said Slim.

"What are you doing here?"

"I volunteered to stay behind. Wait for you two to come out of that cave. We sure as hell weren't going to come in after you."

"Why did the others leave?"

Slim shrugged. "I reckon most of 'em are aiming to quit

the Shamrock. They would have done it a long time ago, probably, except not many men want to stand face-to-face with the likes of Mr. Blake and tell him they're haulin' freight. The rest just flat out didn't want to tangle with you, Mr. Payne. They wouldn't have been here at all were it not for Mr. Blake, you understand."

Ethan nodded. He harbored no ill will toward any of the Shamrock cowboys. They had just been following orders. He nodded at the two dead men.

"So what happened here?"

"I was standing right close, so I heard it all," said Slim. "When the shooting started, Mr. Chappell told Mr. Blake he was gonna have to stop, that he couldn't let Miss Blake get killed. Mr. Blake told him to shut up and start shooting. Well, Mr. Chappell's face turned real dark, and he drew his pistol, and pointed it at Mr. Blake, and told him to order us to stop shooting. Mr. Blake called him a yellow son of a bitch and turned his back on him. That's when Mr. Chappell shot him. I honest to God didn't think he would. But when he did, several of the boys turned their rifles on him. Guess they figured he might try to kill them next." Slim was keeping an eye on Kathleen. "I'm truly sorry, miss."

"Thank you," she said, solemnly, but Ethan didn't think she was sorry at all.

"You aimin' to shoot me, Mr. Payne?" asked Slim.

Ethan holstered the Colt, and the Shamrock cowboy lowered his hands.

"Then I reckon I'll load these two onto their horses and take 'em on home, if it's okay with you folks."

Kathleen nodded. "Yes. Do that."

Slim hefted Seamus Blake's corpse onto a shoulder and started for the canyon bottom. He was a short and wiry man, but endowed with surprising strength and endurance. He handled the heavier dead man without visible difficulty.

Once he was out of earshot, Ethan turned to Kathleen and said, "It turned out just the way you wanted, didn't it?"

"I don't know what you mean." It wasn't a very convincing denial.

"Sure you do. That's why you were seeing Chappell. You didn't love him. That's plain to see. The only other reason is that you figured sooner or later your father would find out, and there would be a confrontation between the two of them, and by that time Chappell would be so hopelessly in love with you that he would do anything to keep from losing you. He'd even go so far as to kill your father. You were counting on that confrontation. And it happened right here."

"You think you've got it all figured out, don't you?"

"I don't think you expected Chappell to end up on the wrong side of grass. Maybe you were thinking about marrying him anyway, just so you could combine the Shamrock with his ranch."

She shook her head. "I thought about it. But the price would have been too high. Besides, it would have made the Shamrock his. As his wife, I would have to surrender all my property to him."

"Right. So you'll just have to settle for the Shamrock."

Kathleen Blake smiled. "I may just buy Tom's ranch and his herd. He doesn't have any heirs. Only creditors."

Grinning, Ethan pushed his hat back off his forehead. "I expect you'll own half the territory before you're through."

She stepped closer, reached out to touch a button on his shirt. "Possibly. And whatever I own, I'm going to need someone to help me hold on to it. There are a lot of dishonest characters out there who will think they'll be able to take advantage of a woman alone. Someone like you, with your reputation, would be of great assistance."

"How much are you offering to pay?"

"I'll give you anything you want," she said, seductively, and it didn't take a genius to figure out she meant more than money. Especially when she slipped two of her fingers between the buttons on his shirt to touch his chest.

Ethan thought it over. He couldn't deny that he was attracted to Kathleen Blake. Any man with a pulse would be. Such an arrangement would be one that most men would give their eye teeth to have. And the fact that he knew what kind of woman he was dealing with wasn't necessarily a deterrent; he'd know better than to fall in love with her, because any man who did was doomed to disappointment if not death. She wouldn't be faithful to him—Kathleen Blake was the kind of person who wasn't capable of fidelity—but then, why would that matter?

But Ethan shook his head and said no.

"You'll have to find some other man. There are plenty with bad reputations, so it shouldn't take you too long."

She actually pouted. "I doubt I'll find another man like you."

"There are plenty better—and some worse."

"Why won't you accept my offer? Isn't it good enough?"

He took her hand and removed it from his shirt.

"It's a very good offer. You're a bitch, Miss Blake. And I'm a bastard. So we'd probably get along. And I expect I'll see you again—in hell. But I'm not staying around Medicine Bow."

"Why not?"

"A bad memory," said Ethan, turning away. "And I've spent my whole life running from bad memories. I'm too old to change."

PART THREE

PART THREE

20

In the spring of 1881, two celebrities rode the Union Pacific rails west out of St. Louis. One was Ned Buntline, journalist, playwright, and ex-Naval officer; a man with rugged, square features and kind, intelligent eyes. He wore a black broadcloth suit, the product of one of New York's most talented tailors, and he carried a malacca cane; an old injury had left him with a pronounced limp. His real name was Edward C. Z. Judson, but what kind of name was that for the author of sensational dime novels?

Buntline, in fact, considered himself the creator of the dime novel, and rightly so. Fifteen years ago he had sought out the old mountain man, Jim Bridger, and persuaded Bridger to tell him his life's story. Taking a liking to the brash young reporter, Bridger took Buntline on a scouting trip across the plains. Buntline remembered fondly how every night as they sat around a campfire, the grizzled old trapper, scout, and Indian fighter would reminisce for hours, providing Buntline with enough material to fill several notebooks. It had been a grand adventure, one that Buntline would always fondly remember, and it had endowed him with a fascination with the West and westerners that bordered on obsession. The civilized East had seemed entirely too tame after that excursion. Buntline had envied Bridger and those like him—men who had dared the unknown dangers of the frontier; stalwart, resourceful, and fiercely independent men who lived by their own rules and—or so Buntline imagined—died without a whimper. He'd wished that he had taken Horace Greeley's advice and gone west as a young man. But he hadn't, and now he lived the life he wished he'd led through the sensational and hugely successful stories that poured from his pen.

About Jim Bridger there were two things that everyone could agree on. The frontiersman was as brave as a lion, and he was well known for his rigorous adherence to the truth. A lie never passed Old Gabe's lips. But that wasn't going to stop Ned Buntline. The writer took the unvarnished truth, twisted it and turned it, exercised plenty of literary license, and employed his own vivid imagination to transform Bridger into the rip-roaringest hero the frontier had ever known. A series of Jim Bridger stories, penned by Buntline, appeared every week for quite some time, and the eastern reading public gobbled them up. The lurid covers of the paperbound editions depicted Bridger fighting grizzly bears and Indians and the cruel elements. Between the covers, Old Gabe leaped from one hairbreadth escape to another with breathless rapidity. They were so successful that a number of other writers, most of whom had never set foot west of the Mississippi River, tried to imitate Buntline by writing their own stories about Bridger and other western legends.

Jim Bridger had never learned to read, but his friends read the Buntline dime novels to him, and the old mountain man would shake his head and comment that a person had to pan that river of pretty words an awful long time to come up with so much as a nugget of truth. It would have bothered Old Gabe that his name and reputation were being associated with such audacious tall tales, except that he'd long ago learned that there was no point in a man worrying over things he was powerless to change. What also didn't bother Bridger—though it did perturb some of his friends—was that he never made a red cent from the sale of all the dime novels that bore his name. His friends told him he would have been a rich man; Old Gabe replied that all the rich men he'd ever known or heard about were vainglorious fools, and he was happy to be spared such a fate.

It also didn't bother Ned Buntline that his stories were more fiction than fact. His readers didn't mind, either. The truth was boring. It didn't sell very well. The truth would not have made Buntline a wealthy man and the country's best-selling author. He made no bones about it. "I do not purvey the West as it truly is, but the way it ought to be," he liked to say. There was nothing glamorous about the life of a mountain man, but Buntline's readers didn't know that. Buntline's imaginary West was as glamorous and glorious as they could ever have hoped for.

Nothing succeeds like success, and Buntline soon found himself with a lot of competition in the dime novel field. To stay ahead of the pack, he searched diligently for another subject like Bridger, whom he could mold into a paperback legend. The man he found, William F. Cody, was his traveling companion on that westbound Union Pacific train.

Buffalo Bill Cody was now the most famous westerner of all, and Buntline was smugly confident that Cody had him to thank for that. Until a few years ago, Buffalo Bill had been an obscure army scout. Born in a log cabin in Iowa in 1846, he'd escaped his poverty-stricken roots by signing up to be a rider for the new Pony Express. There wasn't a more glamorous job for a young adventurer than that. Nor a more dangerous one. It was a life fraught with peril and hardship for many, but Bill Cody seemed to thrive on peril and hardship. He became one of the most reliable riders the company had. During the Civil War he'd served as an army scout, and proved himself reliable in that vocation as well. The army had come to depend on him as they had no other—General Philip Sheridan believed him to be the best scout who had ever lived—and Cody had even been awarded the Congressional Medal of Honor in 1872. But it was Buntline who'd made the name of Buffalo Bill Cody familiar to every household in America.

Cody was not yet forty years old, but he looked older. His life, one of constant struggle and danger, had quickly aged him. Tall and rangy, with shoulder-length sandy hair and a luxurious mustache and goatee, he wore tawny buckskins adorned with long fringe and colorful Indian beadwork. His long frame was draped across the hard wooden bench facing Buntline's, and he was snoozing beneath the floppy brim of his plainsman's hat, oblivious to the rocking and the racket of the train as it chugged down the iron road at thirty miles an hour. It felt, thought Buntline, as though the train was going to jump the tracks at any moment. Cody, mused the writer, could sleep through anything. "I learned a long time back to catch forty winks whenever I could," a drawling Buffalo Bill had told him, "even if it meant doing it in the saddle, or up to my neck in a cold mountain crik."

In Buntline's opinion, Bill Cody was a little on the simple-minded side. Not that he was stupid. Far from it. He had a certain native intelligence. But at times he could be awfully naive. Case in point—Cody's first trip east. In New York City, he had ordered a special dinner put on at Delmonico's for a dozen of his acquaintants, people who had shown him kindness during his visit. Buntline, who had met Cody during a recent excursion west, was one of the guests, and the dinner seemed to be a great success.

But the next morning, when Cody proudly sauntered into Delmonico's to pay his bill, he was astonished to find that the total far exceeded the fifty dollars he had to his name. It had never occurred to him that fifty dollars would not be more than adequate to feed a dozen men. "Out where I come from," he explained, shame-faced, to Buntline, "all you need is an ounce of lead and a charge of powder and you can feed two dozen."

Cody had turned to Buntline for help. Ned had recently written a play, one that was currently being performed in New York City's premier theatre. It was based—loosely—on Cody's career. Having seen the play, Cody told Buntline, "You manage to get me out of a great many ticklish situations in that drama, Judson. So I was hoping you could get me out of a real one with this danged tavern bill."

Buntline had been more than happy to oblige. In return, he asked Cody to present himself before the audience attending the play's next performance. Cody had faced hostiles bent on taking his scalp and not batted an eye, but to answer a curtain call, to stand in the footlights before a packed house, proved far more petrifying than any peril he had faced on the frontier. Still, Bill Cody had guts, and he honored Buntline's request. He faced a storm of applause and a standing ovation. The theatre manager offered him five hundred dollars a week to stay in New York and play himself. Cody had never made that much money in a year, but he declined. That was one thing about many of the westerners he'd met that Ned Buntline could never understand—they seemed to think there were a lot of things in life more important than money. In his opinion, you'd be hard-pressed to find very many people in the East—and particularly in New York City—who thought that way.

That night, seeing how the crowd of usually reserved New Yorkers responded to Buffalo Bill's appearance, Ned Buntline had a stroke of inspiration. A few months later he arranged to meet with Cody and another frontiersman by the name of Texas Jack in Chicago.

"I have written a drama called *The Scout of the Plains*," Buntline announced. "Bill, I would like for you to play yourself in the title role."

"I'd rather be stuck in the path of a herd of stampedin' shaggies with both legs broke," declared Buffalo Bill.

Buntline would not be denied. He was confident that this project would result in fame and fortune for them all. He explained how the play would be composed of authentic scenes that would not only entertain but also educate the public about what life on the frontier was really like. He sold that play more earnestly and with more determination than he had ever sold anything in his life. Eventually the two scouts agreed, reluctantly, to try it for a while. Cody made one stipulation.

"If the Indians go on the rampage, Judson, me and Texas Jack will have to drop everything and get back to the army. They'll need our help, especially with them Sioux."

"And they're going to make trouble, mark my words," said

Texas Jack solemnly. "Yes, sir, them Sioux are not going to go quiet, like so many other tribes have. We've had an easy time of it so far with the redskins. But that's about to change."

Buffalo Bill nodded gravely. "I'm afraid you're right on the money, Texas Jack. So that's the way it'll have to be, Judson," he told Buntline. "If you want us to make fools of ourselves in your extravaganza, you better know that when the Sioux hit the warpath we're hitting the trail."

"We'll put that in the contracts," said Buntline, confidently. He very much doubted that the Sioux or any other tribe would cause the United States Army too much trouble. And even if he was wrong, he could already imagine the sensation their departure for an Indian war would cause. *"Ladies and gentlemen, I regret to inform you that the stars of our show, Buffalo Bill and Texas Jack, have bid the comforts of the East adieu. Those stalwart frontiersmen have rushed to join their comrades in blue in a fight to the death against the savage Plains Indians. We can only hope and pray that they return covered with glory. But if they fall as gallant heroes in battle, at least we had the rare privilege of knowing them."* Yes, it would have to be something along those lines, something dramatic enough to stir the thin blood of his fellow easterners.

"And I'll do you one better," added Ned Buntline. "If you're called back to the frontier to fight Indians, then by God I'll go with you."

Buffalo Bill and Texas Jack laughed, delighted with Ned Buntline's spunk.

Buntline had written his new play in four hours flat. He schooled both plainsmen on their parts with relentless energy. When he believed the men were sufficiently familiar with their roles, the play opened in a prestigious Chicago theatre. But as soon as the curtains rose, Cody was struck by a monumental case of stage fright, and forgot all his lines. Buntline rushed to the rescue.

"What have you been doing with yourself lately, Bill?" he asked, joining Cody on stage.

Cody had spotted a familiar face in the crowd—a wealthy

gentleman named Milligan, whom Buffalo Bill had once guided on a hunting trip. Serving as a guide for easterners, and even some foreign royalty, had been a profitable sideline for the scout in between Indian campaigns. The Milligan hunt had been written up in the Chicago papers.

"Why, I've been out on a hunt with Milligan," replied Cody. It was all he could think to say.

The audience roared with approval and laughter. Milligan's pathological fear of hostile Indians had made him the brunt of many a joke.

"Tell us about it, Bill," urged Buntline, realizing that the play he had written was of no use now—those four hours had been wasted. They were going to have to make this up as they went along.

"We ran up on the meanest passel of redskins I've ever had the misfortune to meet," answered Cody, becoming more at ease. If there was one thing he and Texas Jack and every other plainsman worth his salt could do, it was tell a good story. A man had to be an accomplished campfire raconteur as well as a crack shot to get anywhere on the frontier.

Buntline feigned alarm. "Good heavens, Bill! What happened?"

"Why," drawled Cody, with a slow grin, "Milligan and I got scalped, of course."

The audience exploded into cheers and applause. Though neither Buffalo Bill nor Texas Jack managed to utter a single line of their prepared parts, the play was a smashing success. The scenes in which the scouts dispatched their redskin foes—played by Chicago professionals done up in garish body paint—were real crowd pleasers.

The Scout of the Plains, though panned by the critics, was a financial bonanza. Buntline didn't mind the critical ridicule. He played a small part, and his character met death in the second act; the newspapers suggested that the theatrical world would be a happier place had the death occurred before the play was written. Buntline had a good laugh at that one. The critics could carp all they wanted; his pockets were fast being filled with gold.

From Chicago the play moved to St. Louis, then Cincinnati. Buffalo Bill and Texas Jack got over their stage fright and actually, over time, remembered their parts. Buntline was quite happy to rake in the proceeds. They performed before packed houses everywhere they opened. The season was scheduled to close in Boston. But they never got that far. Texas Jack had been right. The Indians did stir up trouble, and another Indian war *did* break out. It started with a national tragedy, the massacre of the Seventh Cavalry, led by the dashing George Armstrong Custer, at a place called Little Bighorn. The very day that news of this defeat reached Cody, he went to Buntline and announced his immediate departure. Buntline had known better than to try to talk Buffalo Bill out of going. He'd said he would, and if Cody said he was going to do something you could bet the farm that he would.

So off went the star of *The Scout of the Plains*, and Buntline was given the opportunity to recite his by now well-rehearsed and quite melodramatic pronouncement to disappointed audiences. Of course, Buntline didn't go west to fight Indians with Cody and Texas Jack, even though he'd said he would join them. And Cody never called him on it, either. Buntline had to assume this was because Bill knew he'd have his hands full without having to watch over some tinhorn easterner.

Buntline prayed that Cody would not only survive the Indian war but also return a hero. And his prayers were answered. Buffalo Bill was with the Fifth Cavalry when it avenged the death of Custer and his soldiers in an attack on a Cheyenne force at Warbonnet Creek in Nebraska. These very Cheyenne had united with the Sioux and the Arapaho at Little Bighorn, so the Fifth Cavalry's troopers showed no mercy. Neither did Buffalo Bill. In the thick of the fight, he was credited with killing the fierce Cheyenne war chief, Yellow Hand, in one-on-one combat. It was said that Cody took Yellow Hand's scalp and held it aloft for the cavalrymen to see, shouting above the din of battle: "This scalp is for Custer!" The troopers roared their approval of this sentiment, and redoubled their efforts to vanquish the Cheyenne. And vanquish them they did, in a most decisive fashion. Buffalo Bill Cody had become a living legend.

He was more than a celebrity in the East now; he was a true American hero, a defender of American values and a warrior for his people. He was, in short, the most famous westerner of them all. And whom did he have to thank for that? Ned Buntline was entirely too modest to be the one to say it, but he thought he'd had a big hand in it, regardless of Bill's heroics at Warbonnet Creek. He could tell, though, that Cody wasn't at all certain that he liked the fame. Though he felt obliged to return to the east following the end of the Indian war and fulfill his contract with Buntline, the scout made no bones about the fact that he frankly couldn't wait for the show to finish its tour so he could go back out West. "Where I belong," he told Buntline. Though the Indians were subdued, Buffalo Bill had agreed to serve as guide to another one of those wealthy English gentlemen who wanted to put on a big safari on the American frontier. Buntline wasn't worried, having elicited Cody's solemn word that he would be back the following year for another season before the footlights. And for a man like Buffalo Bill Cody, his word was his bond, no matter how many second thoughts he might have in the meantime.

The second season was an even bigger success than the first. When it was over, Buntline had a new proposition for Buffalo Bill. Inspiration had struck again, this time on a much grander scale.

"We've done well, Bill, but we can do better," Buntline told him. "You're a big hit in the East. And yet even if we played every night the year round, we couldn't pack all the people who want to see your show into the theatres."

"What do you suggest, Judson?"

"An outdoor extravaganza. A Wild West Show. Horses, buffalo, wild Indians—I mean the genuine article, Bill, not bit players painted up to look like redmen. We'll travel from place to place in a great caravan of wagons. We'll set up in the great outdoors, and play to thousands at a time, instead of hundreds the way we do now. Best of all, we'll be able to give the people what they really want—the sights and sounds and taste of the West as it really is."

Bill Cody was cautiously enthusiastic. He liked Buntline, and appreciated what the man had done for him, but he didn't entirely trust the man. Still, a Wild West Show sounded a damned sight better than a theatre show. Especially if Buntline was sincere in that last part. One thing that had been bothering Cody was the likelihood that many of the easterners who had come to see *The Scout of the Plains* were getting the wrong impression of what life out West was like. It would be good to bring them the authentic article— real Indians, real cowboys, real mountain men. And best of all, it would be a way for Cody to spread some of the wealth around. He'd felt more than a little guilty profiting from the story of the West while so many of his friends—men who had, in some cases, played a much larger and more important role in that story than he—had not.

"Sounds like a possibility," he murmured, trying not to sound at all excited, knowing that if Buntline sensed he had his hook in Buffalo Bill Cody, he would proceed to take control of the whole enterprise. Though he'd been one of the stars of *The Scout of the Plains,* Cody had at times felt like little more than a stage hand. It was Judson who ran the show. Buffalo Bill was determined that it would be different this time. "Thing is, I won't put my name to such an endeavor unless I have the say-so in who gets hired for the show."

"Well, I . . ." began Buntline.

"I know the best shots, the best horsemen, the best trackers, the best rope artists, and the best bullwhackers in the wild country," said Cody. "If you want this Wild West Show to be a big success, Judson—and I'm sure that you would settle for nothing less—then you'll want the best people. And I know where to find them. Then there's the little matter of talking them into it. A lot of these men I'm talking about will be reluctant to give up life in the wide open to go traipsing around this neck of the woods showing off in front of big crowds of city folk."

Buntline smiled. It seemed Buffalo Bill Cody had learned a thing or two about the business end of things.

"All right, then. You'll do the hiring, Bill."

"Fine. When do we start?"

"This will take some time to organize, and a lot of money. We'll have to play another season or two and put back as much money as we can. Meanwhile, when we are able, we must go west and recruit our cast."

"We?"

"Well, you know me, Bill. I can't pass up a chance to visit *your* neck of the woods. But not to worry. I won't interfere."

And that, mused Ned Buntline, as he gazed out at the rolling prairie from the Union Pacific passenger car, was what he and Buffalo Bill were doing now. At the moment they were looking for a particular man, in part as a favor for a friend of Cody's. The man's name was already well known in the East, and in that respect he would make a perfect addition to the show. But his reputation was what bothered Ned Buntline. By all accounts he was a hired killer, a dangerous man. More dangerous even than Wild Bill Hickok, who had joined his friend Cody for a few performances during their recent tour after Texas Jack's departure.

Wild Bill had proven to be too wild to handle. He was forever getting into trouble. He seemed to go out and look for it. In Titusville, Pennsylvania, he got into a fight with a pack of roughnecks from the oil fields. When on stage he would sometimes whirl, draw his six-shooters—which were loaded with blank cartridges—and blaze away at the crowd. Blanks or not, the audience inevitably reacted by scattering like quail, much to Wild Bill's amusement. He also liked to shoot his blanks so close to the bodies of the imitation Indians he was battling in the play's fight scenes that the discharge would singe the actors and sometimes ignite their clothing.

On one occasion, after an altercation with the manager of one of the theatres, Wild Bill had grabbed the man by the shoulders and hurled him over the footlights into the orchestra pit. A policeman was summoned, the manager lodged a complaint, and Wild Bill was informed that he was being placed under arrest.

"How many of you are there?" Wild Bill wanted to know.

"I'm alone," said the peace officer dubiously.

"You'd better get some help," replied Hickok amiably.

The policeman decided that this was excellent advice and took his leave, returning a short while later with another officer of the law.

"How many of you are there now?" queried Wild Bill.

"Two of us."

Wild Bill shook his head and fastened a steely gaze upon the constable. "I think you need more reinforcements, amigo."

The policeman nodded. "I think I do, too."

When he returned the third time he brought a dozen men with him, and Wild Bill, amused by the entire affair, surrendered himself peaceably into their custody.

Such shenanigans finally convinced Cody that his unpredictable friend could not remain with the show. That suited Wild Bill just fine. His contract annulled, he returned to his beloved frontier, only to be killed in Deadwood a short while later by the coward Jack McCall, who shot Hickok in the back of the head, apparently without provocation. Wild Bill had been playing poker, one of his favorite pastimes. His hand, at the moment of death, had been two pair, aces and eights—the winning hand. McCall had recently been hanged in Yankton, Dakota Territory.

"What I'll never understand," Cody sorrowfully told Buntline, "is how Wild Bill could have let somebody sneak up on him from behind. I can't believe he didn't know McCall was stalking him."

Buntline kept his opinion to himself. He was convinced that Wild Bill Hickok had harbored a death wish. But he saw no point in trying to persuade Cody that his self-destructive friend had grown weary of life.

As far as Buntline was concerned, the man they were going to Denver to find was made from the same mold as Hickok. Buntline had grave reservations about signing him on. But Cody was insistent. And Ned Buntline remembered that he'd promised not to interfere in the hiring of the Wild West Show's cast. Still, in this case Cody wasn't being reasonable. Hadn't he learned anything from trying to handle Wild Bill? Why did he have to go out and recruit more trouble? It was just bad for business. So Buntline wrestled with the problem of whether he should violate the arrangement he had with Cody and put his foot down. He had no illusions with regard to how difficult it could be to change Cody's mind. Buffalo Bill had never met this man, yet he had given his word to a lady that he would find Ethan Payne and recruit him for the show.

And Buffalo Bill always kept his word.

21

Clad in his buckskin garb, with his weathered face and shoulder-length mane of sandy hair, Buffalo Bill Cody could not go anywhere in the East without attracting a lot of attention. But Ned Buntline noticed that west of the Mississippi Cody could travel in relative obscurity. The frontier was brimming with picturesque characters, a manifestation, the New Yorker supposed, of the rampant individualism that life on the wild frontier encouraged. Then, too, it was simple frontier etiquette to leave a man alone and not ask too many questions. You could inquire after a man's identity if you had a demonstrably valid reason for needing to know, but if you asked about his business you risked giving offense. And in the West that was sometimes a dangerous thing to do. This was one of the many aspects of western life that Buntline truly appreciated, because it had been his experience that "back east" people tended to involve themselves in the affairs of others. This nosiness, he supposed, was just an offshoot of civilization, but it was hardly civilized behavior, in his book.

Since Buffalo Bill Cody did not attract undue attention because of his appearance, they were able to travel from St. Louis to Denver by rail without causing a ruckus. It was clear that for his part Cody appreciated the anonymity. He had never been comfortable with all the attention and the adulation foisted upon him by the eastern public. He didn't cotton to being a celebrity.

At Cheyenne they left the Union Pacific line and switched to a "short" line that took them on into Denver. The city sprawled across a high plain ringed by mountains—a peaked and scalloped line of blue or snow-clad green, depending on their distance. Unlike many other mining towns, Denver had an air of permanence about it. A great many of the buildings had been constructed of granite or red sandstone. The residential areas looked quite respectable. The "bad" side of town was limited to a couple of streets where the gambling halls were located above saloons. In the past few years Denver's population had doubled, and its citizens were brashly confident in the future of their adopted home. They adhered to a "thousand-mile theory" of progress to prove that Denver was destined for greatness. Chicago was a thousand miles from New York, Denver was a thousand miles from Chicago, and San Francisco was a thousand miles from Denver. Obviously Denver was perfectly located to become one of the premier metropolitan areas of the nation. It was the only real city that existed west of the Mississippi, at least in Ned Buntline's experience.

Leaving the train depot, Buntline and Cody walked to nearby Brown's Palace and paid for a pair of the best rooms in the house. Buntline had long since grown accustomed to luxury in his accommodations. He felt the best of everything was his due. Cody knew that the writer had grown up in poverty, and that he had climbed the ladder of success and made a name for himself despite such humble beginnings was something that Buntline had every right to be proud of. For his part, Buffalo Bill would have been happy with an empty stall filled with relatively clean straw in the local livery. But he understood that even though he didn't particularly care for the role of celebrity, his friend and business associate insisted that he play the part.

Noting that the desk clerk was avid in his perusal of the local newspaper, Cody asked him if he knew where a Mr. Ethan Payne could be found.

"Ethan Payne!" The clerk recognized the name, and he doused it with stern disapproval as he spit it out. "Yes, indeed, I *do* know where you can find him. Behind bars. Which is *exactly* where a man like that belongs."

Buntline groaned. "I'm almost afraid to ask. What did he do? Kill somebody?"

"Nope. He was arrested for vagrancy. Owes some people a lot of money. Some of them are people you don't want to owe money to."

"I don't follow you," confessed Cody.

"I mean people like King Letcher. He runs a gambling hall. Not a man you want to short-change. From what I've heard, Payne can't pay his gaming debts. Folks who can't pay their debts to King Letcher usually wind up with their skull broken, or worse. Of course, in Payne's case, we would have ended up with a lot of dead bodies, because Letcher wouldn't have gone after him alone, and everybody knows Ethan Payne is a cold-blooded killer."

"Cold-blooded?" asked Cody. "What makes you say that? What has he done?"

The clerk peered at Buffalo Bill. "You don't know?"

"No. I don't know much about the man, frankly. I'm looking him up as a favor for a friend."

The clerk put the paper down and peeled off his spectacles and began to clean the lenses on the sleeve of his coat. "Well, let's see. Way I hear it, he got his start over in California, in the Gold Rush days. Gun guard for a mining outfit. Killed a bunch of road agents who were trying to steal the gold. He might have captured them and brought them in, but not Payne. No, sir, he gunned them all down. That would become a habit with him."

"Killed a passel of road agents," murmured Cody. "That doesn't sound so bad."

"It would get worse. Then he worked as a troubleshooter for the Overland Mail Company. They say he murdered a station manager in order to steal the man's wife. He was let go, and wound up in some Kansas trail town—Abilene, I think it was."

Cody nodded. "He was a town marshal in Abilene. That much I do know."

"He married some whore there, and got into so many gun-fights that the good people of the town finally sent him pack-ing. They decided he was more dangerous than the Texas cowboys he'd been hired to keep an eye on. He showed up next in Wyoming, and became the hired killer of a cattle baron by the name of Seamus Blake. They had a falling out, and some say he killed Blake. Shot him in the back. Others say it wasn't him who did the deed. But I wouldn't be surprised if he had."

"Sounds like you have a bone to pick with Payne," remarked Cody.

The clerk shook his head. "Never met him, myself. I just don't like his kind. And we sure don't need gunslingers of his caliber in Denver. This is a respectable town. Not like it was in the early days, when it was just another wide-open mining camp. In those days maybe Ethan Payne would have fit in. But there's no place for him these days."

Cody glanced at Buntline. "You see, we're trying to get civilized out here, just like folks back east."

The clerk nodded vigorously, oblivious to the veiled sar-casm in Buffalo Bill's comment. "That's absolutely right. It's why the sheriff arrested Payne and put him in a jail."

"To protect him from this King Letcher fellow?" asked Buntline.

"One way or the other, somebody was destined to die." The clerk shook his head again. "Letcher and Payne are a couple of cards from the same crooked deck if you ask me. Person-ally I wouldn't care if they did kill each other. And I doubt the sheriff would, either. The thing is, when there's gunplay, inno-cent people sometimes get hurt. We've got a bad element here in Denver, and I reckon it can't be helped, but we're trying to make our town a good, decent place to live, and, like I said, we don't need the likes of Ethan Payne around."

"Well, I'll certainly sleep better knowing that you folks take keeping the peace so seriously," said Buntline.

Buffalo Bill suppressed a smile. He knew that the writer wasn't being sincere. The last thing Ned Buntline wanted was a tamed West.

"You see," said Cody, as they walked away from the hotel

desk, "that's the reason I want to do this Wild West Show. To capture the spirit of a frontier that is vanishing right before our eyes. That man was right about one thing. There really isn't room out here anymore for men like Payne."

"You know more about this Payne fellow than you let on," said Buntline. He had done his homework prior to leaving Chicago, checking newspaper sources to find anything he could on Ethan Payne. This information he had shared with Cody, in hopes it might dissuade Buffalo Bill from carrying out his plan to hire Payne. It hadn't worked.

Cody nodded. "I know what you told me, which is what got written up in some big-city newspaper. Which doesn't necessarily make it true. But I wanted to find out what the rumors were. It isn't always the truth that matters, you know, Judson. What matters is what people *think*, true or not."

"If he's done everything the clerk said he's done, then he strikes me as a pretty bad character."

"Maybe," allowed Cody. "I say we cache our possibles in our rooms and go to the jailhouse to see for ourselves."

"Sounds like a good idea."

They arrived at the Denver jail a quarter of an hour later. A young man with a tin star on his brown broadcloth coat and a flourishing mustache that covered most of the lower portion of his angular face was at his desk going through a stack of wanted posters. He peered suspiciously at his two visitors as though he was trying to remember if he had recently studied their likenesses.

"We'd like to see Ethan Payne," said Cody. "We understand he's a guest here."

The lawman wasn't amused. "Who wants to see him?"

"This is Mr. Ned Buntline," said Cody, "and I am William F. Cody."

"Buffalo Bill," added Buntline helpfully.

The young peace officer's eyes widened and his face became animated. He shot to his feet and stuck out a hand. "It's an honor to meet you, Mr. Cody."

"My privilege, sir." Cody gave Buntline a sidelong look; he didn't like it when Ned Buntline tossed his name around like that, as though it were some sort of currency. It was a little too much like bragging.

"You a friend of Payne's, Mr. Cody?" asked the young lawman.

Cody sighed. "Nope. I've never met the man."

He fastened his steel-blue eyes on the fellow behind the star, daring him to violate western etiquette by asking him specifics about his business with Ethan Payne. He could tell that the lawman was thinking about it, and his curiosity almost got the better of him. Almost.

"I guess that'll be okay," he said. "But I'll have to ask you to leave any weapons you have right here on the desk."

Cody placed his pearl-handled Colt revolver on the desk, and noticed that Buntline wasn't producing any weapons of his own. With a devilish smile, Buffalo Bill drawled, "Well, Judson? I guess you've forgotten that over-and-under you keep in your right-side coat pocket."

Startled, Buntline glanced guiltily from Cody to the lawman, who was suddenly looking at him suspiciously.

"Who did you say you were, mister?"

"Ned Buntline. I'm a . . . writer."

"Can't say that I've heard of you. What do you write?"

It was all Buffalo Bill Cody could do to refrain from laughing out loud at the expression on his associate's face.

"I can vouch for him, deputy," he said.

"Well, that's good enough for me, Mr. Cody."

Buntline put his derringer on the desk beside Buffalo Bill's six-shooter.

They were allowed into the cellblock. According to the lawman, Ethan Payne occupied the first cell on the left. The deputy locked the cellblock door behind them. Ned Buntline wasn't sure what to expect, but he wasn't at all prepared for what he found. The man sitting on the narrow iron bunk in the five-by-eight cage of strap iron looked like a Bowery bum. Payne hadn't shaved in more than a week, and by the smell of things he hadn't bathed in at least a month.

He seemed lost in thought, and didn't bother looking up to see who was entering the cellblock.

"Ethan Payne?" asked Cody.

Ethan raised his head and fastened bloodshot eyes on his visitors. "Who wants to know?"

"I am William F. Cody. This is my friend and business associate, Ned Buntline. We've come to make you a proposition."

"Go away."

"Is it true, Mr. Payne, that you stood up against fifty Texas rowdies in Abilene, Kansas?" asked Buntline.

"Fifty?" Ethan smirked. "Why not make it a hundred?"

"Are you not the Ethan Payne who singlehandedly tracked down and brought to justice the vicious Wesley Grome gang of road agents in your capacity as troubleshooter for the Overland Mail Company?"

"Wesley Grome never robbed a stage in his life that I know of," said Ethan, bitterly. "But I let him hang, all the same."

"Didn't you clean out a gang of rustlers, at least twenty in number, up in the Wyoming Territory, leaving none of the desperadoes alive to tell the tale?"

"I didn't kill anybody in Wyoming. That includes Seamus Blake. Though I planned to. Somebody else got to him first."

Buntline glanced at Cody. "Are you sure you want to go through with this, Bill?"

"I gave my word, Judson."

Buntline sighed.

"Mr. Payne," said the famous Indian scout, "I want you to come to work for me. Mr. Buntline and I put on a play for the folks back East. We've been very successful, and we've got big plans for the future. I can offer you a thousand dollars a month to start."

"A thousand dollars?" Ethan was stunned. "That's a lot of money."

"All you have to do is sign a contract and portray yourself in an extravaganza," explained Buntline.

"An extravaganza," said Ethan, sounding extremely skeptical.

"I can write a scene that I believe will replicate your heroic stand against the Texans in Abilene. I am confident it will be very well received."

"The East must be chock full of fools if you think those folks will buy me standing up alone against fifty men."

"Well, we might not be able to manage fifty," confessed Buntline, his businessman's mind immediately calculating the costs involved. "How about a dozen?"

"This extravaganza. What's it about?"

"It consists primarily of Buffalo Bill's exploits on the frontier. We portray the glamour and glory of the Wild West for the enjoyment and edification of our fellow countrymen."

"Glamour and glory?" Ethan laughed. "Who are you trying to kid?"

"We just give the people what they want," said Buntline, defensively.

"So how 'bout it, Payne?" asked Cody. "Are you game? Or would you rather sit here and rot in this iron cage?"

Ethan stood up and came to the cell door. Buntline could hardly refrain from backing up, the stench of the man was so great.

"Sure," said Ethan. "Why not? My life's been one big lie anyway. Problem is, I owe a man a lot of money, and I haven't got two bits to my name."

"King Letcher," said Cody, nodding. "We know about that."

"He cheated me out of my last dollar."

"I'll square things with Letcher, and pay your fine. It will come out of your first month's wages. Fair enough?"

"It's come down to more than money where Letcher is concerned," said Ethan.

Buntline thought he saw a fierce gleam in Ethan Payne's muddy brown eyes. Yes, he thought, this man is indeed a killer of men. It's the only way he knows. It's how he resolves matters, even though you can look at him and tell he knows that it doesn't actually resolve anything.

"He has this notion that it would do his reputation a lot of good if he killed me," added Ethan, as though he found the concept amusing. He didn't look at all worried that there was a man out there somewhere who wanted to see him dead.

"Well," said Cody, "maybe I can smooth things over with him."

Ethan gave Buffalo Bill a long look. Behind the fancy get-up and the showmanship there was a real westerner, a man who was straightforward and honest.

"What have I got to lose?" asked Ethan dryly.

22

Outside the Denver jailhouse, Buntline pulled Cody aside, out of the flow of foot traffic on the busy boardwalks. It was time, he'd decided, to level with his companion.

"Bill, I know Hickok was a friend of yours, but you have to admit he made trouble for us. This man Payne will make Wild Bill look like a saint by comparison."

Cody laughed. "You're awful quick to judge, ol' pard. But what can I do? I gave—"

"I know, I know," sighed Buntline. "You gave your word. I wish you'd stop doing that, Bill. And why didn't you mention that fact to Payne? Maybe he'd be interested to know that he has a friend back East."

Cody shook his head. "I was asked not to." It was all he intended to say on the subject. "Come on, Judson, let's pay this feller Letcher a visit."

"Sounds like fun," said Buntline dubiously.

King Letcher proved to be everything Buntline had expected, and more. He ran a gambling den and saloon in Denver's red light district, and by all appearances he'd done very well in his chosen profession, which was fleecing the miners and cowboys who ventured into his establishment of their hard-earned wages.

The saloon downstairs was virtually indistinguishable from hundreds of others in the West—a long mahogany bar, a few tables, misty oil paintings of voluptuous nudes on the walls, a well-stocked back bar, a trio of bartenders of servicing the patrons. Percentage girls in gaudy dresses and heavily rouged faces worked the clientele. One of them accosted Buntline as soon as he entered the saloon, brushing her breasts against his arm as she tried to entice him into buying her a drink. Ned Buntline knew how the system worked. The girl would hold out the promise of sex to lure him into buying her a drink, which would wind up costing him three or four times what it should cost, considering that the bartenders would be under orders to water down the drinks issued to the girls. Then another drink, and another. And when she decided she'd gotten all she could out of him, she'd leave him. The girl would get a percentage of every drink she sold, so it was in her best interests to work as many of the saloon's patrons as possible. If any of her marks made trouble, King Letcher had several burly men stationed in strategic locations around the establishment whose only job was to keep an eye peeled for trouble and to dispose of it as quickly as possible. This usually involved bloodshed and broken bones.

The percentage girl was persistent, but Buntline finally managed to rid himself of her. Scowling, he joined a chuckling Bill Cody, who had moved on, unmolested, to the bar.

"Have you met the love of your life, then, Judson? If so, I'd wager they have rooms in the back where such things can be consummated. But you won't believe how expensive these women can be."

"Very funny, Bill. You're a barrel of laughs." Buntline considered expressing his opinion that the high-priced courtesans in Chicago and New York were, as a rule, far more beautiful and certainly more sophisticated than these western whores. But he refrained from doing so, if for no other reason than to spare himself from having to elaborate on how he knew this to be the case.

Cody fingered the lapel of Buntline's exquisitely tailored jacket. "It's the duds, ol' pard. You fairly reek of money."

"You've got money, too."

"But I don't look like I do. That's the secret. No sir, I look like just another hidehunter or scout in town after six months in the big lonesome who's spent his whole bankroll on some new duds."

Buntline caught a barkeep's eye. "We're looking for King Letcher. Is he around?"

The apron pointed at the ceiling and moved on.

They went upstairs to the gambling hall. Letcher's poker tables, wheels of fortune, and faro and chuck-a-luck operations were all doing a very brisk business. Two lookouts, one at each end of the long narrow room, sat on their platforms and from these vantage points watched the goings-on with steely eyes that missed nothing. They were armed with scatterguns and looked like they knew how to use them and wouldn't mind being given the opportunity to demonstrate their skill.

Letcher was running his own table, playing high-stakes poker with a trio of well-heeled gentlemen, an attractive floozy in a purple dress that could barely restrain the magnificence of her snow-white bosom by his side. Letcher was huge and powerfully built, with jaws like a bulldog's and the eyes of a ferret, dark and feral. His chubby fingers, adorned with rings, were dexterous as he shuffled a deck of cards and then flicked the pasteboards to the other player, dealing the new hand. They were playing five-card draw, and Cody and Buntline stood by and observed as Letcher won a hundred-dollar pot with a straight. This cleaned out one of the gentlemen, who morosely took his leave. Cody sat down in his place.

"Ten-dollar minimum bet at this table, friend," said Letcher in a deep rumbling voice, and with a disinterested glance in Buffalo Bill's direction. It was obvious he thought the buckskin-clad Cody lacked the wherewithal to play the game.

"Oh, I haven't come to gamble," drawled Cody.

"Then go about your business," said Letcher gruffly, deftly shuffling the pasteboards.

"I'd be obliged for a few minutes of your time."

"I'm busy. Now you go on. Get."

Cody kept smiling. He did not seem offended by Letcher's curt brush-off. But Ned Buntline was offended. Bristling, he stepped forward.

"Perhaps you don't realize who you're talking to, sir."

"Judson, don't—." But Cody didn't get the chance to finish the admonition, and in hindsight he figured it wouldn't have done much good anyway.

"This is Buffalo Bill Cody," finished Buntline, as though he were introducing commoners to a member of royalty.

"Yeah, right," said Letcher. "And I'm Calamity Jane."

He looked at the other players, who quickly realized that they were expected to laugh at his attempt at humor, which they proceeded to do. Buntline thought they were good actors all, and considered suggesting—sarcastically—to Cody that they hire the whole lot for the Wild West Show. But Buffalo Bill was off on another tack.

"Oh no, you're not Calamity Jane," said Cody. "I know Calamity, and she don't smell half as pretty as you do. You must bathe in that French cologne, Mr. Letcher."

Letcher stopped shuffling and glowered at the scout. "You're starting to annoy me. And people who annoy me wind up in a world of hurt. I don't care who you are. You'd better haul your freight."

Cody didn't budge. He just kept smiling at King Letcher as though the two of them were the dearest of friends. "This won't take long. I've come to pay a debt owed you—a debt incurred by a friend of mine. Ethan Payne."

With hooded eyes, Letcher put down the cards, sat back in his chair, and peered across the table at Cody. Buntline couldn't read the expression on the man's face, but he didn't fail to notice that Letcher's right hand dropped below the level of the table. He hadn't spent much time out West, but Buntline already knew that in a confrontation of this sort you had to worry about the other fellow's hands, and their proximity to his six-shooter. Not that he knew for certain that Letcher was heeled. But it was a pretty safe bet that he was. Buntline glanced warily at Cody, wondering if Buffalo Bill was aware of this development.

"You ought to be more particular about the friends you make," sneered Letcher.

"How much does he owe you?"

"Three hundred dollars. He called and raised a bet and said he was good for it."

"I'd have thought you only played table stakes."

"That's usually the case. I knew he didn't have it," smirked Letcher. "But then, I also knew he wasn't going to beat my full house, either."

"So you gave him enough rope and he hanged himself."

"Something like that."

"Why would you do such a thing?" asked Buntline.

Letcher shrugged. "I like to see men crawl."

"I'll wager Ethan Payne surprised you. I doubt he crawled," said Cody.

Letcher's beady eyes glittered as hard and cold as the diamonds on his fingers. "He called me a cheat. That was a big mistake."

"But it was true, wasn't it?" asked Cody. "Your decks are marked, aren't they?"

One of Letcher's poker opponents made a small sound, as though he were choking on something caught in his throat, and hastily stood up. "Excuse me," he said in a strangled voice, and discreetly slipped away. The other player seemed to be frozen in place. He leaned way back in his chair, looking nervously from Cody to Letcher and then back again. As for the girl who was almost coming out of the purple dress, Buntline noticed that she took two backward steps and glanced at the nearest lookout. Buntline was much relieved to see that the vigilant shotgunner's attention was focused on some loud action at a chuck-a-luck table on the other side of the room.

"Are you really Buffalo Bill Cody?" asked Letcher.

"Yep."

"Well, I don't care if you're Jesus Christ. Nobody calls me a cheat and gets away with it."

As he spoke, Letcher reached under his coat with the right hand that was concealed beneath the table.

"Look out, Bill!" Buntline saw the movement of Letcher's arm and issued the warning softly, trying to avoid drawing the attention of the lookouts. He assumed Letcher was reaching for a hideout pistol. To his surprise, Letcher froze. His beady eyes seemed to bulge from their sockets. Bewildered, Buntline noticed that Cody was leaning forward in his chair, a benign smile on his weathered face. Buntline bent over to peek under the table. Cody had planted the barrel of his six-shooter in Letcher's groin area. The writer felt like laughing out loud. He'd been so worried about what Letcher was doing with his hidden hand that he'd failed to notice what Buffalo Bill had been doing with *his* hands.

"Now, King," said Cody, employing the tone a man would use when he was trying to reason with an old friend, "that's a mighty pretty lady you got there. If you ever want to do more than look at her from now on, I'd advise you to keep your hands where I can see them."

Slow as molasses, Letcher removed his hand from under the coat and placed it alongside his other hand on the table, palms down, chubby, diamond-bedecked fingers splayed.

"Let me tell you what I want you to do," said Cody. "I came here with every intention of paying Ethan Payne's debt. But I can see that you cheated him, so I no longer consider that debt to be a legitimate one. I'm sure you agree."

Letcher nodded.

"Fine. I knew you were a reasonable man. So this is what I want you to do. You're to write a letter to the sheriff saying that, being the generous fellow that you are, you've decided to drop any charges or complaints you might have against Payne."

Letcher was fuming, but he didn't say anything, and he didn't move, either. Didn't so much as twitch. Buntline knew Cody still had his pistol lodged in the vicinity of the gambler's private parts.

"In return," continued Cody, "I'll do you a favor. Soon as Payne gets out of the calaboose, I'll keep him from coming over here and ventilating you. How's that for fair?"

"Sounds fair," said Letcher through clenched teeth.

"Judson, you're never without pencil and paper, I believe," said the famous scout.

Buntline produced his notebook and a stubby charcoal pencil from his coat pockets and gave them to Letcher, who promptly wrote the note to the sheriff. Cody read it and nodded in satisfaction.

"That should do the trick." He stood up, and the pistol was back under his belt. "We won't take up any more of your time, Mr. Letcher. Come along, Judson."

Buntline followed Cody out of the gambling hall, fully expecting King Letcher to order his lookouts to stop them, and fully prepared to dive to the floor as soon as he saw one of those scatterguns swinging in his direction. But King Letcher just sat at the table, unmoving, watching Buffalo Bill Cody leave with those cold, hooded eyes. Buntline would have been willing to bet that they couldn't get out of the saloon without some mishap. But he would have lost that bet. When they reached the street, the New Yorker remembered to start breathing again.

"That was the damndest thing I ever witnessed, Bill," he gushed, heady with the joy of being alive. His hands were trembling, and he laughed self-consciously as he showed them to Cody. "Why, it was just like something out of a dime novel!"

"I'm sure it will be," replied Buffalo Bill wryly.

"You're an honest-to-God hero."

Cody winced. "Not at all. A man never knows how big a shadow he casts until he stands all the way up."

Buntline raised a brow. "What does that mean?" Buffalo Bill had a funny habit of spouting off like that, coming up with these sayings that, most of the time, left the writer baffled.

"Damned if I know, Judson. But it has a ring to it. Maybe you can use it. Come on. Let's spring our new partner out of jail."

As they angled across the bustling Denver street, Buntline said, "One thing, Bill. Was King Letcher really using a marked deck?"

Cody just shrugged.

"He must have been, the way he acted."

23

Ned Buntline had written about dozens of gunfights. An untold number of men had perished violently in his dime novels. But he himself had never been so close to violence of the sort he wrote about as he had been that night in Denver, and it took a little while to smooth out his nerves. Without making any comment about how frayed around the edges the writer looked, Cody suggested that they drop by another saloon on the way back to the jailhouse and have a drink. Buntline gratefully accepted. He ordered a whiskey and knocked it back in one gulp. Then he beckoned the bartender over and asked for another shot. Meanwhile, Cody sipped his whiskey and then looked at the note that King Letcher had written at his request.

"You're not thinking of springing Payne out of jail tonight, are you?" asked Buntline.

"I was thinking about it."

Buntline shook his head. "I wish you wouldn't. One more night behind bars won't kill the man. And it's just . . . safer that way. The next train out won't be until morning, anyway. And as long as Payne is in jail, there's less likelihood of trouble."

"Trouble from who?"

"Whom. From Letcher, that's who."

Buffalo Bill thought it over. He couldn't deny that the possibility existed that Letcher might still try to start something with Ethan Payne. Cody had always been one to live his life by that old maxim of "live and let live." But there were a lot of men in the West who weren't like that. Men who knew how to nurse a grudge, who believed in an eye for an eye, and who took offense at the smallest thing. It was usually a bad thing to be known as a man who backed down from trouble, or who did not endeavor to collect payment for some real or imagined slight. He had to assume that King Letcher was of that breed.

So he nodded, folding the letter and putting it away. "All right, Judson. We'll do it your way. We won't go fetch Mr. Payne until tomorrow morning."

Buntline breathed an audible sigh of relief, and reached for his second shot of who-hit-john.

The next morning bright and early, Cody arrived alone at the Denver jail. The same young badge toter—Buffalo Bill assumed he was a deputy—was on duty. So he had a feeling that getting Ethan Payne out of his cell would take some time. He was right. When he produced the letter by King Letcher, the deputy read it, and shook his head.

"I don't know how you managed to get Letcher to write something like this. It sure ain't like him."

"He wrote it, all right. That's his signature."

"Oh, I believe you, Mr. Cody. But I don't have the authority to let Payne go."

"Of course not."

"I'll have to go get my boss."

"You go on ahead. I'll wait here."

The deputy hesitated, wondering if he should leave the jail unattended when a friend of one of the prisoners was loitering in the office. But he wasn't about to offend Buffalo Bill Cody. So he hurried out, taking the key to the cellblock door with him. Cody took a chair over by the potbellied stove and whiled away the time leafing through a day-old local newspaper. He didn't have to wait long. In ten minutes the deputy was back with his boss, the town marshal, a man who curtly introduced himself to Cody as Ty Lanniger. The marshal shook Cody's hand and then produced the Letcher letter.

"How did you get this?"

"I just made Mr. Letcher see that it really was in his best interests to drop the whole thing."

Lanniger looked skeptical. "It's not like King Letcher to let bygones be bygones—especially when money's involved." The marshal thought it over, then folded the letter and stuffed it in his pocket. Cody surmised that the lawman was savvy enough to realize that this could be the answer to his prayers. He'd done what he could to prevent—or at least, postpone—violence by locking Ethan Payne in jail. But he didn't have a charge that would stick when the circuit judge rolled in, and he knew it. Sooner or later he would have to let Payne go. And here came Buffalo Bill Cody to take him off his hands.

"When are you taking Payne out of Denver?" asked Lanniger.

"Right now. On the next eastbound train."

Lanniger fished a timepiece out of a vest pocket, consulted it. "It's scheduled to roll out in less than an hour."

"Right. So, if you don't mind . . ."

His mind made up, Lanniger turned to the deputy. "Cut Payne loose."

The deputy nodded. He unlocked the cellblock door, entered, and a moment later emerged with Ethan Payne. When he saw Cody, Ethan looked relieved.

"I was beginning to wonder what had happened to you," he admitted.

"Just had to get a few things straightened out first."

Ethan eyed Lanniger warily. "Are they straight?"

By way of an answer, Lanniger went to the desk, opened a bottom drawer, and brought out Ethan's gunrig. He tossed it across to Ethan, who caught it readily. Instead of buckling it on, he draped it negligently over his shoulder. He didn't even check to see if the Colt in the holster was still loaded.

"Don't come back here," Lanniger told Ethan. His steely gaze switched to Cody. "And don't miss that train."

"We won't," said Buffalo Bill, pleasantly. "Come on, Payne."

They stepped outside. Ethan paused in the shade of the boardwalk, squinting at the bright sun. He looked like a shaggy old grizzly that had just come out of hibernation. And, mused Cody, smelled just about as pungent. The other passengers aboard the eastbound train would not be pleased to have him for a traveling companion, but there wasn't time to get him cleaned up.

"If you're thinking about paying King Letcher one last visit, forget it," warned Cody. "I've spent a lot of time getting that smoothed over."

"It never crossed my mind," replied Ethan.

Cody looked skeptical. "Sure. Let's get to the station. If we miss that train, I have a feeling you'll end up right back here."

They headed north along the street. Ethan wasn't sure where he was going, but he was pretty certain it wouldn't be with Cody, at least not after they put Denver behind them. He was just glad to be out of that cell, and he felt a certain sense of obligation to the buckskin-clad man who walked beside him. Not enough so that he would participate in any Wild West Show, however. At some point between here and there, he would part company with Buffalo Bill, and he would take his leave owing the man a favor.

Ned Buntline was waiting for them on the station platform. The train was loading—a Baldwin locomotive chuffing a plume of black smoke in the crisp morning air, a coal car behind the mogul, and several passenger cars behind that, with two freight cars and a caboose bringing up the rear. They were still putting luggage in one of the freight cars, people were still climbing aboard the passenger cars, and the engineer was still inside the depot, but Buntline had been getting progressively more nervous. He was sure that if they didn't get out of Denver on this train, this morning, there would be hell to pay. It made him edgy just knowing that he was in the same town as King Letcher. He'd been expecting the man to show up at any moment. For that reason he'd been keeping his eyes peeled. Which was why he saw a man he recognized immediately as one of the shotgunners in Letcher's saloon as soon as the man stepped out of an alley across the street between an assayer's office and a general store. The man wasn't looking at the station, though. His gaze was directed south along the main street. Buntline looked that way and saw Cody and Payne coming toward him. The writer realized that they couldn't see the shotgunner; a wagon was parked in front of the general store, blocking their view. The shotgunner wore a long yellow duster. A cold morning wind was gusting down off the snowcapped peaks to the west, across the sagebrush plain and through the alley, and it whipped the duster away from the man's body. That was when Buntline spotted the scattergun that the man held braced against his body beneath the coat.

"Lord Almighty," breathed Buntline.

It was just like something out of one of his dime novels.

"Bill, look out!"

Cody looked sharply toward the station, recognizing Buntline's voice, and trying to spot his friend. But Ethan didn't look that way. As he dropped instinctively into a crouch, his eyes quickly scanned the street, searching for danger. He saw the shotgunner step around the back of the wagon, saw the scattergun coming out from beneath the yellow duster. Other people saw the gun, too. He heard a woman scream, and a man ran directly across the line of fire in a panicked effort to get out of the way.

"Get down!" Ethan grabbed Cody as he shouted the warning, swinging Buffalo Bill roughly around, because Cody was in the line of fire, too. Buffalo Bill lost his balance and sprawled in the muck of the street. Ethan yanked the Colt out of the holster—the gun rig was still draped over his left shoulder—and threw himself sideways as the scattergun came up and flame belched from one of the barrels. The buckshot whistled over his head. He hit the ground and rolled and came up on one knee, firing a split second before the shotgunner could cut loose with the second barrel. When Ethan's bullet struck him, his aim was thrown off, not by much, but enough so that the buckshot went wide. A woman screamed—it sounded to Ethan like the same woman who had screamed a moment before—and he glanced in that direction in time to see a man on the boardwalk in front of a barber shop go down. The plate glass window behind him was shattered. Ethan checked the shotgunner; he was down, but still alive, writhing in the mud. Rising, Ethan brought the Colt up, took careful aim, and fired a second time. The shotgunner's body jerked, and then was still.

Ethan felt lancing pain in his right calf, and his legs were knocked out from under him before he heard the next shotgun blast. He landed poorly, knocking the air out of his lungs. Another of Letcher's men was coming from another alley on the opposite side of the street. He'd fired both barrels, and as he came forward to finish Ethan off, he broke open his scattergun and dropped in two fresh loads. Then he stopped, seeing that Ethan wasn't as badly hurt as he'd expected. Ethan triggered the Colt, thumbed the hammer back and fired a second time. A few feet away, Cody was shooting, too. Three slugs hit the shotgunner; he performed a jerky pirouette and went down.

Ethan sat up and checked his leg. He had three or four shots in his leg, and it hurt like hell, but the wounds weren't serious. With one good leg he was able to stand. He checked the street. It had been bustling with activity a moment before; now it was virtually empty. Except for Marshal Lanniger and his deputy. The lawmen were running toward them, guns drawn.

"You okay?" Ethan asked Cody.

Buffalo Bill was getting up, looking with dismay at the mud on his buckskin coat.

"Only my dignity has sustained any damage," he said.

"Good. You go on ahead. Thanks for getting me out of jail, and offering me a job, but I've got some business to finish."

He started to hobble away. But he'd spent too long inquiring after Cody's well-being. Before he could get very far

Lanniger had stopped running and was pointing his pistol at him.

"That's far enough, Payne. Drop the gun."

"It was self-defense, Marshal," said Cody. "These men came out of nowhere and started shooting at us."

Lanniger was too old a hand to be distracted. He kept his eyes—and his pistol—on Ethan. "I said drop the gun." His voice was pitched lower and flatter, and Ethan knew that he meant business. If he didn't do what the marshal said, he'd have one more person shooting at him.

He threw down the Colt. Expecting no further violence, the deputy holstered his six-shooter and ran across the street to render aid to the wounded bystander. People were beginning to emerge from their hiding places, venturing cautiously out of doorways and alleys, gathering in small groups to discuss in whispered tones what had just transpired.

Cody spun his pearl-handled pistol around to extend it, butt-first, to Marshal Lanniger.

"If you're taking him into custody," said Buffalo Bill, "you might as well take me, too. He didn't do anything different from what I did."

Buntline arrived on the scene. "It was a clear-cut case of self-defense, Marshal," said the writer. "I saw the whole thing."

"Really," said Lanniger. "And just what did you see?"

Buntline told him everything, from the moment he had first seen Letcher's shotgunner coming out of the alley across the street from the train depot, to the arrival of the marshal and his deputy. He concluded with some supposition. "Those two men were bent on killing Mr. Payne here. And they would probably have killed Mr. Cody, into the bargain. Obviously King Letcher sent them to do just that."

Lanniger swept the scene with his narrowed eyes. His gaze came to rest, briefly, on the fallen bystander, tended now by a doctor, with the deputy lending a hand. The marshal muttered an angry curse.

"This is just what I was trying to avoid," he rasped. "By God, I'm going to have Letcher's hide for this."

"I'll take care of that for you," said Ethan.

"Don't press your luck," growled Lanniger. "I'll handle Letcher."

"Will you?" said Ethan. "Then I suggest you hurry. Because I don't think he'll stay around here very long once he finds out what happened. And I'll tell you, Marshal, I don't particularly care to wonder if he's still on the loose and still gunning for me. Don't want to spend the rest of my life looking over my shoulder."

"Really? I would have thought you've been doing that for quite a while now. But like I said, Letcher is my problem. Your only problem is with me. If you're not on that train this morning, I'm putting you back behind bars, and it'll be a cold day in hell before you see the light of day again."

Cody picked up Ethan's pistol and stuck it under his belt. "I'll make sure he gets on that train, Marshal."

Ethan glared at Buffalo Bill. He didn't cotton to the man confiscating his gun, and acting like his keeper. But he was smart enough to keep his mouth shut. The prospect of more seemingly endless days locked in a dark cell was enough to send chills down his spine.

Cody's assurances seemed to satisfy Lanniger. The marshal lowered the hammer on his six-shooter and holstered the gun. He didn't say anything. He didn't have to. He just turned away, crossing the street to check briefly with the doctor on the condition of the wounded man before heading back whence he had come. Ethan watched him go, wondering if he would find King Letcher—and if he did, whether he could handle the gambler. Letcher was a hard man, but then, so was Ty Lanniger.

Accompanied by Buntline and Cody, Ethan went to the train station. They boarded the last passenger car. When they were settled into their seats, Buffalo Bill returned the Colt to Ethan.

"I didn't ask you if you had any belongings you wanted to bring along," said Cody.

Ethan shook his head. All he had to his name was the shirt on his back and the pistol in his holster. He'd had to sell his rifle some time ago just for money to buy food, and he'd lost the mountain mustang in a poker game.

"Well, Bill," said Buntline, feeling oddly elated now that the danger had passed and he'd survived. "Doesn't appear as though the West is *entirely* tamed."

Cody glanced pensively out the window beside him. He could see part of the street where the shootout had taken place. Men were carrying away the dead shotgunners.

"Not yet," he allowed. "But it won't be long. There are enough men like that marshal around to see to it."

Buntline gazed curiously at Ethan. "When was the last time you went back east?"

Ethan had to pause a moment to calculate the answer. "It's been almost thirty years since I left Illinois, and I haven't been back since."

Buntline let out a low whistle. "That's a long time. No family?"

"No. Not to speak of."

"You mean you don't have anyone?"

Ethan fastened a cold stare on the writer. "No." His expression and tone of voice made it plain that he did not care to discuss the matter further.

"That's odd," said Buntline. "Because Bill here was—"

Cody shifted on the hard bench and in the process kicked Buntline, hard, in the shin.

"Ow!" yelped Buntline, reaching down to rub his leg. "Watch out, Bill."

"You, too, Judson."

Buntline stared at him—then realized that Buffalo Bill didn't want him to pursue the topic any further, either.

"Well," said the writer, "let's talk about your part of the new show, Mr. Payne. I could use your input. . . ."

Ethan put his head back, pulled his hat down over his face, and pretended to go to sleep.

24

He was billed as Ethan Payne, the Most Famous Town Tamer the Wild West Had Ever Known.

Which was absolute nonsense, as he was quick to point out to Ned Buntline. There were numerous other star packers who were much more dedicated to the proposition of law and order than he, and who'd done a lot more to tame the frontier and rid it of the bad elements. He went so far, in fact, as to explain his true motives for getting involved in the shooting of his predecessor in Abilene, Happy Jack Crawford, who had died unhappily at the hands of Tell Jenkins. "Frankly, I couldn't have cared less about whether Abilene had law and order," he said. "I just saw an opening, and took it."

But, of course, Buntline wasn't interested in his confession, not in the slightest. He tried to smooth things over, and undermine Ethan's objections to the way he was billed, by explaining that Ethan wasn't really playing himself as much as he was representing all the brave men who pinned a badge on their shirt and took on the lawlessness that ran rampant in the Old West. In the end, Buffalo Bill intervened, and the title was pared down to simply Town Tamer. Ethan could live with that, even though it gave a completely false impression of what he'd been doing in Abilene.

He wasn't even really sure why he was doing the show at all. Back in Denver he'd made up his mind to use Cody to help him get out of jail, and after they put Denver behind him he'd part company with Buffalo Bill and Ned Buntline. But then his conscience started bothering him. A real annoyance, having a conscience, and he wondered why he still had one, after all the things he'd done and all the people he'd hurt, intentionally or otherwise. But there it was—an inner voice scolding him for being such a cad to even consider backing out on Cody after all the effort the man had expended trying to get him out of the Denver mess. Buffalo Bill was a good man—brave, forthright, a straight talker, and a man who could be a steadfast friend. Unless you betrayed him. So Ethan had agonized over what course to take all during the train ride east, and by the time they'd reached St. Louis he'd made up his mind to stick to it for a while. It wasn't as though he had pressing business elsewhere, and he could sure use the wages they were prepared to pay him. And how hard could it really be, acting like a hero in some silly performance?

If he'd only known the answer to that then, he might have jumped the train in St. Louis.

His scene opened against a painted backdrop of an Abilene street at dusk, with two rows of dark buildings, the lights of the windows spilling out onto a dusty street beneath a star-spangled purple sky. A two-sided prop, stage left, was made up to look like the front and side of the jailhouse—a fact made obvious by the bars on the window and, for the truly obtuse, a sign proclaiming it to be the Sheriff's Office of Abilene, Kansas. He had to give Ned Buntline credit. The man had spared no expense in setting up the scene. That Abilene did not have a sheriff, but rather a town marshal, was a small matter that Ethan didn't think worth bringing up. He doubted anyone in the audience would know enough to call them on this inaccuracy.

The stagehands were all laborers from eastern cities—Irish, most of them—a burly, not to mention surly, lot who seemed united in their ill-concealed contempt for the westerners who had been hired as performers. Ethan figured this had to do with what the Mexicans called *machismo*. The Irishmen prided themselves on having a collective reputation as hard-drinking, hard-fisted, hard-living buckos who never flinched from danger and never walked around a fight. As it happened, westerners had a reputation that was markedly similar. It was like putting two young bulls in the same pasture. There was bound to be violence sooner or later. But violence had long since ceased to worry Ethan.

The best part of it all was that most of the men employed to play the scene with him were honest-to-God westerners. That made it somewhat easier for Ethan, playing opposite men who knew their way around horses and guns and the ways and customs and speech patterns of frontier denizens. He couldn't imagine some puffed up, dandified eastern actor giving a convincing rendition of a Texas cowboy. And he seriously doubted that he could have kept a straight face had some eastern dandy tried to portray a range rider opposite him.

Act One portrayed the cold-blooded murder of Happy Jack Crawford, who emerged from the jailhouse in response to the drunken antics of Tell Jenkins, played by a big-shouldered actor with a thick Texas drawl who was hired because of his very convincing leer and an ability to perform the "border roll" with his pistol. He didn't look at all like Tell Jenkins, noted Ethan, but then that didn't matter because Tell hadn't lived long enough to make a reputation for himself and get his face known far and wide. When the too-trusting Jack Crawford tried to reason Tell Jenkins into surrendering the six-gun with which he had been shooting up the street in a drunken spree, the leering "Texas ruffian" pretended to give up his charcoal burner butt-first, only to execute the border roll and pump four bullets into the hapless Happy Jack, who expired in fine melodramatic form. Ethan soon learned that there was at least one problem with hiring real westerners rather than professional actors; some of the former tended to ham it up when their big scene came along. It wasn't that they took themselves seriously as actors; on the contrary, they rarely took any of it seriously enough to suit Buntline. It took the man who played Happy Jack at least three times longer than Buntline had envisioned to die. An exasperated Buntline informed Cody after opening night that he'd seriously considered shooting the man for real just so the show could proceed.

Then it was Ethan's turn to make an appearance, entering from stage right to face down Tell Jenkins with his pistol still holstered. The dastardly "cowboy" tried the same trick on Ethan, but before he could carry out the border roll a second time, Ethan had drawn his gun—a lightning-quick draw. He got the drop on Jenkins who, in the best tradition of bullies everywhere, was transformed into a sniveling coward begging for mercy. The performance never failed to elicit boos and catcalls from an unsympathetic audience, and a rousing cheer of approbation when Ethan deposited Jenkins in the hoosegow with a rather too-flowery speech about how justice would be served, and cold-blooded killers would always get their comeuppance. Ethan felt downright stupid speaking the lines, but the audiences seemed to love it, and pretty soon he ceased being embarrassed.

After locking Jenkins in the jailhouse—he would appear from time to time at the cross-barred window to leer and hiss at Ethan and the audience—Ethan was presented with the badge recently worn by Happy Jack Crawford, who was carried off, stage right, by a pair of mournful extras. A woman, presumably Jack's wife—he hadn't been married in real life—wept inconsolably over her beloved's corpse. Ned Buntline played the Abilene mayor who persuaded Ethan to accept the job, appealing to the hero's desire to see justice done. For his part, Ethan played hard to get—he was reluctant to take on the job. Of course, the reality had been altogether different, but once again the facts had absolutely nothing to do with a good story, and should not be allowed to interfere, as Ned Buntline never hesitated to point out. The Ethan Payne of Buffalo Bill's Wild West Show was a man who loved the freedom of the open plains, of living with the big sky above him and a good horse beneath. He hated to give up that freedom and lock himself into the responsibility of bringing law and order to wild and woolly Abilene. Not that he was afraid, or doubted his ability to make the Texas rowdies toe the line. So, initially, he resisted the mayor's blandishments.

And then *she* came onto the scene—an actress by the name of Molly Renwick, who hailed from Albany, New York. She was as pretty as a picture, with a peaches-and-cream complexion and a delicate, heart-shaped face, big, doe-like eyes, and a very fetching lilt to her angelic voice. She played Alice, Abilene's sweet-dispositioned schoolmarm, who just happened to be in the wrong place at the right time; she was set upon by a pair of leering Texans even as Ethan was leaving town. Naturally, he rescued her. Naturally, they fell instantly in love. And before long, Ethan was wearing the tin star.

Act Two presented the arrival of ten more Texas ruffians, bent on breaking their friend Tell Jenkins out of jail, and obviously all too ready to fill Abilene's brave new badge toter full of lead. They rode into town in a thunder of hooves punctuated by Rebel yells and shooting their smokemakers at the moon. Ethan's noble attempt to talk them out of their scheme was futile. They warned him that he had one hour to let Jenkins go, or they would return and "curl his toes." That gave Alice time enough to plead with her beloved to give up his prisoner, to surrender the badge to Abilene's mayor. She could not bear to lose the man she had waited her whole life to meet. But Ethan could not bring himself to do as she asked. He had taken on a grave responsibility when he'd accepted the badge, and it was his solemn duty to see it through, no matter what. And as he walked out to meet the Texas outfit bent on filling him full of lead, he paused long enough to embrace Alice, and tell her that if he did perish on that day, he would die a happy man for having had even so brief a time to spend with her. Occasionally, at this point in the performance, one or more of the women in the audience would burst into tears. The first time it happened Ethan was so startled that he very nearly lost his composure; it was all he could do to keep from laughing. That intelligent people could actually take such melodrama seriously was just completely beyond his comprehension.

Ethan pointed out to Buntline that, with regards to his showdown in Abilene, the truth was that there had not been a shot fired, because he had rigged the jailhouse with enough dynamite to blow it, Tell Jenkins, himself, and all the Texas cowboys who were confronting him to kingdom come, and possibly back again. Ned Buntline merely shook his head. "It's called literary license, my friend, and there's nothing wrong with partaking of it from time to time. The main thing is to entertain the crowd. They pay good money and they deserve a good show, don't you agree? The end result will be the same—you will vanquish the villains, Tell Jenkins will get his just reward, and you become the hero of the day, the man who tamed the town they said could not be tamed."

"I didn't kill ten Texans doing it, though," said Ethan. "If I had, half the cowboys from the Lone Star State would have come gunning for me. Those range riders are not the sniveling cowards you make them out to be. No braver men ever walked the earth."

"A brave villain is not a concept an eastern audience will readily grasp," replied Buntline.

There was a lot that easterners couldn't grasp, mused Ethan. But he didn't press the issue. He just reminded himself of the handsome salary he was making. This wasn't his show, anyway. It belonged to Buntline and Cody, and if they wanted to play fast and loose with the facts, so be it.

In the shootout that followed, with guns going off like firecrackers and a cloud of acrid powdersmoke drifting into the first few rows of the audience, lending authenticity to the scene, Ethan stood tall in front of the jailhouse door, resolutely gunning down his adversaries, who skulked around the stage like a pack of wolves. Several of the cowardly cowboys turned tail and ran, ignoring Tell Jenkins' pleas to save him from a Kansas rope, his gaunt face pressed between the bars on the small window of his cell. The last Texas hooligan to fall gasped with his dying breath, "I cannot believe you got the better of us, Sheriff Payne."

To which Ethan would solemnly reply, "When a man is in the right, he can beat tall odds. There's no room for lawbreakers out here anymore. Either you walk the straight and narrow or you end up on the wrong side of grass."

And then, with Alice flying into his arms, and the powder-smoke hanging heavily in the air around them, the curtain would descend, and after a breathless moment of silence the audience would burst into enthusiastic applause, and Ethan would take one curtain call to cheers and, more often than not, a standing ovation. And of course he thought it was all quite ludicrous. His final oration was a paraphrase of comments made by none other than Denver's marshal, Ty Lanniger. And in reality Ethan Payne had been the lawbreaker, the wild one who represented the kind of troublemaker real lawmen like Lanniger were determined to get rid of. The irony didn't escape Ethan when he spoke those words.

Ned Buntline delightedly proclaimed Ethan a natural. He seemed to suffer not at all from stage fright, and was surprisingly adept at remembering his lines, which he delivered in a laconic style that made for a refreshing change from the melodramatic deliveries of the other players, and that complemented his portrayal of a dauntless, soft-spoken hero. Even the critics were kind to him. One wrote that Ethan Payne was the living embodiment of the courageous spirit so admired as an attribute of the Western hero. Ethan had a good laugh at that one.

What Buntline failed to comprehend was that Ethan's calm dependability before the footlights was a result of massive indifference on his part to the whole undertaking. Ethan didn't care what the audience thought about him. He had a role in what he considered to be a monumental farce, and he couldn't take himself or the play very seriously. Like a trained animal in a circus, he did what was expected of him, took his wages, and let others worry about the future of the show. And he continually told himself that once he had a decent grubstake stashed away, and felt that he had fulfilled whatever obligation he had to Cody for helping him out of that trouble in Denver, he would be on his way. Not that he had any idea where to go. The West had been shrinking rapidly for this particular yonder man. He was viewed with pervasive malice among Texas cowpunchers because he *had* in fact made a fool of an entire Lone Star outfit in Abilene. And Wyoming was out of the question, too, since the rumor persisted that he was responsible for the death of the great cattle king, Seamus Blake. He couldn't go anywhere near a Rocky Mountain gold camp because the memories of Julie and how she had died were still too strong for him to willingly endure. So he wasn't sure where he would go. But that uncertainty had ceased to worry him. He'd been a drifter too long to let it.

Ethan knew that Buffalo Bill was committed to portraying the true West for the edification of eastern city folk, and at first he thought that Ned Buntline shared his partner's vision. Buntline certainly talked a good game. He spoke enthusiastically and often about their grandiose plans for expanding on the Wild West extravaganza. Eventually, though, Ethan realized that this was partly an attempt to elicit a commitment from Ethan to invest part of his earnings in the future of the enterprise.

"Bill intends to put on a stagecoach holdup for the audience," said Buntline one day. "You could ride in and save the day, Ethan, just like you used to do as the Overland's troubleshooter."

"One of the passengers, no doubt, would be a pretty damsel in distress," said Ethan wryly.

Buntline was completely oblivious to the thinly veiled sarcasm. "Of course. You would arrive just in the nick of time, saving her honor, rescuing her from defilement at the hands of the despicable road agents."

Ethan shook his head. Buntline was sounding more and more like his dime novels every day. Ethan had taken the time to read a couple of them, which Ned had given him, gratis. He'd found them extremely amusing, not to mention outrageously unbelievable, and absolutely nothing like the real West. "I've agreed to stay for one season, Ned, and I'll stick to that. But afterward, I'm leaving."

"Oh, I see. Do you have any specific plans?"

"Not really. Who knows, I might even want to try my hand at farming."

"You're a pretty old dog to be learning new tricks, Ethan."

"Actually, I was born a farmer's son."

When Buntline told Cody about Ethan's plans, the famous army scout chuckled. "Well, there is a certain romance to it. The most famous gunslinger of the Wild West—now that Hickok has met his Maker—hangs up his guns and gets behind a mule and a plow. But I'm pretty certain Ethan is pulling your leg, Judson."

"I certainly hope so. Next to you, he is the most popular member of the troupe."

"Well, I hope he pulls it off," said Cody. "I like Ethan Payne. I'd hate to see him end up like Wild Bill."

"You know what they say happens to those who live by the sword, Bill."

"He's not a bad man, Judson, though he's done some bad things."

Buntline shrugged. "I'd like to know why you haven't told him about your mutual lady friend."

"This is the way she wanted it done. Far as Ethan is concerned, it was our own idea to go to Denver and recruit him."

Buntline was intrigued. "Sounds like a great story. I wonder how it will end. Who is this woman?"

"Maybe you'll meet her when we get to Chicago."

25

Though he believed Cody to be hopelessly naive about the authenticity of his Wild West performances, Ethan took a liking to Buffalo Bill. The man was a true hero.

Bill had moved from Iowa to Kansas with his family at the tender age of six. "Bleeding Kansas" was in turmoil over the issue of whether it would be admitted into the Union as a free or a slave state. Bill's father, Isaac, was an ardent anti-slavery man, and was stabbed in the back by a proslavery "border ruffian." Isaac survived that attempt on his life, and barely escaped another when a proslavery mob marched on his house. Young Bill Cody, learning of the mob's intentions, jumped on a horse and, though shot at by his father's enemies, managed to reach Isaac in time to warn him.

When Isaac died—of natural causes—the support of the Cody family was left in Bill's hands. Eleven years old, Cody went to Leavenworth and talked his way into a job with the firm of Russell, Majors & Waddell, who were employing a fleet of Conestoga wagons to haul westbound freight. In a single season the company had hired four thousand men to ship sixteen million pounds of freight.

Cody's first job was with a wagon train carrying supplies to federal troops putting down the Mormon Rebellion in Utah. On this trip he met the legendary Kit Carson at Fort Laramie. Kit's stories about his mountain man days fired Cody's imagination. The boy fell in love with the West.

When Russell, Majors & Waddell opened their Pony Express, they advertised for "young skinny wiry fellows not over eighteen" who were expert riders and willing to "risk death daily." Cody fit the bill perfectly. The pay—twenty-five dollars a week—seemed a princely sum to him. He earned every penny of it.

Carrying a *mochilla,* a mail sack with four pockets, a Pony Express man rode half-breed California mustangs from station to station along a route that stretched from Leavenworth to Fort Laramie across the Nebraska Territory, over the plains of southern Wyoming Territory to Salt Lake City, thence to Carson City via the arid wastes of Nevada, through the northern reaches of the Sierra Nevada to Sacramento and San Francisco. There were one hundred and ninety way stations along the route. The express reduced the time it took to transmit a letter between New York and San Francisco by ten days.

Time and time again Bill Cody proved his mettle as a Pony Express rider. He outraced fifteen hostile Indians on one run. He once rode three hundred and twenty miles in twenty-one hours and forty minutes, setting a record for the longest ride in the shortest time. He established himself as the most reliable and resourceful rider in the company. And he loved every minute of it.

But the Pony Express was destined to be short-lived. In 1860, the United States Congress passed an act to "facilitate communication between the Atlantic and Pacific states by electric telegraph," and stipulated that the project had to be completed by July 1862. It was, and the Pony Express was doomed. In that same year, the Pacific Railway Act provided for the construction of a transcontinental railroad. The Central Pacific would build eastward from California while the Union Pacific would start laying rails westward from Council Bluffs, Iowa. Work on the railroad began in earnest after the Civil War, and Bill Cody got a job with the UP as a hunter. Charged with supplying meat for the naddies who built the iron road, Cody once again set a record, killing 4,280 buffaloes in a seventeen-month period. In so doing he earned his nickname, Buffalo Bill.

Later, Cody became a scout for the army in its campaigns
against the Indians of the northern plains. He fought in
numerous engagements and earned the undying admiration
of General Phil Sheridan, as well as a Congressional Medal
of Honor for his role in the rescue of an army patrol surrounded by a vastly superior force of hostiles.

Ethan figured his own life was a pretty sorry spectacle by
comparison.

In addition to Ethan's scenes, the show consisted of three
acts in which Buffalo Bill was the principal player. In
between acts, Buntline hired performers to entertain the
audience while the curtain was down and the stage was
being set. He believed variety was the spice of life, and that
a paying customer should never be bored. These performers
included a rope artist from Texas who called himself the
Brazos Kid and who could perform amazing feats with
thirty-three feet of hard twist, an old Sac and Fox Indian
who did a ceremonial dance, and a trick-shot artist by the
name of Albert Pierce.

Pierce was a New Yorker who had never been west of the
Mississippi, and who, in fact, had absolutely no desire to
sample the dubious pleasures of frontier life. He was something of a fop, a vain and pleasure-loving sort, and Cody
didn't have much good to say about him as a person, though
there was no question about his uncanny skill with the brace
of pearl-handled, silver-plated, .32-caliber Smith & Wesson
revolvers he used. He could strike a match at twenty paces
with a bullet fired from one of his pistols, and he could do
this ten times out of ten, blindfolded. Buntline had insisted
on hiring him.

Most cities enforced ordinances prohibiting the discharge
of firearms loaded with live rounds in public houses. But
Ned Buntline could be very persuasive when he needed to
be. Precautions were taken: Pierce used special cartridges that
he prepared himself, and that carried small powder charges,
so that when the bullet struck the cotton batting that backed
the props used during his performance it was already pretty

well spent. After an exhibition of Pierce's marksmanship, city officials were confident that the sharpshooter never hit anything he didn't mean to.

The highlight of Pierce's act was when he used his sister for target practice. Annabelle Pierce was a tall, graceful, and extremely attractive woman, with hair the color of corn silk and big blue eyes, a "perfect blushing flower of feminine pulchritude," as one smitten reviewer writing for a penny press put it. Pierce would shoot silver dollars that Annabelle coolly held out between thumb and forefinger. Annabelle's steely nerves were as remarkable as her brother's accuracy.

The relationship between Annabelle and Albert did not go as smoothly offstage. Pierce was obsessively protective of his sister. A young woman so blessed in every respect as Annabelle Pierce was bound to draw her share of male attention. Hardly a night went by that she did not receive flowers and a card from some smitten admirer. This never failed to incense Pierce, and if a gentleman was so bold as to call on Annabelle to compliment her personally, he would inevitably find Albert acting as a scowling chaperone. Considering Albert's skill with the Smith & Wesson pistols he carried, no one was willing to go very far in courting Annabelle. Rumors began to circulate in the show's company that Albert's feelings for his sister were more than brotherly.

Ethan felt sorry for Annabelle, the shy, sweet, lovely girl with an overbearing brother, and he got the impression that she was terrified of Albert. But he made up his mind not to get involved. It was none of his business. The situation was a powderkeg waiting to explode.

The brash young Texan who called himself the Brazos Kid provided the spark by falling head over heels in love with the beautiful Annabelle Pierce.

Late one evening after the show in the Cleveland Opera House, Ethan was sound asleep in his hotel room when a frantic knocking on the door roused him. Pulling on his trousers, he opened the door to find Annabelle standing in the hall, her dress torn and her bruised face streaked with tears.

"Please, you must help me, Mr. Payne!" she gasped, shooting a frightened glance along the hallway. "I don't know who else to turn to."

Against his better judgment, Ethan let her into his room.

"Who did this to you?" he asked.

"Albert," she sobbed.

"Why?"

"He discovered that I have been slipping out of my room at night," she confessed, blushing.

"Really? Why were you doing that?"

"I . . . I don't know that I care to say," she stammered.

"I'd have thought you were too afraid of your brother to do such a thing."

"I *am* afraid of him. But I—I am also in love."

"Oh, I see. Someone in the company?"

"Yes, that's right."

"Let me guess. The Brazos Kid."

Her violet blue eyes widened. "How did you know?"

"Like I said, just a guess." Ethan wondered if the girl even knew what love was. No doubt she was infatuated with the Brazos Kid because the Texan was the first man willing to risk Albert's wrath to spend time with her. Maybe she believed him to be her salvation. As far as Ethan was concerned, the Kid was just a brash young fool. He had two things working against him. He was from Texas, and he wasn't old enough to understand that he was as mortal as the next man. He'd seen plenty of young cowboys like the Kid during his stint as Abilene's town marshal. They strutted and crowed and thought they were tough as old whang leather, and they seldom exercised caution. There was a certain romantic image associated with being a cowboy, and they were all too aware of the role they were supposed to play. The Brazos Kid would never back down from a man like Pierce, even though he was no match for the quick-draw artist. It would destroy his own self-image to do so. And his apparent fearlessness, suspected Ethan, had nothing to do with his feelings for Annabelle. Ethan doubted the Kid was in love with her, but naturally she would mistake his bold resolve to be with her, despite the threat posed by her brother, as evidence of love.

"But Albert doesn't know I've been seeing The Kid," said Annabelle. "He . . . he thinks I've been spending time with someone else."

"Who?"

"He thinks—oh, I'm so dreadfully sorry, Mr. Payne!"

Ethan's skin crawled. "What did you tell him?"

"That—that it was you." She covered her face with her hands. "I am so ashamed. I didn't know what to say. I knew Albert would kill The Kid. I couldn't bear for that to happen."

"Oh?" Ethan smiled dryly. "So you'd rather Albert killed me instead? Well, I guess I can understand that."

"No, Mr. Payne! It isn't like that at all. The Kid wouldn't stand a chance against Albert. But . . . but you would."

"I see." Ethan couldn't help speculating that perhaps Annabelle Pierce wasn't as innocent as she made herself out to be. Was it possible that she had schemed to create a confrontation between him and Albert? Maybe she was so desperate to escape her brother that she was willing to see him dead. Or maybe, mused Ethan, I'm just a hopeless cynic. "Well," he said, "I suppose I ought to be flattered. Where is Albert now?"

"I told him you were downstairs, in the bar room."

"Quick thinking." Ethan donned his shirt and boots and took the Colt out of its holster to check the loads. Annabelle watched him breathlessly. "I hope you'll forgive me, miss," he said dryly, "but I'm no knight in shining armor. I'd prefer not to get killed over you. So we're going to go visit Bill Cody, and you're going to tell him the whole story."

Buffalo Bill's room was down the hall. Cody quite often was out late, socializing alongside Ned Buntline with the locals, mingling with the money men and drumming up investors for the Wild West Show. But tonight Ethan was in luck. Cody answered the door, and Annabelle told him her story, leaving nothing out. When she was finished, Cody glanced at the Colt stuck in Ethan's belt.

"What are your plans?" asked Buffalo Bill.

"Well, I don't plan to use this unless I have to."

Cody nodded. "I'd prefer that you didn't."

"It all depends on Albert Pierce, doesn't it? And, speaking of the devil . . ."

At that moment Pierce appeared at the other end of the hall, returning from the wild goose chase his sister had sent him on. When he saw Annabelle and Ethan together he quickened his pace, reaching under his coat for his pearl-handled pistols. Ethan took one look at the young man's expression and knew Pierce was in a killing frame of mind, so he pushed Annabelle aside and stepped forward to shield her with his body. But Cody stepped between him and Pierce.

"Don't do it, son," warned Buffalo Bill.

"Stand aside," rasped Pierce. "This damned scoundrel will pay for ruining my sister's reputation."

"You'll have to go through me," said Cody.

Ethan didn't think that would deter Pierce, and he knew Cody was unarmed. "Better let me handle this, Bill," he said.

Cody ignored him and advanced to meet Pierce. "Don't draw those pistols. You're young, and you've yet to learn that passion is the most erring of all pilots on the voyage of life."

"There you go again, Bill," said Ethan, shaking his head.

Pierce hesitated—a fatal mistake—and then Cody lashed out and hit him in the jaw, and Pierce went down, half conscious. Before he could recover, Buffalo Bill had relieved him of the Smith & Wessons. A sullen Pierce got to his feet, rubbing his jaw.

"I'm not finished with you, Payne," he said.

"Yes, you are," said Cody. "Pierce, you're fired. Come morning I want you packed and out of here."

Pierce's eyes were like hot coals. "Fine. Come along, Annabelle."

"I'm not going anywhere with you, Albert."

"Yes, you are. You're my sister and it's my job to look out for you. I'm not going to leave you here with *him*. I promised our mother on her death bed that I would take care of you."

"And you've certainly done that," she said angrily, tears welling up in her eyes. "If our mother only knew how *well* you took care of me, Albert."

Cody glanced at her, and Ethan could tell by the expression on his face that Buffalo Bill was thinking along the same lines as he was. There had been something about the attention Albert Pierce had paid his sister, the looks he gave her, that had made Ethan wonder also if his feelings for Annabelle went beyond those a brother was expected to have for his sister. And Annabelle's words seemed to imply that his suspicions were not unfounded.

"You heard the lady," said Buffalo Bill, turning back to Pierce. "Get going."

"We'll meet again, Payne."

"Better give that a second thought," advised Ethan coolly.

"No, you can count on that."

When Pierce had gone, Cody turned to Annabelle. "Well, Miss Pierce, you are welcome to remain with the company as long as you wish. I'm sure we can find something for you to do. Some part for you to play, perhaps."

"I'm so sorry I caused all this trouble."

"Too late for sorry." Cody glanced at Ethan. "You'll have to watch your back from now on. Pierce is the kind who'll bushwhack you and not blink an eye."

"He'll cool down."

"I wouldn't bet the whole she-bang on it, pard."

"I'm not running," said Ethan. "So if that's what you're fixing to suggest, don't bother."

Cody grinned. "Knowing you, it would be a waste of time."

The next morning, Albert Pierce was gone.

Thinking herself free at last from her brother, Annabelle went at once to the Brazos Kid and let him know that they could pursue their love affair openly and without fear. Later, Ethan would look back and see that it was at this point that he should have intervened. But he didn't want to get involved. He didn't think it was his place. Even though Annabelle had dragged him into it, he could get himself back out again by minding his own business.

They went from Cleveland to Cincinnati and from there to Louisville, and somewhere along the way the Brazos Kid and Annabelle Pierce consummated their love. Only it turned out not to be love, at least on the Texan's part. Poor Annabelle, being an old-fashioned girl, assumed that they would marry. But when the Brazos Kid failed to broach the subject she grew impatient and mentioned it to him. At that moment she discovered the truth. He had made his conquest and was swiftly losing interest, and he certainly wasn't going to get tied down, and had no intention of marrying her.

In Louisville, Fate brought Ethan back into the situation from which he had gone to great pains to extricate himself. On the afternoon before the opening show, he visited the city's brand new opera house. Buffalo Bill's show would have the honor of being the first performance on that stage. Ethan was impressed by the opulence of the theatre, with the rich damask on the walls, the comfortably upholstered rows of seats, the gold brocade curtains that concealed a stage made of teak that shined like gold itself. On either side were ornately carved and luxuriously appointed private boxes. He sat in the back row so that he could admire the entire interior. It was, he decided, the finest building he'd ever seen. And tonight the people of the city would come, filling up the theatre, eagerly hanging on every word and action of the players on that stage. They would be thrilled by the exploits of an Ethan Payne who had never really existed. They would go home thinking of him as a hero who had lived a life of grand adventure in a wild West that had never existed, either. His mind wandered back across the years to those days as a boy in Roan's Prairie when he had dreamed of going west and striking it rich and having grand adventures. The frontier he had dreamed of then was not far removed from the frontier portrayed in Buffalo Bill's extravaganza. The real West, the West that he knew, would be forgotten; it was the mythical West of his boyhood dreams and the show they would put on tonight that would be forever remembered. And maybe, thought Ethan, that was just as well.

He saw movement in the corner of his eye, and glanced up at one of the private boxes. There was someone up there. At first he couldn't see who it was—could see only a dark shape moving in the shadows at the back of the box. But then she came to the edge of the balcony, and he recognized Annabelle. She was looking down at the stage, and did not see him at the very back of the theatre. He was wondering what she was doing up there when she climbed up to stand on the rim of the balcony, fifty feet above the floor of the opera house, clinging to the gold draperies that framed the box. Ethan's heart skipped a beat. He shot to his feet.

"Annabelle! No!"

He startled her, and she nearly lost her balance, teetering on the rim. If she let go of the drapery, she would fall to almost certain death.

"Annabelle," he said, speaking calmly. "Please. Get down from there."

She stared at him, and though he couldn't see her face clearly in the dimly lit hall, her despair and uncertainty were palpable. All she had to do was let go. It was such a simple thing, really.

"I'm coming up," he said. "Wait right there. Please."

He was afraid to leave her sight, as though his very presence there kept her from doing what she had come here to do. Her intentions were plain enough. She had come to kill herself, but she'd expected to be alone, to perform her final act without an audience. Still, there was no way he could save her from down here. He had to get to the box. He had to take the chance.

Turning, he entered the lobby. The stairs were to his left, and he took them three at a time, reaching a corridor adorned with a plush crimson carpet, paintings in gilt frames, shiny brass gaslights, gleaming mahogany settees. He reached the door to the private box where Annabelle was—where he *hoped* she still was—and, taking a deep breath, opened it and went inside.

But Annabelle Pierce was no longer balanced precariously on the balcony's rim, and for a brief instant Ethan's heart sank—until he heard a muffled sob and saw her, huddled in a dark corner of the box, her face buried in her hands. Relieved, he went to her, sitting down beside her, and putting an arm around her trembling shoulders. She lay her head on his chest and wept inconsolably. He didn't say anything, just sat there and held her, and felt a kinship with her, an understanding, that seemed odd to him at first, until he realized that Annabelle Pierce had contemplated suicide because her dreams had turned to dust. And he knew what that was like.

26

They sat there in the shadows of the private box for quite some time, and after a while Annabelle stopped crying. But she didn't move her head from his chest, and he didn't stop holding her. Eventually they heard voices—the show's Irish crew was arriving to set up the backdrops for the night's performance. Only then did Annabelle stir, lifting her head to look at him, her violet-blue eyes swollen from crying.

"They mustn't see me like this," she whispered. "Some of those men, they've . . ."

"They what?"

"They've been . . . saying things to me. Horrible things. I think he's been bragging about. . . ." She shook her head, unable to bring herself to tell Ethan what he already knew.

"You mean the Brazos Kid has been bragging."

She nodded. "And now there are some in the crew that think . . . that just because I . . ." Another tear escaped down her cheek.

"That's enough crying," he said firmly. "You have nothing to be ashamed of."

"Oh, don't I?" Her voice was filled with self-loathing. "I was such a naive fool!"

"We all make mistakes. You're talking to someone who's made more than his share."

"What am I to do?" The query was edged with panic

and despair. "First Albert, and then . . . how could I have been so stupid? All I ever wanted was to be loved, to find a good man to whom I could be a good wife. To have a home and children. To put down roots. To live a quiet, happy life. And now that's not possible. I'll never have any of those things."

"Why not?"

She looked at him as though he were joking. "Why not? What man would have me? Now, after everything that has happened? No good, decent man would want anything to do with me."

"Well, I think you're wrong."

She gave him a curious look. "Would you? Honestly."

"Yes. Though I don't consider myself either a good or decent man. But I believe there are many men who fit that definition who would realize, as I do, that none of this is your fault."

She pulled away from him, wiped the tears from her cheeks, and heaved a deep sigh. "I am ashamed. You must think me a coward, for wanting to take my own life."

Ethan shook his head. He was beginning to think that he and Annabelle Pierce had a lot in common. They'd both made mistakes—the kind that young, naive people tended to make and subsequently they'd tried to run away from those mistakes, she by contemplating suicide, and he by doing essentially the same thing, taking perilous jobs and reaching the point where he didn't really care if he lived or died. And, of course, that was what had made him so dangerous, and had contributed to his reputation. Overland troubleshooter, Abilene marshal, range regulator—high-risk occupations all. He should have been dead long ago. On more than one occasion he had cursed God or Fate or whatever it was that determined such things for keeping him alive so that he could continue to suffer.

"It's harder to live sometimes than it is to die," he said, more to himself than to her.

She looked at him sharply, in surprise, her eyes wide. "Yes, that's so true."

"As to what you should do—you should stay with the company."

"Oh, I couldn't."

"Because of the Kid. Well, you can, because he won't be with us much longer."

"What are you going to do, Mr. Payne?" she asked, her voice an even softer whisper than before.

He got to his feet and held out a hand to help her up. "Stick around, why don't you? See for yourself."

She managed a tremulous smile. "I think I will."

That night Buffalo Bill Cody found Ethan in the wings, watching the Brazos Kid, who was one of the opening acts, performing his rope tricks to the amazed appreciation of a full house. Ethan wondered if Cody had a gut feeling that there might be trouble in the offing; a man didn't survive as long as Bill had done plying the perilous trade of army scout without developing some pretty impressive instincts.

"That boy's quite a hand with a rope," remarked Cody. "I've never seen better."

"I reckon," said Ethan.

"Quite a hand with the ladies, too, I understand."

Ethan refrained from even looking in Buffalo Bill's direction. "So I've heard."

"That's why I've decided to cut him loose after we finish our stint here. He's not going to be a part of the Wild West Show." Cody paused, expecting Ethan to comment on this news, but when he got no response, he took a piece of paper from under his coat, unfolded it, and handed it to Ethan. "Judson and I have put our heads together, trying to come up with some sort of promotion for the show that we're planning. We've got enough money now to finance the whole she-bang. Anyway, I was wondering what you thought of it."

Ethan had a lot of things on his mind that he considered much more important than a Wild West Show that didn't even exist yet, but he took the paper and read what it contained:

**Reasons Why You Should Visit
BUFFALO BILL'S WILD WEST . . .**

1. Because it is a LIVING PICTURE of life on the
   FRONTIER!
2. Because you will see INDIANS, COWBOYS, and
   MEXICANS as they live!
3. Because you will see BUFFALO, ELK, WILD HORSES,
   and a multitude of curiosities!
4. Because you will see an INDIAN VILLAGE, transplanted directly from the Great Plains!
5. Because you will see a GENUINE BUFFALO HUNT in
   all its realistic details!

These words were enclosed in an elaborately scrolled border that included renderings of cowboys, Indians, teepees, and buffalo. And at the center top was a character in long-fringed buckskin with long, flowing pale hair. Presumably, this was meant to be Cody himself. Ethan read it twice. Then he looked up at Cody, amazed. "I had no idea you had all this in mind."

Buffalo Bill beamed. "I must confess, amigo, it has become something of an obsession for me. What I envision will be the most spectacular entertainment the world has ever seen."

Ethan shook his head. He couldn't imagine how Cody would be able to pull off some of the features he had just read. A buffalo hunt? An entire Indian village transplanted directly from the Plains? "You mention a multitude of curiosities," he said, glancing once more at the flyer. "You mean like two-headed calves and such?"

Cody laughed. "No, no! I mean characters like you!"

"Well, I'm not sure . . ."

"If you choose to stay with us, that is," said Cody. "Personally, I hope you will. We can duplicate your scene with the Texans at the Abilene jailhouse. And I was also thinking of putting on a stagecoach robbery. Into which, of course, you would ride, in the knick of time, to rescue the innocent travelers and do in the owlhoots. You would be an important part of the show, Ethan. And, if it is as successful as I expect it will be, you'll make a lot of money in the bargain. More than you are being paid now, I assure you."

Ethan had to smile and shake his head again.

"What is it?" asked Cody. "What do you find amusing?"

"The irony of it all. You know I've got more money now after a couple of months on your payroll then I've ever had in my pockets at any one time, my whole life. More money than I really know what to do with. And the irony is that I went west in the first place to get rich, so I could marry the girl I'd always been in love with. But I never got rich."

"And the girl?"

Ethan hesitated. He had never spoken to Buffalo Bill of Lilah Webster, and he was reluctant to do so now. But he owed the man an answer.

"She couldn't wait forever."

"And now it's too late," said Cody.

Ethan laughed softly, but there was bitterness in his laughter. "I'd say. About thirty years too late. I had my chances."

Cody chose his next words with care. "Well, amigo, you never honestly know about these things. Sometimes we get that one last chance."

"I've been told that before," said Ethan. He noticed that the Brazos Kid had finished his routine, and was now basking in the enthusiastic approbation of the crowd that filled the new opera house to overflowing. "Excuse me, Bill," he said, abruptly, and, to Cody's astonishment, walked right out on stage, heading straight for the Brazos Kid.

The Kid saw him coming and looked puzzled, initially, and then annoyed, as he assumed Ethan was trying to steal some of his applause. And indeed, the volume of the applause rose to a crescendo as Ethan appeared. He was clad in his stage outfit—black trousers, white shirt, and a black frock coat with a shiny five-pointed star pinned to the left breast. Though he had not yet performed his act in Louisville, the people knew who he was. His reputation had preceded him, and the word was out that his part in the program was touted as one of the highlights.

Reaching the Kid's side, Ethan glanced back into the wings. Cody was still standing there, staring at him, perplexed. Smiling, Ethan bowed to the crowd. The Kid tipped his hat.

"What the hell are you doing?" asked the rope artist out of the side of his mouth.

"Oh, I'm here to beat the hell out of you, Kid," replied Ethan.

"What?"

Straightening out of another bow, Ethan brought his right elbow up and drove it, as hard as he could, into the Brazos Kid's face. The Kid staggered backward and sprawled, blood spurting from his nose. Some of the men and women in the front rows gasped, startled by the violence. But most of the crowd thought it was just part of the performance. Ethan hadn't thought it possible, but they were cheering and clapping more loudly than before.

"Why, you son of a bitch!" railed the Kid, bouncing to his feet. The coiled lariat was in his right hand, and he struck Ethan with it. Ethan threw up a left arm, trying to protect himself, but the hard twist laid open his cheek. He drove a right into the Kid's midsection. The rope artist doubled over, wheezing. Ethan brought his knee up into the man's face as it arced downward. This time he heard the cartilage cracking. With more blood spewing from his broken nose, and now from his mouth as well, the Kid reeled sideways and fell, sliding a few feet across the shiny teak flooring.

Aware that suddenly the crowd had fallen silent, Ethan stood over the Kid, fists clenched. "That was for Annabelle, you bastard. If you lay a hand on her again, I'll put a bullet in your brainpan."

Then he brought the heel of his boot down hard on the Kid's right hand. Once again he heard the snapping of bones. The Kid's scream was blood-curdling, and mingled with the screams of several of the women in the audience. Ethan bent down, grabbed a handful of the Kid's hair, and lifted his head up.

"Now you're going to have to find something else to do for a spell. Something that only requires one hand."

He let go of the hair, and the Kid's head bounced off the floor. He was mewing like a dying kitten. Ethan turned, saw one of the Irish stage hands moving as though he intended to rush out onto the stage and intervene. But one cold glance from Ethan stopped him dead in his tracks. Ethan kept turning then, to face the audience. He could see several uniformed constables coming down the aisles.

"Ladies and gentlemen, you've just witnessed the final performance of the Brazos Kid, who has a bad habit of taking advantage of innocent young ladies."

The constables reached the stage. They had their billy clubs out, and they approached him warily. He threw back the frock coat and drew the Colt pistol, and they lurched backward, fearful that he might use the six-shooter. But he rolled it, and offered it butt-first to the nearest officer. An instant later the other two had a firm grip on his arms. Ethan didn't resist. He allowed them to march him off the stage and up the center aisle of the opera house.

And as he was escorted out, in custody, a most unexpected thing happened. A man stood up and began to clap. Then another. Then a dozen more. And by the time he'd reached the back of the house, the entire audience was on its feet, giving him a standing ovation.

At that moment Ned Buntline arrived at Buffalo Bill's side. The writer was as white as a ghost. He watched several of the Irish stage hands carry the half-conscious Brazos Kid off stage.

"Good God, Bill!" gasped Buntline. "I knew it! I knew that man was trouble! I tried to talk you out of hiring him."

Cody put a hand on Buntline's shoulder. "Simmer down, Judson. Ethan Payne has just made the headlines—and so did our show. I can see it now. 'Genuine western justice, rough and ready, was dispensed last night. . . . ' "

"Why yes," breathed Buntline. "Yes, of course! But . . . but what of the Kid?" He watched as the stagehands carried the bleeding man right by him.

"I'll pay his doctor's bill, and I'll buy him a one-way train ticket to wherever he wants to go."

"Where will that be?" wondered Buntline aloud, always solicitous of the bottom line.

"As far away from Ethan Payne as a man can get, I'd imagine," murmured Buffalo Bill.

27

Once again Ethan Payne found himself inside a jail cell, and the experience brought back bad memories of his unpleasant sojourn in the custody of Denver's Marshal Lanniger. At least this time he was prepared to pay the price for the privilege of beating the hell out of the Brazos Kid. He wasn't sure that Buffalo Bill Cody would bail him out this time. Cody was a good man, and slow to anger, but it was quite possible that Ethan's conduct on stage at the Louisville Opera House had burned Bill's bacon. And of course Ned Buntline would say "I told you so" and probably try to persuade Cody that they could find someone less troublesome to play the part of the Town Tamer. In that case, Ethan was prepared to wait it out, to serve his sentence for doing what needed to be done where the Brazos Kid was concerned. And when he got out, he'd have enough money to go anywhere he wanted. A few weeks or months in jail would give him time to figure out where that would be.

The last thing he expected was the first visitor he got. He heard her voice in the office beyond the cell block door, loud and strong and insistent. It was Annabelle Pierce, and she clearly wasn't going to take no for an answer, even though the constable in charge was doing his best to convince her that she couldn't see the prisoner. Annabelle's forcefulness surprised Ethan—she'd always struck him as a shy, reserved young woman. But not today, and the constable eventually waved the white flag. A moment later she was in the cell block, clutching the bars of the door to Ethan's cell, and the constable was going down the line, wielding his billy club in a menacing fashion to silence some of the other prisoners—all males, of course—who were inclined to make ungentlemanly comments to the pretty female in their midst.

"What are you doing here?" asked Ethan, rising from his bunk to go to the bars, speaking in a whisper so that the others couldn't hear.

Her eyes were bright as she looked at him. "I came to say thank you. I know you did that for me. And I feel so badly that it's because of me that you're in this awful place." She looked apprehensively around the dark cell block, and moved her body a bit closer to his, as if he could protect her from the half-seen dangers that surrounded her.

"Don't worry about it," he told her. "Go see Bill Cody. He'll take care of everything."

"I found out just today that Molly Renwick is leaving the show. I asked him if I could take her place, and he said yes. Did you know that?"

"No, I didn't."

"Which means I would have been on stage with you." She looked at him earnestly, and then suddenly the color came to her cheeks and she glanced away, embarrassed. "But if you're not with the show when it leaves Louisville, I won't be either," she said, barely loud enough for him to hear.

Now he knew what that light in her eyes was all about. She was in love with him.

And somehow he knew, as well, that her instincts were on the mark. He *would* protect her. He *would* take care of her. He didn't need to ponder where he would yonder next. He was right where he was meant to be, with Annabelle.

Ethan took one of her hands from the bars and lifted it to his lips and kissed it. Surprised and pleased, she looked up quickly, inquisitively and hopefully searching his face for assurances that he was sincere in what that small act implied. And what she saw reassured her. Her smile was warmer than the sun.

It was at that moment that Mr. William F. Cody entered the cell block, the hapless constable who had failed so miserably in keeping Annabelle at bay trailing along behind. Ethan noted that Annabelle did not pull away from him—and he didn't let go of her hand, either. There was no need to keep up appearances, because it really didn't matter to either of them at this point what anybody else thought about them.

Cody looked at Annabelle, then at Ethan, and almost smiled. But he caught himself and cleared his throat and tried to look very stern and businesslike.

"How are you, Ethan?"

"Never been better."

Cody nodded and glanced again at Annabelle, because he knew why Ethan looked so uncommonly content for a man behind bars. "Miss Pierce here told me everything that happened. I wish she had come to me earlier, but I can understand her reluctance. As for you, well, I don't fault you for what you did. If you hadn't done it, I probably would have had to."

"It was my pleasure."

"Yes, I could tell you took immense satisfaction from it," said Cody dryly. "At any rate, I just want you to know that I am going to do all in my power to get you out of here as quickly as possible. I'm on my way to see a judge. Hopefully we can at the very least persuade them to acquiesce to my offering a bond for your release."

"Thanks, Bill. I have the money to—"

Cody raised a hand to silence him. "No. You're my employee. I'll provide the bond. But it might take a day or two to make the arrangements, you understand."

"There's no hurry," said Ethan, his gaze captured by Annabelle's.

"I'll look after him, Mr. Cody," she said.

"Then you'll be in very good hands, Ethan."

"Miss," said the constable, "you can't be staying here long."

"You'll either let me stay here as long as I like," she replied, with that forcefulness that had so surprised Ethan earlier, "or I will go commit a crime, and you'll have to put me in one of these cells. Preferably, this one."

Cody laughed. "By God, Miss Pierce, I knew you had strong nerves. You had to, to stand there and let your brother shoot a coin out of your hand. But I didn't realize you had such a strong spirit to go with them!"

"From now on, Mr. Cody," she said, with a simple earnestness that touched Ethan's heart, "wherever you find this man you'll know I'm not far away."

Cody stopped laughing and nodded, clearly moved by this expression of devotion. "Yes," he said, humbled in its presence. "Yes, I know that's the case." He started to turn away, thought of something, and turned back to her. "By the way, thank you."

"For what?" she asked.

"In spite of all his bad habits, I've come to consider your man a friend—a friend I've been worried about for some time now, as far as his future is concerned. And now, I don't have to worry about him anymore."

He nodded to them both, and left the cell block. The constable started to say something to Annabelle. Realizing the futility of it all, he just shook his head and walked out, too.

Ethan spent two nights in the Louisville jail, but it wasn't an ordeal. Annabelle was there nearly all the time. Only at Ethan's insistence did she leave when it got dark, and the following morning she was back again, bearing a plate of food from a nearby restaurant. The constables explained to her that they were responsible for and fully capable of feeding their prisoners, but she quickly won them over. They could tell she posed no threat to them, that she wasn't part of some clever conspiracy to bust Ethan Payne out of jail. She was just a woman in love who was sticking by her man, and they respected her for it. So did Ethan's fellow prisoners. There were no ugly comments aimed her way after that first visit; they, too, understood, without Ethan having to spell it out for them, that Annabelle Pierce was a good woman who shouldn't be subjected to that kind of abuse. And, as one old man in a cell two doors down from Ethan's explained, her presence actually brightened his day. They were glad to see her come and sorry to see her go.

Bill Cody finally arranged bail, and Ethan was released with the understanding that he had to remain in Louisville for his appearance before the judge, which was scheduled for the following week. The show had to move on, but Cody offered to stay for the trial. Ethan told him it wasn't necessary. Besides, Buffalo Bill had retained one of Louisville's best lawyers, Rutherford Bond, to represent him. Ethan promised to pay him back for any expenses he'd incurred. Cody dismissed all of that, and elicited a promise from Ethan that as soon as the Louisville matter was cleared up he and Annabelle would rejoin the troupe.

"We have a handful more performances," explained Buffalo Bill, "and then we're going to start putting the Wild West Show together. I'm counting on you to be a part of it."

Ethan assured him that they would rejoin the troupe as soon as possible. He was still ambivalent about remaining with Cody and participating in the Wild West Show, but on the other hand he felt he owed the man.

As for Annabelle, Ethan not only desired to be with her, he also desired her physically—but there were a couple of problems to attend to. Since they were required to stay in Louisville for a while, accommodations had to be seen to, and Ethan told her that in his opinion it would be best if they had separate rooms and even preferable if those rooms were in separate hotels. Talking about sex was not something that came easily to Ethan, and he didn't expect it would be any easier for Annabelle. In fact, she *made* it easy to address the issue.

"I love you," she said, "and I *want* you, too. But I know that will have to wait."

"Yes. Until . . ."

She just smiled at him. "Until you make up your mind whether you're going to marry me or not."

"You've made up your mind?"

"Oh yes. I want to be Mrs. Ethan Payne, if that suits you."

"Well, we'd better wait and see if I'm going to be spending the next few years in jail," he said ruefully.

That wasn't the only reason, but he didn't want to dredge up the past—the Brazos Kid and Annabelle's own brother. This time it would be different. When they shared a bed, it would be with a firm commitment, so that there wouldn't be even the shadow of a doubt in her mind that it was forever.

"There's something else," he said. "My reputation. What happened at the opera house the other night will only make matters worse. As soon as they hear I'm out of jail, I suspect there'll be a lot of people—reporters and otherwise—dogging my tracks."

She suddenly looked anxious. "Oh. You don't know, do you? Well, you'd have no way of knowing."

"Knowing what?"

"A local newspaperman has already written about me. About us. He saw me going into the jail all the time, and yesterday, when I came out, he confronted me. He asked me who I was and if I was there to see you, and I told him the truth. And it came out in yesterday's edition of the newspaper."

"What, exactly?"

"That you and I were . . . lovers." She blushed. "That what you did to the Kid was because he had made advances toward me. I didn't say that. I guess he just made the assumption."

Ethan nodded. He didn't question her further. Of course, he could hardly have expected her to tell a newspaperman the details of her relationship with the Brazos Kid. And it would be altogether natural for a correspondent to make the assumption that he had. An assumption, mused Ethan, that wasn't completely off the mark. Because it occurred to him that the reason he had reacted that way—punishing the Kid for his transgressions—was because he'd had feelings for Annabelle Pierce even then, even though he hadn't been able or willing to admit it to himself.

"In that case," he said, "we'll have different rooms, but in the same hotel." He smiled at her. "And the closer the better."

28

As Ethan had feared, as soon as Louisville's newspaper reporters got wind of the fact that he was out of jail and facing a trial, they began to hound him. In fact, reporters from the newspapers of several nearby towns arrived to join the hunt. They began by knocking on his hotel room door. He deterred the first few by slamming the door in their faces. The next one made the mistake of trying to prevent the same fate from befalling him by inserting his foot across the threshold. Ethan took him by the front of the shirt and threw him halfway down the hall. The very next day one of the Louisville daily papers carried an article about his violent proclivities, cataloging the career of one of the most notorious mankillers in the history of the Wild West. Most of what was written was complete fiction, and the few elements of the story that had any basis in fact were grossly exaggerated. But there it was, and Ethan doubted it would do his cause much good when time came for him to appear in court. It occurred to him that maybe he'd spent too many years reacting to situations with quick and effective violence. That was a habit a man needed to acquire out west, where a second's hesitation or a perceived weakness could be fatal. But just how dangerous was a newspaperman? Maybe a good habit to have on the frontier was a bad one to have in the civilized part of the country. And pretty soon—a lot more quickly than he had ever imagined—the frontier would be civilized.

He'd heard Bill Cody say as much on more than one occasion. This was why, after all, Buffalo Bill was so intent on seeing his dream of a Wild West Show become a reality. It was a tribute to a place and a way of life that would soon be no more.

Even though he was capable of this sort of soul-searching, Ethan still responded in the old, instinctive ways when the reporters found out where Annabelle Pierce was and began to hover around her door like vultures. Twice Ethan had to venture forth with pistol drawn to scatter them. He wasn't surprised when he had a visit from one of Louisville's constables.

This fellow was a big, burly, mustachioed man with a sergeant's stripes on the sleeve of his uniform and a heavy Irish brogue. Unlike the constables who had appeared at the opera house to take Ethan into custody, this one didn't appear to be the least bit intimidated by Ethan's reputation.

"Well, now," said the sergeant, sizing Ethan up across the threshold. "I hear we've been having a spot or two of trouble here lately. We've had a number of complaints leveled against you, Mr. Payne. Several members of the press claim to be in fear for their lives when they come round here."

"Then they shouldn't come around here."

The sergeant smiled bleakly. "Aye. I know they can be a real pain in the neck. But under the circumstances, it just won't do for you to go waving that hogleg around, y'see. That's why I'm here. I'll have the pistol, if you please, and any other firearm you might be carrying."

Ethan had already taken note of the fact that the sergeant was armed only with a billy club, and it was stuck under a broad black leather belt. He admired the man's courage. It wasn't bluff or bluster. This was a man who fully intended to leave with Ethan Payne's gun, whether it was handed over willingly or not.

He produced the Colt.

The sergeant thanked him. "I'm told those fellows have been botherin' the lady across the hall, and I suspect that's the reason you've been wavin' this smoke-maker around. We will post a man at the top of the stairs, and try to see to it that the two of you have a bit of privacy."

"Thank you, Sergeant. I appreciate that."

The sergeant nodded, started to turn away, then thought of something else. "Oh, and I'll be certain that you get this weapon back when you leave town."

"I hope that'll be soon."

"No offense," said the constable, "but so do I."

The sergeant was as good as his word. Within the hour there was a constable posted at the head of the stairs leading down to the lobby. He stood where he could see the entire hallway, and the doors to both Ethan's room and Annabelle's. He was replaced four hours later by another constable, and that one was replaced four hours later, as well. Ethan no longer had to worry about reporters on his doorstep, or on Annabelle's.

But he hardly had time to enjoy the peace and quiet. The lawyer Buffalo Bill had retained, Rutherford Bond, came calling the next morning. Bond was, like the sergeant, a big man, but where the former was all brawn, Bond was one of the fattest men Ethan had ever seen. He was tall and round and well dressed, carrying a staghorn cane and wearing a gold vest and bowler hat, and his snow-white beard and mustache were closely trimmed. He had pale blue eyes in a ruddy face, and looked quite jovial. But Ethan was soon to learn that, where Bond was concerned, looks were deceiving.

The lawyer had barely squeezed himself through the doorway before he rounded on Ethan and snapped, "I under-stand you've been playing hell with the press."

"Well, I—."

"Refusing to talk to them. Threatening them with bodily harm. And now you've even managed to have a constable guarding the hallway." Bond grimaced, and shook his head. "My God, man. What were you thinking? You and the young lady are holed up here as though you have something to hide. And your behavior is certainly not going to go far in convincing the judge that you aren't, as the newspapers are making you out to be, a violent, half-civilized brute who is a danger to society."

"Well," said Ethan, taking a deep breath and trying to remain calm, "I gave up my gun to the constabulary. So I guess I won't get a chance to kill anybody before my day in court."

Bond fastened those iceberg-blue eyes on him. He wasn't the least bit amused. "You've been having your meals sent up, I take it."

"That's right."

"Not any longer, you aren't. You are going to breakfast with me. And so is the young lady."

"I don't want Annabelle—Miss Pierce—subjected to—"

"As soon as you talk to the newspapermen, they'll leave both of you alone."

"And what am I supposed to say?"

Bond looked surprised. "The truth, of course. That's all I deal in, Mr. Payne. The truth. It is my stock and trade. The whole truth and nothing but the truth. Remember that."

"Not this time."

"What do you mean?"

"The truth is I beat the hell out of the Brazos Kid because of what he did to Miss Pierce—but you're not going to bring that up in court."

Rutherford Bond turned away from Ethan and went to the window. He looked down at the street for a moment, then glanced at a nearby chair—the only chair in the room. Judging it to be too small to hold him, he settled on the edge of the bed, hands resting atop his cane, and looking, Ethan thought, like a fox that had just found a henhouse.

"Very well, Mr. Payne. No mention of whatever it is that the Brazos Kid did to Miss Pierce, and that so provoked you, will be made."

Ethan was startled. He hadn't expected the lawyer to give in so easily. "I don't much care if I get a jail sentence, Mr. Bond," he said.

"Really. Most men would."

"I've been in jail before, and I didn't like it. But this time I can handle it."

He didn't bother trying to explain to Bond that he could handle it because now he knew he had something to look forward to—someone waiting for him when he got out. No matter how long it took. And somehow that made all the difference. It endowed him with a serenity that he'd never felt before, the knowledge that he could endure anything as long as Annabelle was nearby. Besides, he didn't see that it was any of Bond's business.

"Well, sir," said Bond, "I rather doubt you'll see the inside of a jail cell, at least not in connection with this case. You see, I'm not going to have to establish your motive, or should I say, your justification, for your attacking the Brazos Kid. You and Miss Pierce are going to be seen all around Louisville in the days to come. And people will see, as I do, that you are in love. I assume that Miss Pierce is in a similar condition. I have never actually experienced it myself, but I have often seen it afflict others. The newspapermen will see it, too. And they will speculate, as newspapermen love to do, that your assault on the Brazos Kid was motivated by your feelings for Miss Pierce. And mark my words, Mr. Payne. You will find yourself transformed from villain to hero almost overnight."

Ethan was dubious. Even though she had never complained, he had sensed that Annabelle was wearying of her imprisonment in the hotel. So he decided that it was worth trying what Rutherford Bond had suggested.

Less than an hour later, they were walking out of the hotel. For Ethan it was akin to being released from jail. The streets of Louisville were bustling with carriages and wagons; the sidewalks were clogged with pedestrians. Everyone seemed to know Bond. Proceeding down the two blocks to the restaurant he had suggested, he exchanged greetings with dozens of people. Ethan was a little surprised that no one seemed to be paying him much attention. Several men, though, did take notice of Annabelle. She was dressed nicely, and the sun was shining in her golden hair, and Ethan felt not only fortunate but proud to have her on his arm.

They were just about to enter the restaurant when a

young man in a tweed suit with wisps of light brown hair that passed for a mustache accosted them. Ethan recognized him as one of the reporters he had chased out of the hotel hallway. The smile he fastened on them was more of a sneer.

"Mr. Payne! What a surprise to see you on the street."

"Mr. Weatherby," said Bond. "How nice to see you again. I read your piece about my client. I never knew you to be so ambitious."

Weatherby stared at him suspiciously. "I don't know what you mean, sir."

"I had no idea you aspired to be judge, jury, and executioner."

"All I said was that your client had a reputation for violence. One, I might add, that I can personally attest to."

"Just this morning Mr. Payne was expressing to me his regret for having acted so precipitously. His principal concern has been the privacy of his acquaintance, Miss Pierce."

Weatherby followed Bond's gesture in Annabelle's direction. It was as though he was seeing her for the first time. His eyes widened as he realized how beautiful she was. And when she smiled at him, he seemed to melt.

"I'm so sorry, Mr. Weatherby," she said. "I feel responsible for any discomfort you may have been caused. Mr. Payne was only trying to protect me. Surely you understand."

"Well, yes, of course, I mean, it's . . ." He stared at her, then at Ethan, and finally at Rutherford Bond. "An acquaintance, you say?"

Bond just beamed. He could tell that Weatherby had taken one look at his client and the lady and seen exactly what he had seen—that they were in love. It was obvious to anyone who had the gift of sight. The attorney wrapped a beefy arm around the reporter's scrawny shoulders.

"Yes, that's right," he said, his tone smooth as silk. "Now, Weatherby, we're all gentlemen here. There's no need to say more on this subject, is there?"

"No. No, certainly not," said Weatherby, and glanced at Annabelle again. And she smiled at him again. And Ethan could tell that the man was completely captivated. The hostility that had been so evident when he'd approached them had vanished completely. He managed to drag his gaze away from her long enough to give Ethan a glance. "I'm sorry, Mr. Payne. I *didn't* understand your motives. Now that I do, I can see why you reacted the way you did."

"I was wrong to threaten you," said Ethan. "I'm the one who should apologize."

"Well," said Bond, benevolently, "I'm very glad that we've cleared this up. Mr. Weatherby, we were just going in for breakfast. Why don't you join us?"

"Thank you, sir, but I just ate. And I . . . I need to get back to my office."

"Some other time, then."

Weatherby was looking at Annabelle again. "It was a pleasure to meet you, miss. And good luck to you, Mr. Payne."

Then he was gone, though not without glancing over his shoulder a time or two for just one more look at Annabelle Pierce.

Bond chuckled. "There, Mr. Payne. You see what I mean?"

"Yes, Mr. Bond, I do." Ethan felt more optimistic about his prospects at that moment than he had in days. He began to think that with Rutherford Bond defending him he might actually get out of this mess without doing another day behind bars. With any luck they would be free to leave Louisville in a week's time, and then he and Annabelle could start their new life together, hopefully without any shadows from the past hanging over either one of them. Right then and there he knew what he needed to do to ensure a happy tomorrow for the both of them.

After breakfasting with Bond, they returned to the hotel. Ethan saw Annabelle to her door. She hesitated crossing the threshold, and the longing in her eyes rendered words unnecessary. Ethan glanced along the hallway. There was a constable, as usual, at the top of the stairs, and he was watching them.

"I'd better not," said Ethan, regretfully. "But very soon, Annabelle—very soon we won't have to worry about what people think. Or about what happened in the past. That is, of course, unless you object to being the wife of a farmer."

"I'll go anywhere. Be anything. It doesn't matter. But what about the show?"

Ethan shook his head. "I owe Bill Cody a few more performances. But then I'm going to quit. And, hopefully, fade quietly out of the public eye."

"But, a farmer? I had no idea . . ."

Ethan smiled ruefully. "It's something I was reluctant to admit for the past thirty years. But I grew up on a farm."

"You're sure you wouldn't mind?"

"I'm sure."

"You've always made your living by the gun."

He shook his head. "And that's bought me nothing but trouble. I think today was the first time I've walked down a street without being heeled since I left Illinois. And I felt . . . free. Unburdened. It was a good feeling. But I won't be able to keep doing that unless I give up the role of Town Tamer."

She glanced down the hallway at the constable, who was no longer paying them much attention. Her hands on Ethan's shoulders, she kissed him softly. The mere brushing of her pliant lips across his was enough to make him dizzy.

"And we'll live happily ever after?"

"Yes, we will."

"A farmer's wife." She was playing coy. "You haven't actually asked me yet, you know."

Ethan grinned. "I will, though. When all this is over. You can count on it."

"Oh, I *am* counting on it," said Annabelle, backing into the room, and with one last seductive smile, she softly shut the door.

29

The trial began a few days later, with Judge John J. Corbett presiding. Rutherford Bond described Corbett to Ethan as a tough but fair-minded man. Louisville's prosecuting attorney, however, a young man named Edward Shellen, was, according to Bond, an ambitious fellow who dreamed of a great political career, and who had made it clear he intended to showcase his talents by bringing to justice "that violent and cold-blooded killer," Ethan Payne. To let Payne go, Shellen had told others, would be to threaten the peace of Louisville. The streets would no longer be safe when word got around that this was a city where law and order did not prevail. Bond warned his client that Shellen would attempt to ignite his temper on the stand. "The worst thing you can do," said Bond, "is to provide Shellen and the judge with an example of violent behavior. You'll play right into Shellen's hands if you do." Ethan promised to keep a tight rein on his temper.

There was no jury—the defendant's fate would be determined by Judge Corbett. But Shellen still had an audience to play to; the courtroom was packed with spectators. With so much press attention given to Ethan, his case had become the talk of the town. When he arrived at the courtroom, Ethan scanned the sea of faces for a familiar one. And there was Buffalo Bill Cody, on the first row directly behind the table where Bond and Ethan were to sit. He had saved a place for Annabelle Pierce beside him, and he gave Ethan an encouraging word prior to the arrival of Judge Corbett.

Shellen rose to inform the judge that he had but one witness to call, since the victim, the Brazos Kid, had refused to testify. The Kid, Shellen added, was still bedridden in one of the city's hospitals, suffering from grave injuries inflicted upon him by the defendant, the notorious gunslinger Ethan Payne. Ethan noticed that Corbett had a poker player's face. He stared at Shellen without expression as the prosecutor made his opening remarks, then turned his gaze upon Rutherford Bond.

"Well, Rutherford?" he asked. "Do you have anything to say to that?"

Bond hefted his considerable bulk out of the chair, tugged on his gold vest, and cleared his throat. The crowd was hushed.

"I'm sorry, Your Honor," said Bond humbly. "I'm afraid I was distracted by Mr. Shellen's eloquence, as I speculated on how well it will serve him on the hustings as he pursues what I'm confident will be a spectacular career in politics."

Shellen rose. He was a thin, dark-haired man, impeccably dressed and clean-shaven, but his gentlemanly dress and demeanor didn't fool Ethan; he knew a predator when he saw one. "Excuse me, Your Honor, but I hope my learned colleague will keep his attention focused on the issue at hand, which is not my political aspirations, but rather the heinous assault inflicted upon a young man by his client."

"I am grateful for the advice," said Bond smoothly, "and will endeavor to do as Mr. Shellen suggests."

He sat down again.

"I am heartened," said Shellen, with a smirk, "that Mr. Bond did not attempt to persuade the court that I had misjudged his client, that Ethan Payne was in fact a man of sterling character who suffered an undeserved reputation as one of the frontier's most notorious of killers."

Bond sighed, and once more, with great effort, arose from his chair. "Certainly not. As the court knows, I am wedded to the truth, and the truth in the case of Ethan Payne is that he *has* killed many men in his time."

He sank with a sigh of relief into the chair, and glanced at Ethan, who was watching him with a wry smile on his face. "I'm sure glad you're on my side," whispered Ethan. Bond just smiled.

Shellen called the defendant to the stand. Corbett asked Ethan to place his hand on the Bible at the corner of the table behind which he sat and asked him if he would swear to tell the truth and nothing but the truth. Ethan did, and upon the judge's invitation, sat in a chair at the end of the table, facing Shellen and the courtroom audience.

"Mr. Payne," said Shellen, standing directly in front of him. "Since we've fairly well established that you are a killer, perhaps you could tell the court exactly how many lives you have taken."

Ethan shook his head. "I don't know. I do know that I didn't intend to kill the Brazos Kid—and I didn't."

"So you say now." Shellen sounded skeptical. "Have you killed so many men that you can't count the number?"

"I didn't try to keep count. I didn't carve notches in my gun."

"So you didn't care how many."

"I tried . . . to forget about them."

Shellen smiled coldly. "Apparently you succeeded. You killed many men, and then you forgot about them."

Ethan sighed. It was clear that Shellen was getting the better of him.

"No comment?" asked Shellen.

"Sorry, didn't think that was a question."

Shellen turned on his heel and walked away. "You're right. It wasn't a question." Arriving at his table, he picked up a sheet of paper and glanced at it. "When you were employed by a mining concern in California many years ago, you were placed in charge of a gold shipment being transported to San Francisco, is that correct?"

"Yes."

"At the time, the company you worked for had been plagued by a band of robbers, who had made off with several previous gold shipments. The plan, as I understand it, was that a decoy would be sent out to draw the robbers off, while you took the real shipment to its destination. However, for reasons that do not concern us here, you were attacked by these robbers. The gold was stolen. You gave chase. And when you caught up with the robbers, you killed several of them from ambush."

"It wasn't an ambush. I tracked them to their hideout and—"

"And you ordered them to surrender."

"No."

"You attempted to retrieve the gold without engaging in gunplay."

"That would have been impossible."

"The truth," said Shellen sharply, "is that you gunned them down without even giving them an opportunity to give up. Isn't that so?"

Ethan was off-balance. How did Shellen know these things? No one else who had been there that night was still alive. The prosecutor was guessing—and it just so happened that he'd guessed correctly.

"Sure," said Ethan. "That's pretty much what happened."

"And why did you do that, Mr. Payne?"

Ethan glanced at Bond, who was sitting there behind the defense table, fingers interlaced over his generous belly, looking quite content with the way things were going.

"I was scared," he replied.

"Scared?"

There was something new in Shellen's voice—uncertainty. Ethan realized that he'd turned the tables on his inquisitor. And he'd done it unwittingly. But clearly Shellen had not been prepared for that answer.

"Yes," said Ethan. "Scared out of my wits. I was hardly more than a kid."

"But if you were scared, why did you go after these criminals?"

"I'd been given an important job, and it was important to me to see it through."

With a grimace, Shellen again referred to the sheet of

paper. "And when you were employed as a troubleshooter for the Overland Mail. Isn't it true that you killed a fellow employee, the husband of a woman with whom you had been having an affair?"

Ethan looked at Annabelle. To pass the time while she'd waited with him in the Louisville jail, he had told her about his life, leaving nothing out, secure in the knowledge that none of it would change her mind about him. It hadn't, and now she was smiling at him, her blue eyes a warm and safe harbor for him.

"That's right," he said. "It was in self-defense, though."

"Fact is, the man flew into a rage when he found out about the affair you were having with his wife. Under the circumstances, that's perfectly understandable, wouldn't you say?"

"Yes, I'd say that."

"So you killed him."

"I did."

"Were you in love with his wife, Mr. Payne?"

Ethan felt his anger on the rise. He was willing to sit here and be subjected to an inquisition about himself, but he didn't think it right for Shellen to drag Julie Cathcott into it.

"She's dead."

"And what does that have to do with anything?"

Ethan tried to tamp down the lid on his temper, but Shellen's indifference rankled him.

"She shouldn't be dragged into this. It has nothing to do with what I did to the Brazos Kid."

"Well, we'll get to that, all in good time. Thank you, Mr. Payne, but I do not need any advice from you on how to conduct this case."

"How about some advice from me, Edward," said Judge Corbett. "I'd like to know where you're going with this line of questioning."

"I'm just trying to establish that Mr. Payne has a proclivity for violence, Your Honor."

"Rutherford?" Corbett looked at the defense table with brows raised.

"I have no objection, Your Honor."

Corbett shrugged. "Then get on with it, Edward."

"Thank you, Your Honor. Now, Mr. Payne. Were you in love with this man's wife?"

"No, not really," said Ethan softly.

"And not long after that, when you had lost your job with the Overland Company due to this killing, you left that part of the country—and left her behind."

"Yes."

"So a man is dead because he found out you were sleeping with his wife, whom you did not really care for."

"I cared for her," snapped Ethan. "We were both . . . lonely. It just happened. I'm sorry that it did."

"You met her some time later, didn't you?" asked Shellen. "In Abilene. She had turned to prostitution, isn't that correct? And she was addicted to opium?"

Ethan's eyes blazed with anger he could scarcely control. "All of which was my fault. And damn you for dragging her into this."

Shellen smiled. "I believe you're the one to blame for that."

Ethan nodded. "You're right."

"At the time you were the town marshal of Abilene. But before long, Abilene wanted nothing more to do with you, and you moved on. Why was your tenure at Abilene so brief in duration, Mr. Payne? Why did the town fathers want you to leave?"

"Because there were men gunning for me, and there was concern that innocent bystanders might be hurt."

"Why were they doing that?"

"It turned out they'd been hired by a man named Marston."

"And why would this Marston fellow hire men to kill you?"

"Because he blamed me for crippling him some years before."

"And were you to blame?"

"Yes, I was. He was a thief. I was working on a riverboat, and caught him trying to escape with things he had stolen from the passengers. We struggled, and he fell into the river. I thought he was dead."

"After Abilene you moved on to Wyoming, and went to work as a range detective for the Sweetwater Company. Would you explain what a range detective does?"

"He deals with rustlers. Gangs that steal cattle from their rightful owner."

"And how do you deal with rustlers, Mr. Payne?"

"Kill them unless they give up. And they don't often do that, because out there a cattle rustler is hanged."

"How many men did you kill during your work as a range detective?"

"None. But the ones I took in were hanged."

Rutherford Bond stood up. As he had done with Annabelle, Ethan had spent the previous days telling his attorney everything he could recall about his years on the frontier, leaving nothing out.

"Your Honor," said Bond, "I believe we can hasten this case to its conclusion if you and Mr. Shellen would permit me to ask the defendant a question or two at this time."

"I am not finished with my examination of this witness," said Shellen.

"There will be no cross-examination if I am allowed to ask a couple of questions at this juncture, Your Honor."

Judge Corbett nodded. "Go ahead, Rutherford."

"Your Honor—" said Shellen, beginning a protest.

"Be quiet, Edward. Stand aside for a moment, if you please. I've seen Rutherford take several days to cross-examine a witness, and if I have an opportunity to avoid that happening in this instance, by God I'll take it."

There was some chuckling from the spectators, swiftly silenced by the judge's stern glance.

"Thank you, Your Honor," said Bond. He came around the defense table and approached Ethan. "Mr. Payne, did you attempt to prevent the hanging of the cattle rustlers you brought in alive?"

"Yes, I did. But I failed."

"Why did you try?"

"Because I wanted to hand them over to the law, and not to Seamus Blake—the cattleman I was working for."

"Is there another reason?"

Ethan looked down, hoping Bond wouldn't see the pain of old memories reflected in his eyes. "One of them was a friend of mine."

"One more question, Your Honor," said Bond.

Corbett nodded.

"Mr. Payne, you have a reputation as a killer of men. As we all know, many other individuals who have lived their lives out west have a similar reputation. The frontier is a violent place. Often there is no law save that practiced at the end of a gun barrel. Did you ever kill a man for any other reason than self-defense?"

"No. But I've done things that I regret, and that led to the deaths of others that might have been avoided. When those men stole that gold in California, I should have gone back to the company and told them. Maybe it was pride that kept me from doing that. And when Joe Cathcott left his wife pretty much by herself to run that Overland station, I knew better than to get involved. I told myself I was in love with her." He looked again at Annabelle. "I finally know, now, what love really is. That's why I know I wasn't really in love with Julie Cathcott. Even if I was, though, I shouldn't have gotten involved. Because then Joe Cathcott came back and he did what any husband might do and I killed him because if I hadn't he would have killed me. And when Tell Jenkins killed the Abilene marshal, I stepped in and put Jenkins in jail. Some people called me a hero, but I knew better. I was just tired of drifting. So I saw my chance to belong somewhere—in that case, Abilene. But the people there soon found out that as long as I was around they wouldn't have any law and order. And in Wyoming I knew better than to take Seamus Blake up on his offer, but he paid me a lot of money, and again, I was tired of drifting. So I became his range detective. Only problem was, I came to see that Blake and I were a lot alike."

"What do you mean, 'a lot alike'?"

"We'd both taken advantage of the fact that out west a man made his own law." Ethan shook his head. "It's not like what folks see in Buffalo Bill Cody's show." He looked past Bond's girth at Cody. "Sorry, Bill, but that's not the West I lived in all these years. The West I know isn't so much about doing what's right. It's more about doing what you have to in order to stay alive. And like I said, I did some things I wish I hadn't."

"Well, Mr. Payne," said Bond, turning slowly away, "so have we all."

He reached the defense table and Ethan thought he was done, and was going to sit down. So did Shellen; the prosecutor began to rise from his chair. But then Bond turned back to Ethan.

"One more question."

"Your Honor!" exclaimed Shellen.

"Sit down, Edward," growled Corbett. "One more, Rutherford, and you're finished."

"When you attacked the Brazos Kid at the opera house, Mr. Payne, did you think he deserved it?"

"Yes, I did," replied Ethan, with conviction.

Bond nodded and sat down. "I thank the court for its indulgence."

Shellen shot to his feet. "When you attacked the Brazos Kid, Mr. Payne, were you doing that in self-defense?"

Ethan looked at Annabelle, and smiled. "In a manner of speaking."

"You were in fear for your life."

"No. I did it in defense of someone who means more to me than life itself." He fastened a stern gaze on the prosecutor. "And that's all I'm going to say on the subject."

"No more needs to be said," said Shellen smugly. "Your Honor, I think it's clear that Ethan Payne broke the law when he assaulted the Brazos Kid. And it wasn't the first time he has broken the law, or visited violence upon another. If Louisville is to remain known as a place where law prevails and disorder will not be tolerated, then it seems to me that this court has no choice but to find Mr. Payne guilty of the charges that have been leveled against him."

"Are you done?" asked Corbett.

"I am, Your Honor," said Shellen, and sat down, looking satisfied with himself.

"Rutherford? Anything further from your side?"

"No, Your Honor."

"Then I'm ready to rule. Mr. Payne, I find you guilty of all charges."

There was a collective gasp from the crowd, and a ripple of murmurs silenced by Corbett's vigorous use of his gavel.

"I hereby sentence you to six months' imprisonment and a two-hundred-dollar fine. I also hereby suspend the prison sentence. But you will be responsible for paying the fine." He slammed the gavel down once more. "Case is closed."

Ethan was vaguely aware of the fact that just about everyone in the courtroom audience was on their feet, talking excitedly. But his attention was focused on Annabelle as he turned to her, and felt her arms encircle his neck and the warmth of her sweet breath on his face just before she kissed him. Because she was, after all, the only thing that really mattered.

30

Their last stop was Chicago, where they were scheduled to play four shows. Since the company arrived two days early, Ethan took the opportunity to catch a train south to Murphysboro. Annabelle want with him, of course. There he rented a buggy and they rode out to the old place, not far from Roan's Prairie.

The cabin had burned down—it was now a pile of charred timbers obscured by tall weeds. The barn still stood, just barely, leaning at a precarious angle, a sad derelict of weathered boards and cobwebs, good for nothing except as a home for the bats nesting in the loft, and looking for all the world as though the next strong wind would knock it down. Ethan was sorry to see it in this condition. One of his earliest and most enduring memories was of his father building that barn.

The fields that he had been so reluctant to work so many years ago were completely overgrown. He and Annabelle walked across them, scattering a host of grasshoppers, and he could feel the furrows beneath his feet, like the ones he had begrudged making. He stopped once, knelt, and picked up a handful of dirt. The smell of the earth was strong in his nostrils. Then a gust of wind rustled the trees that stood around the charred remains of the house, and swept across the fields and reached him, and he thought of the wind as it blew down off the snow-capped Rockies and across the seemingly endless Great Plains. He thought about all the places he had yondered and all the things he had seen. And he was glad to be back home. He preferred the smell of the earth.

They went down to the river, the cool green shade of the willows, and watched the water rush by in its race to reach the mighty Mississippi. He hadn't intended it—or maybe, subconsciously, he had—but the route they took brought them to the old tree where he had last seen Lilah Webster, where he had told her of his plans to go west with Gil Stark, where he had promised her he would return, and they would be married, and live happily ever after. That had been so long ago, and yet he could remember it quite vividly.

Somehow he felt as though a bond existed between himself and this place. For a long time he sat there and listened to the river's song, and thought about dreams never realized and promises never kept. Annabelle sat close beside him, silent, allowing him room for his private thoughts, aware, as women are always aware, that his thoughts were dwelling on someone else. But she wasn't troubled by that, and he knew that she wasn't, and he drew comfort from that knowledge.

Eventually he roused himself, and they went back to the farm and climbed into the buggy and rode on to Roan's Prairie in the hot dusty afternoon heat. The town had grown a great deal since he had last been here. He hardly recognized this place as the sleepy little country hamlet of thirty-odd years ago. He passed by the house where Gil Stark had been born. A woman was coming out the front door with a pair of tow-headed boys, and Ethan didn't recognize her. He checked his horse and tugged at the brim of his hat and she smiled kindly up at him.

"I'm looking for the Starks," he said. "They used to live here."

She nodded. "Yes, they did. But Mr. Stark died many years ago. His widow lived here for quite a long time after that, but then she sold the place to us, and moved away. I'm afraid I don't know where. Were you a friend of theirs?"

"I had some news for them, about their son."

"Oh, you mean Gil Stark? I've heard of him. He was an outlaw, wasn't he? They say he was hanged a year or so ago, out in Montana."

"Wyoming," said Ethan. "And I guess he *was* an outlaw. But in the end he gave his life to save a friend." He thanked her and went on, stopping at the bank. He was surprised to find Mr. Shalhope behind the president's desk. Shalhope was a paunchy old man, with a ring of bushy white hair around his bald pate, and thick muttonchop whiskers in the fashion of the day. He still had that pinched, sour expression on his face that Ethan remembered from his childhood, when Shalhope had been a much younger man with a much less-prosperous belly and much darker hair.

"Good afternoon, Mr. Shalhope."

The banker looked up from his ledgers and peered short-sightedly at Ethan over the pince nez perched on the tip of his nose.

"Do I know you, sir?"

Ethan smiled. "You have no reason to remember me. My name is Ethan Payne. This is my fiancée."

Mr. Shalhope—thoroughly charmed by Annabelle, as all men were—smiled warmly at her, then turned his attention to Ethan.

"I confess you looked familiar to me, and now I know why. You remind me of your father, God rest his soul. The last time I saw you, you were just a lad. You went west with that other boy—what was his name again?"

"Gil Stark."

"They said the two of you had gone off to California with the intention of striking it rich."

"I did strike it rich, but not in California." Ethan's arm was curled around Annabelle's narrow waist, and he pulled her closer to him, and Annabelle couldn't help but laugh softly, and blush. Shalhope looked momentarily confused, and then he understood what was happening. He chuckled, a bit uncomfortably, as he was one of those people who were embarrassed by public displays of affection.

"The reason we're here, Mr. Shalhope," said Annabelle,

"is that we're interested in the farm where Ethan grew up. We were hoping you'd know who owns that property now."

Settling back in his chair as she spoke, Shalhope was gazing at her as though she were an angel descended from heaven. Belatedly he realized that he was expected to answer, and leaned forward, startled. But Ethan spoke before he could.

"I'm interested in buying back the farm. Do you think there's a chance that the owner might be willing to sell it?"

"I doubt it very much," said Shalhope. "Because *you* own it, Mr. Payne."

"There must be some mistake."

"No. I handled the transaction myself. The bank did take possession of the property after your father passed away. And we sold it to a fellow by the name of—oh, what *was* his name?—Sherman, I believe. Yes, that was it. Sherman. But he didn't have much luck; we had several years of very bad drought, and he pulled up stakes. As he had purchased the farm outright, it remained in his name, of course, but he had informed me that if anyone expressed an interest in the property that I was to sell it for whatever I could get for it. Several years passed, and then I heard from the attorney of someone who lived in Chicago. The attorney would not divulge his client's name, but the purchase of the property was made, and I must say it was more than a fair price. The title was placed in your name."

"Lilah," said Ethan. "Lilah Webster. Though that's not her name now. But it had to have been her."

"Lilah Webster?" exclaimed Shalhope. "Well, I'll be. I remember her! But it never occurred to me that—"

"This won't do," said Ethan firmly. "She did that for me. But it's a gift I can't accept."

"Well, now, hold on." Shalhope put some glasses on and began to rifle through a drawer of his desk. "The possibility that you would not feel right accepting such a gift did come up, as I recall. Let me see. . . . Ah yes, here it is." He brandished a sheet of paper. "Yes, as I thought, it says so right here. Arrangements can be made for you to repay the amount given for the property. There is an account provided here, at a Chicago bank. I am permitted to secure any terms you wish to abide by."

Ethan looked at Annabelle. "It doesn't have to be that place. If you'd rather not, I mean."

"No. It's your home. It will be *our* home."

"We can find a place that doesn't need so much work. . . ."

She smiled and touched his lips with her fingers. "We'll make it work. Together, there isn't anything we can't do, you know."

"I know."

"So let's come to terms with Mr. Shalhope."

Shalhope beamed. "That is always music to a banker's ears."

When they were finished with their business in the bank, Ethan waited until they were outside on the boardwalk before turning to face Annabelle. He took her hands in his and looked her in the eye and asked her to marry him.

"Annabelle."

"Yes, Ethan?"

"Will you marry me? Now. Today. Right this minute."

Tears brimming in her eyes, she stepped into his waiting arms. "Yes. Oh, yes, Ethan. We've wasted enough time."

They found a justice of the peace, and were married, and spent their wedding night in Ethan's hotel room back in Murphysboro. In the early morning hours, when Annabelle was fast asleep, he slipped out of bed to sit in a chair pulled up near the window. There he was haunted by the ghosts of his past—Julie and Manolo and Gil Stark, and even Joe Cathcott and Wesley Grome and Frank Sellers. All dead now. All dust. In the morning, though, when Annabelle awoke and smiled and kissed him and put her arms around him, the ghosts were gone, and somehow Ethan knew it

wasn't likely they would ever haunt him again. He could put
it all behind him now, and concentrate on the future, because
now he *had* a future.

"Are you happy, Ethan?" she asked. "I'm the happiest
woman in the whole world."

He was almost surprised to discover that, indeed, he
was happy, and experiencing a rare contentment. It was as
though the last thirty years had been a long nightmare from
which, at last, he had awakened. But he couldn't regret all
the time he'd spent yondering, because it wasn't time he had
lost; it was the road he'd had to travel, for if he hadn't taken
it he would not have met Annabelle Pierce. All those years
of wandering in the wilderness, he had reflected on what
he'd left behind, on the kind of life he could have led with
Lilah Webster, had he'd been wise enough to never leave
Roan's Prairie. Now, though, he had to accept that leaving
Roan's Prairie with Gil Stark hadn't been the mistake he'd
thought it to be—and staying *would* have been a mistake,
after all. He'd thought that Lilah had been his one true love,
and he'd been tormented by the loss of that love, and of the
happiness he'd assumed would have resulted from their
being together. But a person had but one true love, and he
knew without the slightest doubt that Annabelle was his.
Which meant Lilah could not have been.

Then, too, he knew now that he'd had to leave home to
arrive at a full appreciation of what "home" meant. He had
been too young to see it before, and he'd been further
blinded to the truth by the death of his mother, and the living
death of his father, who had drowned his own sorrows and
regrets in jugs of moonshine. Abner Payne had tried to run
away from his problems, and most of all from his self-
perception as a failure, by drinking himself into oblivion
every day. Ethan had chosen another course, but it was still
running away. One lesson he had learned was that it didn't
help at all to run away from problems.

Annabelle loved him for who he was, an unconditional
love. He hadn't needed fame and fortune to win her love, or
keep it. Lilah had told him as much, on that day, by the river,

when he'd said his good-byes. He'd thought she was talking only about herself, and she'd probably thought so, too. But it was Annabelle who had proved it to him.

Buffalo Bill's show was opening that evening, and Ethan and Annabelle arrived at the theatre an hour before the curtain was to rise. Buffalo Bill Cody was relieved to see them both.

"I was beginning to think you'd run out on me, Ethan," he confessed.

"I wouldn't do that, Bill. Oh, by the way, I believe you've already met my wife," said Ethan wryly.

Buffalo Bill was delighted. "This couldn't have worked out better if Ned Buntline himself had scripted it," declared the scout.

They had four shows to do, and on the fourth night Ethan stepped on stage for the last time. For once, he was a little self-conscious. When the scene was over, he made his curtain call to vigorous applause, which subsided when he raised his hands in a gesture for silence.

"This is my last chance to set the record straight on a few things," he told them. "What you just saw might pass for good entertainment, I reckon, but it's not what happened. Unlike Bill Cody, I'm no hero. I wasn't fighting for justice in Abilene. I was a drifter. A yonder man. I saw a chance to make a place for myself, and I was so desperate I was willing to die to make it. I stood by and watched Tell Jenkins gun down Jack Crawford. I knew he was going to do it, and I might have been able to stop it, but I didn't. I stood by and let it happen because I wanted Crawford's job. Tell Jenkins got rid of him for me."

A current of gasps and murmurs ran through the crowded house. Ethan glanced into the wings and saw Cody and Buntline there, staring at him.

"When those cowboys rode into town to spring Jenkins from jail, I didn't stand up to them for the sake of law and order. I did it for myself. And I was scared. Not of dying, but of failing—again. I knew if I ran I'd just be a worthless drifter the rest of my life. I guess I had a couple of things going for me. Those cowboys were just as scared as I was. Maybe more. Most of them were just kids. Most of them couldn't have hit the broad side of a barn from the inside. And I reckon most had never been in a real shooting scrape before. They didn't want to die.

"So you see, ladies and gentlemen, there was nothing heroic or glorious about what I did in Abilene. It was a dirty business and I take no pride in my part of it. There are a lot of things I've done that I'm not proud of. Some worse than I've described to you today. No, I'm no hero. I'm just a man who made his share of mistakes, and then some. The frontier is full of men like me. There are heroes, but you don't hear much about them. They don't get written up in the dime novels. They're the common folks, who try to make a good, decent life for themselves, who play fair, in a land where it's too easy to resort to this."

Ethan drew the Remington Army from his holster, and laid it on the boards at his feet. Then he walked off the stage.

After a moment of stunned silence, the audience began to applaud. One by one they got to their feet, until the entire house was standing.

Cody and Buntline was waiting for Ethan in the wings.

"Sorry, Bill," he said. "I had to come clean."

Cody grinned. "Sounds like the people appreciate a little honesty." He glanced wryly at Buntline. "Judson, ol' pard, we might ought to keep that in mind."

"What about that pistol of yours, Ethan?" asked Buntline.

"I won't be needing it anymore. You keep it. It's all that's left of the Town Tamer—a man who never existed."

Annabelle arrived. Her eyes shining, she put her arms around his neck and kissed him. "You were a little hard on yourself, dear," she said. "You've been *my* hero since the day I first saw you."

"Let's go home," he said.

"Payne!"

Ethan whirled and caught a glimpse of Albert Pierce and the Smith & Wesson in his hand. Annabelle saw her brother in the same instant. She pushed Ethan aside, trying at the same time to place herself in the line of fire. A heartbeat later, Pierce fired.

As Ethan staggered and fell, and Annabelle fell, too, Cody instinctively turned on Pierce, but Pierce swung his pistol around to cover Buffalo Bill.

"Don't make me kill you, too," he rasped. He glanced at Annabelle, concerned. "Sis? Annie! No, it couldn't—"

Buntline saw his chance. Pierce was so worried about Cody and his sister that he paid the New Yorker no attention, and Buntline struck with his malacca walking stick, knocking the Smith & Wesson out of Pierce's grasp. Before Pierce could draw his second pistol, Cody was on him, smashing an iron fist into his face, knocking him down, and hitting him twice more when Pierce tried to get up.

Relieving the unconscious man of his second pistol, Cody tossed the gun to Buntline. "Keep an eye on him, Judson."

Buntline nodded. "Go find a constable," he barked at a stage hand who stood nearby, frozen in place. The man took off running.

Cody turned to see Annabelle bending over Ethan's sprawled form. "Good God," muttered the plainsman, sick at heart. He just knew Ethan Payne was dead. Because Albert Pierce never missed.

So he was astonished when, groaning, Ethan sat up, with Annabelle's help, clutching at his shoulder with bloody fingers.

"Well, that beats all I ever saw or heard tell of," said Cody. "I thought you were deader than a rotten stump, pard."

Putting his good arm around Annabelle and holding her close, Ethan said, "He hit me high, Bill. Besides, I've got too much to live for to die now."

"I think your luck has finally changed," said Buffalo Bill. "He was after you, not his sister. And I think she threw his aim off when she jumped in front of you."

Annabelle wasn't the least bit squeamish—she ripped open Ethan's shirt and checked the wound. "We've got to get you to a doctor."

Cody barked orders, and a couple of the brawny Irish stage hands arrived to lift Ethan and carry him off, Annabelle right beside him.

"As much as I hate to admit it," muttered Buntline, "I'm going to miss having him around."

Cody smiled. "Yeah. Too bad he won't be in the Wild West Show."

"Well, he'd certainly add a touch of realism to it," said Buntline dubiously. "But you realize, Bill, that reality doesn't sell tickets."

"We'll see."

"Aren't you ever going to tell him why you went to Denver to recruit him in the first place? About his mysterious friend?"

"No. Never. She made me promise not to."

Ned Buntline shook his head. "It has to be that girl Lilah—the one he left so many years ago. If I'm right, it would make a great story. I just can't figure out why she wouldn't want to see him again, after all this time, and after what they meant to each other."

"That's one story you'll never write," predicted Buffalo Bill.

Buntline shrugged. He could hear the audience; the people were growing restless. They had heard the shot, and were wondering why the stage was empty.

"I'd better get out there and make a speech," said the journalist.

"Go ahead," said Cody, and as he watched Ned Buntline walk out into the light, he wondered what sort of fanciful fiction his partner would weave in retelling the last chapter in the saga of Ethan Payne, the yonder man.

Or was it the first chapter of a new beginning?